Introduction

Tiff hates her job, where her boss tears her down every chance he gets. Her mother always has something to say about how she lives her life. Running is her escape from her constant anxiety, until four hot landscapers howl at her from the side of the road and disrupt her only peace.

Leon, Jace, Quinn and Eli insist that she smells wonderful, and all four of them are inexplicably drawn to her... and they're more than happy to share. Can Tiff really date more than one guy at a time?

But the brothers are hiding something, something big. Even worse, Tiff's boss is meddling in dangerous business, and dragging her in along with him. What will she do when everyone's secrets come to light?

Content Warnings

May contain spoilers.

- Graphic depictions of sex

- Sex in human form as well as werewolf form
- Stretching and stuffing
- Knotting
- Three-ways and spit-roasting
- Primal chasing and primal play
- White-collar crime
- Violence
- Dismemberment
- Off-screen death
- Anal play
- Double penetration
- Breeding kink
- Pregnancy
- Birth

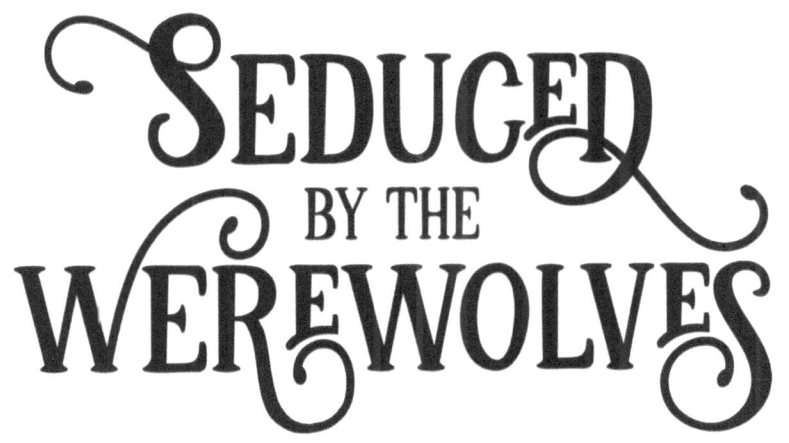

SEDUCED BY THE WEREWOLVES

LYONNE RILEY

Chapter One

"Ms. Dockett, where's my coffee?"

My head jerks up at the sound of Mr. Bosley's irritated voice floating out from his office.

Shit. I completely forgot to stop at the coffee shop on my way into work today. My mind was on tonight's dinner with Mom—specifically, how much I'm dreading it.

"It's coming, Mr. Bosley," I say as I hop out of my chair and grab my purse. He doesn't have any meetings for twenty minutes, which should be enough time for me to run there and back.

"My coffee is supposed to be on my desk when I come in," he growls, still not leaving his office.

"I promise I'll have it soon!"

I sprint out the front door, hop into my car, and drive recklessly to the coffee shop. The line is long at the drive-thru, so I park and run inside instead. It's busy this time of morning, and I stand there tapping my foot much too fast while the barista works. Then I've got the caramel crunch latte in my hand and I'm speeding back to the office.

I manage to get the cup onto Mr. Bosley's desk moments before his first appointment is due to walk in. Mr. Bosley scowls at me as I leave. Back at my desk, I'm patting down my ruffled hair and straightening my skirt as a visitor enters.

"He's expecting you," I tell the woman, who looks even younger than I am, wearing a skintight dress with hair piled on top of her head in a severe bun.

She doesn't even glance at me as she walks into Mr. Bosley's office and closes the door. I sit back in my chair, breathing hard, trying to shake out my trembling hands. Sometimes this job makes me want to cry.

Actually, it does. Often.

I take a few calming breaths. *Remember, you have health insurance and a steady paycheck.* I can tolerate Mr. Bosley's shit if it means I can afford food and rent. I just have to squeeze myself down small and do what he wants, and maybe someday I'll get it all right.

Finally, when I feel composed again, the phone rings.

"Orland Bosley's office," I answer, pulling out a pad of paper and gripping my pen tight to still my shaking hand. "How can I help you?"

I only have a few minutes at home to clean up before meeting Mom for dinner at Red Robin. We try to see each other weekly, just to "catch up." Usually it's an hour or two of my mother telling me all the things she thinks are wrong with me and how *she* would fix them if she could just be me for a day. Then I receive a nice, thorough summary of all her work and friend drama, until my liquefied brain is nearly spilling out of my ears.

These weekly dinners are just another reminder that I don't fit in this world, that I'm unacceptable the way I am.

When Mom and I sit down at a booth at the restaurant, I can already hear the words coming out of her mouth before she says them.

"How's that diet going?" she asks predictably, surveying the menu.

She's such a hypocrite, inviting me out for burgers and shakes while insisting I'm on a diet I never once expressed interest in. These days I've learned to wear baggy clothes around her so she won't remark on how tight they are, how they show off too much of my big boobs, how my rounded tummy or my thick thighs are too pronounced.

"It's not?" I don't even look at the menu because I plan on ordering the bacon burger with barbecue sauce and fried onions.

"And what about the exercise plan?"

Again, a plan that doesn't exist. I already jog every single morning and go hiking on the weekends. I've invited her along on hikes before, but she has no interest in "tromping through the woods." I don't even do it to lose weight—I just like the clarity of mind it gives me, how focusing on the steady beat of my feet and the thrum of my heart centers me in a world that's so noisy and demanding. Plus, I have killer thighs.

"There is no 'plan,'" I say evenly. "I'm just living my life, okay?"

My mom only sees me as a college dropout. And maybe she's onto something, because it's not like I've done much since I realized higher education wasn't for me. I'm just not a book-learner, as hard as I try. I need to be on my feet, picking things up as I go. When I told her I wasn't going back to college, Mom said I'd just end up working for someone higher up the food chain, doing their bidding like a dog.

She was absolutely right, of course, and she loves to hold that over my head.

Mom sighs like she's running out of patience.

"You need to make a change," she declares, setting the menu down. "You're just a lackey for that Chad Bosley or whatever his name is. And you're still single!"

I can't even hold her gaze as she says this. Yeah, I am single. So what? I don't need someone else's validation to know my life is worth living.

I don't say any of these things to my mom, of course.

"Yep," I say, hoping the waiter will stop by soon. "That's all true."

"Aren't you going to do something about it?" Mom asks, clearly annoyed that I've dodged her pointed insults.

I gave up on online dating a long time ago. I did my best to represent myself accurately in my photos, to be open and interesting in my profiles, but guys would still walk into the bar, see me waiting and turn right around. The ones who did show up—who did stick around—usually only wanted one thing: a hookup with a big-titty girl.

"No, I'm just going on like usual, Mom," I say, turning my gaze on her. "And I'm doing fine."

She lets out an impatient breath. It always goes this way: she aims barbs at me, and I do my best not to let them under my skin. But sometimes the burn gets so intense that I want to scream, to snap and let her know just how much it aches.

At last, the waiter arrives, and I ask Mom about her work instead. She can go on and on about her coworker gossip, and sure enough, once I open the floodgates, I spend the rest of the meal learning all about how Paula from accounting is sleeping around with the sales guys.

I'm mentally exhausted by the time I get back to my apartment. I drop my purse onto the floor and stumble to the couch, then flick on the television to watch something mindless before bed.

Despite what I said, there are times I wish I could come home to someone, a person who would kiss away all my mother baggage, all my anxiety about Mr. Bosley, and take me off to bed. But that person hasn't appeared yet, and I doubt they will anytime soon. Not when this world doesn't fit me. Not while it demands so much, while never truly letting me belong. No matter how hard I try, I just can't seem to mold myself into a shape that's acceptable to other people, not to my mother or Mr. Bosley. And I know it means I'll be alone, maybe forever.

But I'd rather be alone than force myself to become someone I'm not.

Every morning before heading to work, I go on a two-mile jog to try to stuff down all my burgeoning uneasiness about the day ahead. What will Mr. Bosley have to say today to tear me down? Where will I fall short of his expectations again?

That's what the run is for. I can forget, just for half an hour, that I'm a pig headed off to slaughter.

There's a nice neighborhood up the street from my apartment where I like to run along the sidewalks toward the park. Rich people live on well-manicured streets in big, three-story houses with sprawling green lawns. Some even have automatic gates blocking their driveways, or big hedges to keep the riffraff out. Whenever I jog past the gated house with the big stone lions posted outside like sentries, I give them a friendly nod. I try to spot the koi fish in the pond someone put in their front yard. At a few homes, harried families load their kids into big SUVs, trying to get to work on time. I feel comfortable jogging here in my shorts and tight sports bra because nobody takes a second look at me. They're too preoccupied with their own lives.

It's hot out, even this early, so I feel bad when I spot a crew truck in front of a house, the workers already digging in the dirt. The side of the truck reads LUPINE LANDSCAPING, and there's a wolf's head in the logo. Four guys are hard at work in the front yard, making huge holes in perfectly good grass to put in who knows what there instead. Maybe another pond.

I slow down as I pass, because two of them already have their shirts off and it's only eight in the morning. And boy, they are not difficult to look at. All four are tanned from working out in the sun all day, and the two shirtless ones—a tall guy and a guy with a baseball cap—are built like tractors. Then I see why when one of them goes to the truck to lift a bag of cement like it weighs nothing. The man's biceps flex as he hefts it over his shoulder, and then when he bends down to drop it... my eyes are drawn to his ass where it strains his jeans.

I think it might very well be the nicest ass I've ever seen.

A gentle wind blows past me, pulling some of my hair free from my ponytail. As I reach up to retie it, the four men freeze. Their eyes shift toward me, their heads turning as if all of them are tied to a single puppet string.

Fuck. The last thing I need is four hotties jeering at me. That's why I stay in this neighborhood—there's less chance of strangers seeing me and deciding I need to hear their opinions about my body.

I turn and jog away as fast as I can, because after meeting with Mom last night, I don't know if I can handle any more rejection. But as I book it in my squeaky sneakers, I hear a sound from behind me.

"*Awoo!*"

I glance over my shoulder to find all four of them calling out the same way. "*Awoo! Awoo!*"

What the fuck? My brain shorts out for a second. They're *howling*? Who does that?

Oh, I get it. They're teasing me. Mocking me.

My face burning, I run away as fast as I can, their howls echoing in the air behind me.

I still haven't recovered from my run-in with the landscaping crew when I make it back home. My legs are trembling, and whether it's from how hard I pushed them or from my anxiety, I don't know.

I hop in the shower, change quickly and head off to work, still thinking about their huge, shirtless bodies, complete with curly, dark hair. They weren't bus stop advertisement models. They were *men*.

My chest constricts. I've never had someone howl at me before, but leave it to the opposite sex to get creative about being shitty. Tomorrow, I'm going to find a different route. Who knows how long they'll be there, working on that yard project? I'll just avoid it until I'm sure they're finished.

When I get to the office, Mr. Bosley is exceptionally irritated, though I did remember to pick up his coffee on my way into work. Around lunchtime, he comes out of his office, his cheeks red with fury.

"Did you take a call yesterday from Archie West?" he demands.

I blink. "No. No one by that name called."

"He says he did, but no one answered. Where were you?"

I was at my desk all day, even during lunch. I usually pack

some leftovers or order in so I don't have to leave the phone, because Mr. Bosley despises it when I miss a call, even on my lunch break.

"I was here," I answer meekly. Archie West must be lying, but there's no way I can tell my boss that. "I promise, I was here for the entire day, and I checked voicemail as soon as I came in."

Mr. Bosley sniffs the air like he'll be able to smell my dishonesty, and I doubt myself. Did I walk away from the desk yesterday? I suppose I did use the restroom, once in the morning and once in the afternoon, but I didn't see any missed calls.

"Now I have to call back and apologize," he snaps, surveying me from top to bottom. "Your makeup is smudged. Go clean up and come back when you can look a little more *professional*."

With that he returns to the office, and my face heats with shame. I must have been flustered this morning when I was getting ready for work. I run to the bathroom as fast as I can to fix it up, but when I get back to my desk, there's a missed call: ARCHIE WEST.

"God damn it," I whisper, ready to smash the phone into oblivion. Maybe I can still salvage this.

I quickly call back, and Archie's assistant answers.

"I'm so sorry I missed Mr. West's call," I tell her frantically. "Can I connect him to Mr. Bosley right now?"

There's a pause before she answers. "Yes. I'll pretend the line got disconnected."

I sigh with deep relief. "Thank you." I announce to Mr. Bosley that Mr. West is on the line, and the assistant patches me through.

That afternoon, as badly as I have to use the restroom, I

don't leave my desk. I know it's not healthy, but I can't risk losing this job.

By the time it's closing time, I snag my purse and sprint to the bathroom as fast as I can, clenching every muscle so I don't pee myself.

I'll have to start drinking less water, I guess.

Chapter Two

I PLEDGED TO SPARE MYSELF THE HUMILIATION AND AVOID THE landscapers, but the next morning, I'm simmering with frustration and ready to pick a fight. I may not be able to say what I really feel to Mr. Bosley, because he controls my paycheck, but I don't owe those shirtless fuckers anything. I deserve to run wherever I want without fearing harassment. And if they howl at me again, I'll call them out. Maybe, if I confront them, they'll back off and shut up. Most men have big mouths but turn into weak little puppies when someone actually stands up to them.

Taking my usual route, I reach the house with the torn-up front yard and find the landscaping truck parked outside again. All four men are digging in the dirt. Once more, the tallest one is shirtless, his tanned body shining in the early morning light with sweat. In addition to the hair on his chest, today I notice he has thick, dark stubble on his chin, too.

Fuck me, he's hot. It's not fair that he's also an asshole.

I focus my gaze straight ahead as I approach, maintaining my normal jogging speed. From the corner of my eye, though,

I notice all four of them look up when I pass, and their mouths drop open.

Shit. Here it comes.

"*Awoo!*" one calls out. When I glance over, they're all staring at me intently. Each of them howls again. "*Awoo! Awoo!*"

I halt as angry heat spreads from my chest into my head. How dare they? Don't I get to exist in the world, to go for a simple jog, and not be afraid of some strangers making fun of me?

I turn around, letting that ferocity fill me up, and stalk over to them. The tallest of the landscapers smiles as I approach and drops his shovel.

"Hey!" I snap. "What the fuck is your problem?"

The grin falls from his face.

"Problem?" he asks, glancing over at the other three men with confusion. "We don't have a problem."

One of the other guys—shorter, with a wide, beefier chest—tips his baseball cap at me. "Well, we have one minor problem," he chimes in with a sultry voice. "There's a beautiful woman distracting us while we're on a deadline."

His gaze travels from my collar down to my waist, then my shoes and back up again. He looks almost... hungry.

I cover myself reflexively, realizing just how much of my big boobs my sports bra shows. Suddenly I feel incredibly exposed, which makes me angrier.

"You're disgusting," I tell him, and he flinches with surprise. "I'm out here just minding my own business, and you think it's okay to harass me?"

The short one's brow furrows. "I'm sorry," he says to me, holding up his hands. "We didn't mean to—"

"Then why the hell are you *howling*?" I interrupt. At the perplexed look on his face, though, my anger flags. He really doesn't understand why I'm upset.

11

"Because we can smell you," another guy says. He has a puka shell necklace hanging from his neck. "And, um... you smell incredible."

At this, all of them nod at once, as if this is obvious.

For a moment, I don't know what to say. They can *smell* me from that distance? Isn't that worse? I sniff my armpits, and sure, I'm sweaty, but my deodorant is doing its job.

The tall one chuckles. "Not like that," he says in a placating tone, but now all I can think about is how much I must reek.

I always take a shower after I run, but what if I smell like that in the office, too? Did I eat something I shouldn't have? Now Mr. Bosley is going to have yet something else to jump on me about.

My breathing speeds up as I look around at their four faces. It's horrifying that they could pick up my scent that far away. Surely they think I'm disgusting.

"I'm sorry," says the one who's remained silent until now. He's skinnier than the others but just as hot, with low-hanging jeans that show off the sleek muscle winding down from his hip to his groin. "We didn't mean to offend you, but you really do smell great."

All of them nod in agreement. This conversation isn't going how I expected. Here I am, surrounded by four incredibly hot guys who all seem to agree they like the way I *smell*.

The tall one, who has shockingly blue eyes, takes another tentative step forward. This time, though, I hold my ground. I'm not going to let these assholes intimidate me. But now, faced with someone so big, I'm breathing too fast—much too fast. The world is swimming.

"Are you all right?" he asks, leaning down to look in my face. I can barely bring air into my lungs, and my heart is racing so fast I think it might escape my chest.

"She clearly isn't," snaps the skinny guy. He appears at the front of the group and puts a gentle hand on my elbow. "You should sit down." I shouldn't be letting this strange man lead me anywhere, but all my focus is on trying to breathe. He guides me to the back of the truck, where the gate to the bed is down. "Here."

I stumble back until I'm sitting on it, and he doesn't let go of my hand—which I didn't even realize he was holding. The other three guys all crowd around me, but the skinny guy waves them off.

"Give her some space," he growls, and maybe it's just the haze, but it sounds like a dog's growl. "She's having some kind of attack."

"Asthma?" asks the younger man with the puka shell necklace.

"Heat stroke," says the short guy in the baseball cap.

"Shut up!" The skinny one rubs the back of my hand with his thumb. "Try to take deep breaths rather than short ones, okay?"

I focus on the words. *Deep rather than short.* I try to bring the air all the way in, even though my throat is fighting it, and then let it back out again.

"I'm Eli," the man says as I close my eyes, trying to focus. "And I'm right here, okay?"

Slowly my diaphragm relaxes, and I can almost breathe properly. When I look up, there are four huge, chiseled dudes hovering over me, all of them looking quite worried.

"I'm fine," I squeak out, pulling my hand away out of the skinny guy's grip and sliding off the truck bed. First they howled at me, and now I'm having one of those *attacks* in front of them. Great start to the day so far!

But they're being so kind to me. No one has made fun of me, or told me to just get it together. Eli's concerned face makes my heart beat faster again, but for a totally different reason.

I should probably go before anything else happens and I make an idiot of myself. When I get to my feet, the tallest guy lets out a heavy, charged breath.

"Damn," he murmurs, almost like he's drugged. "You really do smell good."

"Leon," snaps the shorter guy in the baseball cap. "You're not helping our case." He looks up at me. "I'm sorry about him. This doof really doesn't know how to talk to women at all."

"As if you do," Leon shoots back.

"Ignore them," Eli says. "We should have introduced ourselves properly before. We already met."

He holds out his hand to me a second time in a more formal handshake. Against my better judgment, I reach out and accept it. Eli squeezes my fingers, and his grip is firmer than I expected. His eyes are brown, but heated and intense. Damn. He has a carved face, with broad cheekbones, a square jaw and a significant chin.

Finally, he releases me and gestures at the other two. They both have earnest, eager looks on their faces.

"That one's Jace." The short guy with the cap nods politely. "That's Quinn." The last one, with the puka necklace, gives me a wide grin. "And you met my idiot big brother, Leon."

The tall guy with the blue eyes clasps his hands in front of him.

"It's wonderful to meet you," he says, without a trace of sarcasm. "I'm sorry for acting like an idiot. What's your name?"

My mouth bobs open and closed. I think there's a chance I misjudged these guys.

"Um," I manage. "I'm Tiffany. Tiff for short. I hate being

called Tiffany, actually." My lack of oxygen has gone straight to my brain.

"Tiff," Leon says, letting the word slide off his tongue. God, even the way he says my name is hot. "I'd like to apologize if we made you feel self-conscious. We just..."

"Are you seeing anyone?" The younger-looking one named Quinn interjects, stepping out in front of Leon. "Would you be interested in going on a date with me?"

I gape at him. What on earth? That came out of nowhere.

Then a creeping anger comes over me. Is that what this all boils down to after all? They just want a piece of ass?

I take a step back and put my hands up. "No. Absolutely not." I give all four of them a dark look. They were never worried about me. They just see me as meat. "I have to get to work."

Leon elbows Quinn hard in the side. "Asshole. You're scaring her off."

"You shouldn't move so soon after—" Eli begins, trying to stop me from leaving.

I shove him away, furious. I don't wait around for anything else to happen before I turn on my heel and take off at a jog back toward home, running much faster than my usual speed.

"Tiff!" one of the men calls to me. As gorgeous as they are, now I know that they're also total creeps.

They don't come after me as I head home, sweating profusely from how hard I'm pushing myself. I promise not to go down that street again tomorrow.

I'm still trembling in the shower, frantically cleaning off whatever those guys smelled on me.

I've had those kinds of attacks before, usually after work,

thinking about things Mr. Bosley did that day or how I might disappoint him the next day. I hate the way my throat closes up so tight I can't breathe and it feels like my heart is about to explode out of my chest.

Today might have been the first time, though, that someone has ever talked me through it. Usually I sit in the bathroom alone, desperately fighting for air as sobs wrack my body. But Eli's hand had been so warm and comforting in mine, his voice so steady and reassuring, that I'd recovered much faster than I usually do.

I groan as I try to get my makeup right with my shaking hands. Finally, I head to the office, making sure I have enough time to stop off at the coffee shop on my way.

Mr. Bosley has nothing to say to me as I deposit it at his desk. Every once in a while, I think how nice it would be to hear a "thank you," but there's no chance I'd ever get that from him.

We're placing new orders today, so I try to put all my attention on adding up wholesale costs. But I keep thinking about this morning instead.

It was so bizarre, I still feel like it was a dream. Why had all four of them looked like they were hypnotized? Am I emitting some kind of pheromone that only landscapers respond to?

Mr. Bosley can't stand it when I'm idling for even a moment, so while he's in the office, I try to look busy. But today he has a lunch meeting, so I finally get a moment to relax.

For the next hour, I think about asking the girls from accounting if what happened was as weird as I think it was, but they probably wouldn't believe me. *You got hit on by four smokin' hot guys at once?* Now that I say it to myself, it feels like the world's tackiest humble-brag.

I have all the numbers ready to present when Mr. Bosley comes back from his lunch meeting, but he's absolutely infuriated and waves me off dismissively. He's pink all over, even down his neck. "Cancel my 1:30 appointment, Ms. Dockett. I have *things* I need to deal with."

"Oh, of course—" But before I can even finish talking, he slams his door closed.

I blink at air. What happened at his lunch meeting?

After postponing his appointment, I hear Mr. Bosley's raised voice booming inside his office. He runs his own small heating and plumbing empire, the "tri-county destination for your HVAC needs." It's working for him, given the Tesla he drives in to work every day, but the business isn't usually so stressful.

After obsessing all afternoon, I text my friends Hannah and Aisling to meet me for drinks—if just to get my mind off of things. They usually have interesting stories to tell about their coworkers at their tech company, one of those places that has work-sanctioned beer nights and free kombucha on tap. We exchange a few messages, and they agree to meet up at our favorite place for chicken wings and beer. Maybe this is just the thing I need.

It's always good to see my high school friends again, even if we've found ourselves in very different places in life. We met when we were fourteen, and they've been my support network ever since.

Once our hands are all covered in hot sauce and our first round is gone, I tell them the story of the landscapers.

"Ew," Hannah says with a grimace. "They were working on a fancy house and *howled* at you? What the fuck does that mean?"

Aisling rolls her eyes. "Men are so gross. It doesn't matter where, they're still gonna be gross."

"Then one of them asked me out," I say. "And I knew what they wanted."

My friends cringe at the same time.

"Disgusting," Hannah says. "Can't even leave a girl alone to exercise."

Then we spend the rest of the night talking about all the nasty things men have done to us over the years. We've all given up on online dating. The last time I went out with someone, it was with Chris. He'd acted so sweet on our first date and was fabulous at pretending to care about my life. At the end of the night, we hooked up, and he didn't even attempt to make me orgasm. Once he was finished, he put all his clothes back on and left my apartment before I could even get his number.

"They just want the T-and-A," says Hannah, scowling. "One and done. Assholes."

When it starts to get late, Aisling and Hannah say goodnight, but I decide to stick around for another drink and take an Uber home. I'll just jog back this way in the morning to get my car, and then I can avoid the landscapers. Maybe I should start running in the evening, or pick another place farther from my apartment.

I'm plotting an alternative route while I toss back my drink, when I hear a familiar voice from down the bar.

"Tiff?"

Chapter Three

I LOOK UP TO FIND ONE OF THE LANDSCAPERS SITTING AT A BAR stool, a foaming beer in his hand. It's Jace, the short one with the baseball cap. Well, shorter than the others, who were all fucking giants. He's got a shirt on this time, thankfully, not that it's doing anything to disguise how his bulky chest stretches the fabric to its limits.

"Damn it," I mutter. I just spent my day trying to forget about these dudes, and now there's one sitting here next to me. "Seriously? I can't get rid of you."

I get up out of my seat, ready to go find a new table elsewhere. I don't need one of these creeps making a move on me right now. Maybe this is my sign I should've gone home already.

"Shit, I'm sorry," Jace says, standing up and grabbing his beer. He looks deeply apologetic as he backs away. "My bad. I didn't even see you there until I sat down." He gestures to the big restaurant behind him. "I'll go find another place to sit."

Jace adjusts his baseball cap to hide his eyes and walks away.

Great. Now I feel like a dickhead. This is a neighborhood bar, and he has every right to be here, too.

"Wait," I call out. Jace pauses, then glances back at me, a tiny spark of hope on his face. "We can both sit at the bar. It's not like I own it."

He hovers uncertainly, like he's trying to be polite by leaving but actually wants to sit.

"It's fine," I reiterate. If I'm uncomfortable, I can always go myself.

Finally, he acquiesces and returns to the bar top. As I take a sip of beer, Jace obediently keeps his own eyes straight ahead and doesn't try to talk to me. He flips over the menu in his hands like he's not really reading it.

The guy seems nice, if a little awkward. It's endearing, actually, how much he's trying to give me space.

Maybe I was too hard on them today.

"Hey," I say eventually. Startled, Jace turns to me. "You seem, um, normal. Normal-ish. So maybe you can explain to me what happened this morning?"

His dark eyes are wide and bright, like I've made his day just by talking to him.

"Oh, yeah! I can try to explain, anyway." He runs a hand through his hair. "We didn't realize we were being creeps until you called us out. And Quinn's the youngest, so he's impulsive. He didn't mean anything bad by it."

"The youngest?" I ask. "Like the youngest guy at your company?"

Jace blinks. "Company? No. The youngest of the brothers." He taps his chest. "I'm the second oldest. Leon's the oldest. Eli is right below me, and Quinn is the baby." With a snort, he adds, "And he acts like it."

Suddenly, so much more makes sense. They look alike

because all four of them are brothers. "So it's a family busi-ness?" I ask, sipping the last of my drink.

"Yeah. We inherited it from our dad when he retired. I'm almost positive my parents had four sons on purpose so he wouldn't have to keep hiring out for more guys."

I chuckle at this. Maybe these brothers aren't so bad. Just... very odd. "So do the four of you, uh, ever interact with women?"

Jace snorts. "Honestly, it's a fair question after today." He tilts his head and frowns apologetically. "I'm really, really sorry. I know that doesn't change things, but I promise, I didn't mean to be an asshole."

I arch an eyebrow at him. "You could have just said hello instead of, I don't know. Howling." Not to mention all that weird shit about me *smelling good*.

Jace abruptly straightens, then holds out his hand.

"Hello," he says. "I'm Jace. It's good to meet you the way normal people meet each other."

His expression is very serious, so I take his hand and shake it.

"Hi." I try to hold in a laugh. "I'm Tiff."

"Hi, Tiff." Jace releases me but slides his fingers through mine on the way. "Can I buy you your next beer?"

I finally let out my giggle, because he's making a sweet attempt. Maybe it wouldn't be so bad to talk to him more. Jace is easy to look at, and I like his good humor so far. "All right. I'll allow it."

Jace calls over the bartender and I tell her what I want. While it's being poured, Jace gives me his full attention.

"So, tell me everything," he says. "I want to know who Tiff is."

I appreciate that Jace doesn't ask about the panic attack I had in the back of the Lupine Landscaping truck. We have a surprisingly comfortable chat about our parents and where we grew up. My childhood was very uninteresting, until Dad suddenly moved across the country to live with some woman he'd met online. Oh, and I was bullied in school for being on the bigger side, but I don't tell him that part.

It sounds like Jace and his brothers come from a pretty average home. They broke a lot of stuff growing up, and they shared two bedrooms among them.

"Not to mention all of our toys, all of our clothes," he says, rolling his eyes. "Poor Quinn always got the clothes last, and by then they were a mess."

"It's cute that you guys shared, though."

Jace hums thoughtfully as he sips his beer. "What about your job?" he asks after a while. "What do you do for work, Tiff?"

It's such a benign question, but it disrupts all the happy feelings I'd been having just chatting with him.

"I'm an assistant," I say, trying to hide my resentment. "Personal assistant. I manage some guy's appointments. Answer the phone. Bring him coffee. Take care of his finances." I can't help but laugh bitterly. "Everything you can think of, I do it."

Jace is quiet at this. I know my job is boring, but he could at least pretend it's not.

"Sounds like you don't particularly love it," he finally says. His dark eyes are inquisitive, not judgmental. I take another long sip of my beer. It's my fourth one, so the alcohol's starting to go to my head. Maybe that's why I let the truth slip out.

"I hate it," I admit. "I go home every day and wish I could

quit. Then maybe pour some gasoline into Mr. Bosley's coffee on my way out."

Jace laughs in the middle of taking a drink and chokes on it. After a few coughs, he smiles at me. "You should quit, then."

"I wish, but I don't have a choice. I'm doing the only thing I'm good at: filing, keeping things organized, tracking vendors —you know, boring stuff."

"Those are all pretty useful skills," Jace says, brow furrowing. "You should see how we run our office. It's a fucking disaster. None of us has any idea about filing or billing or whatever. We do everything in cash."

My eyes bulge out of my head. "Do you record your payments? Are you even paying taxes on them?"

He looks at me blankly. *Oh, no.*

"This is what I'm saying," Jace goes on. "People like you, who know how to run things, are really valuable." He offers me a sympathetic smile. "I'm sorry you feel that way about your job."

I shrug. "That's life. I didn't have these, um, *attacks*, until I started working for Mr. Bosley."

I shiver at exposing this part of myself to a relative stranger. But talking with Jace tonight, well, he doesn't feel like one.

"Like this morning?" There's a dark frown on his face. "That's messed up, Tiff. You shouldn't have to feel that way about a job."

I pull my shoulders protectively up to my neck. It's not like I have a choice in the matter. I have no education, like Mom is always reminding me, and I get good healthcare. So I steer the conversation back to the landscaping company and ask Jace how he likes working outside all day.

"I love it," he confesses. "The fresh air, the sun and the sweat? I could never function in an office."

I have to admit the rest of my evening is enjoyable, and I

stay much too late at the bar getting to know Jace better. He's never inappropriate—not even his hand wanders when I pick up my purse and move to the barstool next to him.

Strangely, though, I wish he would make a move. He's thick and stocky, like he could pick me up without trying too hard. His dark hair has a cute wave to it. When the bartender tells us it's last call, Jace pays the bill, even for my wings earlier.

"It's the least I can do for the way we all treated you. Plus, that job on Work Street is paying well enough."

A warm feeling bubbles up inside me. "Thank you."

When we get up, I almost expect him to invite me back to his place. Would I want that if he did?

I call an Uber, and Jace insists on waiting with me for it to show up. I think I like him. I think I'm disappointed he didn't try to do more tonight. But maybe he's not interested in me like that, and this was just a very kind apology.

Still, I can't help but feel there's more to it. Am I imagining that electric energy between us, something that feels bigger than just politeness?

The Uber finally pulls up, but I signal to the driver to hold on. I want to know if Jace is vibing with me the way I am with him.

"Jace?" I ask.

A grin lights up his face. "Yeah?"

"Do you want to, um... do this again?"

He has a hopeful look that reminds me of a puppy. "Yes! I mean, yes, if you do." He takes my hand in his. "Tiff, would you go out on a date with me?"

A pulse of excitement radiates out from the place he's holding my hand. "I would love to."

There's plenty of beer coursing through my veins right now, so I don't think twice before I rise on my toes and kiss him. I probably should have asked first, but it suddenly doesn't seem like a problem when Jace wraps his arms fiercely around my waist, pulling me against him.

He doesn't try to stick his tongue down my throat like the last guy I went out with. Instead, he tastes my lower lip, taunting it, savoring it. His thick body, with that strong chest and taut belly, presses against mine, and it triggers a mountain of filthy thoughts. I wonder what he would feel like without clothes between us?

His hand travels down my back, pausing just above my ass, and I wish he'd venture even lower. Heat bubbles up inside me, ready to boil over the top. It feels like both forever and only a second passes before he pulls away. I'm breathing heavily, and I can feel the impatience rolling off my Uber driver.

Eventually, I slide into the car, but Jace takes out his phone.

"Number?" he asks. I hastily list it off to him through the open window, and he gives me his before the car drives off.

When I finally make it home, my whole body is buzzing. That was only a taste, a hint, of what could happen between us, and I'm intoxicated by the idea of what might happen next. I'd love to breathe in even more of that wonderful scent of his, to feel those hands wander over the rest of my body.

I wonder whether he'll make an advance next time we go out. Would a guy as sweet, sexy, and smart as Jace want to go all the way with me?

By the time I get in bed, I can't think about anything but Jace shirtless and sweating under the morning sun. I wonder what it would be like if he were on top of me, how his bare skin would feel under my hands. If his kiss was any indication, he knows what to do with his mouth and tongue—and that triggers even filthier daydreams. I imagine his lips wrapped around my nipple or, even better, around my clit.

My hips rock at the thought, and I know what I have to do if I'm going to get any sleep tonight. When I pull out my vibrator, I imagine the long shaft is Jace's instead. What would his cock look like? While picturing him kneeling between my legs, I lube up the vibrator and gently work it through my swollen, wet folds. All it takes is closing my eyes to see Jace there, sliding inside me.

I'm halfway to my orgasm before I can blink, ripples of pleasure echoing across my body. In my fantasy, Jace leans down to kiss me, just like he did tonight. I push the vibrator deeper and stroke it in and out, just like I imagine Jace would fuck me. But where the toy is hard and unforgiving, he would be soft and thick in all the right ways.

Fuck. All my muscles go tight as a drawn string as I climb higher and higher until finally, I break. I'm glad I have my apartment to myself as I can't hold in a sharp cry. This is better than any orgasm I've had in a long time.

I withdraw the vibrator, panting, and lie there boneless for a good few minutes. Jeez, I only *kissed* Jace and I'm already thinking about him like this? I'm hopeless. And maybe desperate.

Feeling a shadow of shame that I just masturbated while thinking about a guy I barely know, I clean the toy in the sink and put it away, then climb into bed, wondering what it would feel like to curl up next to him under the blankets after he fucked me silly.

I hope I get to find out.

Chapter Four

I'm a whirlwind of emotions the following day. Going to get my car at the bar means no time for a regular run, but I don't mind. All my anxiety has been replaced by a seed of thrill that, while small, is growing quickly, and it has my blood running hot.

I can't wait to see Jace again.

I don't tell Aisling and Hannah what happened last night, not after all my ranting about the brothers. Instead, I hoard my secret over the weekend, eagerly anticipating a text message or a call from Jace. I don't hear from him by Monday, but I assume he's busy having fun with his brothers.

He's all I can think about as I try to focus on work. Mr. Bosley jumps on mistakes like a fox on a mouse, and the last thing I need is for him to bring down my good mood. By the time work ends, though, I still haven't heard from Jace. I find I'm disappointed, even though it's only been a few days. It seemed like we had something, but now I'm not so sure. I'm probably just being insecure and should give him time to reach out to me.

Still, I've been ghosted so many times, it also wouldn't surprise me if I never heard from him again.

On my drive home, I find myself passing the landscaping project on Work Street. Maybe I'm just hoping to see Jace, and he'll tell me he's been busy but wants to take me out again. I want to feel his lips on mine again—and maybe, if I'm lucky, even more of him.

I hope he doesn't think it was a mistake to kiss me.

To my surprise, the Lupine Landscaping truck is still parked out front of the huge house, but only one of the brothers appears to be working. It's getting late, and surely he's been at it for ten hours now. He must be exhausted.

I slow down when I drive by, wondering which one of them it is. The man working glances up at my car, and when he sees me in the driver's window, he grins. It's Leon, the oldest one, with the bright blue eyes. They're stark against his dark hair and tan complexion.

He waves at me and jogs over, so now I feel compelled to stop. I shouldn't have come past here. Now who knows what kind of awkward conversation I'm in for?

"Tiff!" Leon's got his shirt on this time, but it's soaked with sweat stains. I've never found sweat stains hot before, but here we are. His broad chest strains the fabric perfectly, and it cuts off just above his jeans, so I can see dark hair trailing down his groin. Holy shit.

When he gets close to the window, I have to admit that strangely, he smells good, too. Really good. It's obviously body odor, which probably should disgust me—but on him, damn. The scent of him wafting into my car is like a drug that immediately fills up my head with warm, airy bubbles.

"What'cha doing here?" Leon asks, leaning casually on the door of my car.

I try to play it cool. "Just heading home for the night."

"Do you live in this neighborhood?"

As if I could. I shake my head and point down the street. "No, I'm over in the apartment building across the road."

Leon leans in farther through my open window with a knowing grin on his face, and that intoxicating smell of his completely envelopes me. "Too bad you're not on foot, because I'd love to walk you home. And apologize for the other day."

I wave a hand dismissively and offer him a smile. "It's fine. I don't hold it against you."

"I'd still like to get to know you better," he says, an almost wicked tone to his voice. And then he *winks*.

Is Leon... hitting on me? Did Jace not tell his brothers we saw each other?

"Um," I say, not sure how to broach this subject. "Did you talk to Jace today?"

Leon squints like he doesn't understand the question. "Yes? We worked all day together."

"Did he tell you that, uh, we..." Shit. Maybe he kept it a secret from them on purpose and now I'm sticking my foot in it.

"Jace told us he met you last night at the bar," Leon says, a quirk in his eyebrow. "Is that what you're asking?"

I breathe a sigh of relief. So he knows. That's a good start.

"He also told us," Leon goes on, his voice dropping low and his eyes going half-lidded, "that he got to taste you."

I stare at him blankly for a moment, processing the words. "What?" I finally ask, my voice cracking. I'm not sure if I heard him right. Who refers to kissing as *tasting*? And Leon said it with such a seductive lilt that I'm tingling. "I... um..." I don't even know how to respond to that.

There's a twinkle in Leon's eye. "Did you like it?"

I swear my face is about to light on fire. What an extremely personal question—and from Jace's *brother*, no less. I'm so flustered I can barely squeeze out an answer.

"Y-yes?" I manage. Not that it's any of his business how much I enjoyed kissing Jace. But Leon doesn't seem uncomfortable at all, not nearly as uncomfortable as I feel right now.

"Good." He leans even closer, and the scent of him rushes into my head—then straight down to the empty space between my legs. Holy shit. He smells *amazing.* "Are you busy tonight?"

I'm genuinely speechless. Is he asking me out? This just keeps getting weirder.

"I thought I would have plans," I begin uneasily, "but Jace didn't text or call."

Leon nods, as if he already knows this information. "I told him it wasn't time yet. And I'm the big brother, so he listens to me."

My heart drops. "You told him not to call me?" Why would he do that? Now I'm annoyed that he interfered, and a little disappointed. Jace is his own person who can make his own choices, so why would he let his brother tell him what to do when it comes to his dating life?

"Jace will call," Leon reassures me. "He's very interested. Now, about the two of us going out." He tilts his head. "Do you like Lucky's? I'd love to buy you dinner."

I wonder if Leon's even heard half of our conversation.

"If I want to date Jace," I say hesitantly, "then I shouldn't also go on a date with his brother." This should be obvious, but apparently it's not.

A massive smile takes over Leon's face. "So you *do* want to go with me?" he asks, and I think if he were a dog, his tail would be wagging. "Jace is the only thing holding you back?"

Of course I want to go out with a sweet, hot guy like Leon. If I had a clone, I'd happily do it.

"I mean..." I begin, then trail off. I'm far too ashamed to say *yes*, even though I'd love to.

"Tiff." Leon's voice is firmer now. "I promise Jace doesn't mind if we go have a night on the town together. You can call him and ask, if you want."

I don't get it. This isn't how I was raised. One person dates one person, the end, over with. There's no "date one person and that person's brother, too."

Still, I find myself pulling out my phone anyway. If I call right now and Leon is wrong, then I'm potentially destroying whatever I had with Jace. Do I really want to risk it?

Leon gives me another one of his big grins, and it makes his full lips look quite kissable. "I think you'll be surprised by the answer you get."

His certainty is rather convincing. My heart racing, I give in and dial Jace's number.

I can't believe I'm doing this.

Jace picks up on the second ring. "Tiff." He says my name as if he's been expecting me.

I swallow hard, dreading what I'm about to ask. "Hi, Jace. I'm with Leon, and, um..." I take a deep breath. "He's telling me something wild. I don't know if I believe him."

"How wild?" Jace asks, an edge to his voice.

"Well..." I trail off. How do I even bring this up? "He says he wants to take me out, on a... uh, on a date?"

Jace breathes a sigh of relief. "Oh, that's all?" He asks this as if it's one of the less surprising things he's heard today.

"He says you would be fine with that." I take a sharp breath. "That isn't true, right?"

"Leon's a great guy," Jace says, sounding upbeat and casual. "I really look up to him. Figuratively speaking. Though I suppose he is taller than I am."

"But?" I ask, waiting for the next part, where he tells me how ridiculous I am for even asking this question.

"No 'but.' I think he'd treat you well and show you a good time." Jace sounds so cavalier about it that it stirs a budding hurt in my chest.

"What about you, though?" I ask. Doesn't he want me just for himself?

Jace is quiet for a moment. Finally, he answers, "I want you to have fun." Now his tone is thick and sultry. "Get to know Leon a little, the way you got to know me."

I think of our kiss outside the bar, and how good his arms felt around me, his lips hungrily lapping up mine.

"What?" I ask hoarsely. "You want me to...?"

"I want you to do what *you* want to do, Tiff," Jace says with a powerful certainty. "Whatever that is, without worrying about me."

"You have to be kidding." Is it not enough that one hot guy expressed interest in me? Now I'm seriously considering two of them?

"I'm not. This could be your and Leon's night, just like we had our night last night. And I shouldn't keep you from it any longer."

I still don't believe what he's saying. "Jace—"

The phone goes dead. I stare down at it, then up at Leon. He looks expectant.

"Well?" he prompts.

"He told me to enjoy myself." I slip the phone back into my purse, still dazed. "Whatever that means."

"What do you want it to mean?" Leon asks. His blue eyes dance with mischief.

I don't know how to process this information. Somehow, for some bizarre reason, they're both interested in me. And they're fine with sharing me.

It's too much. I have no idea what to make of this situation.

"I can't do this." My hands are trembling now, and I feel like I'm caught in a storm. "I don't know what's going on with you two, but I have to go." The urge to flee is so strong, so overpowering, that I put my car's transmission into drive.

Leon's smile fades. "What's wrong?"

I can sense my heart starting to race, my throat tightening up. This is all too strange, too foreign, too... exciting. And I hate myself for wanting it.

My voice is trembling as I say, "Whatever you guys are after, I'm not going to be a part of it." I need to get out of here before I even consider Leon's offer.

"We're not after anything." He furrows his brow. "Well, except going on a date with a super-hot, sweet woman."

This must be some kind of alternate dimension. There's no way a drop-dead gorgeous guy like Leon really feels that way about me.

"Sorry." I put my foot on the gas. Leon jumps back as the car starts to move, surprise—and hurt—on his face. "I have to go."

"Wait!" he calls out, but I'm already driving away, my pulse racing. But there's also an ache in my belly, like I'm making a mistake.

I'm still shaking when I get home, thoroughly conquered by my tangled mess of emotions.

What Leon was asking me was crazy, right? I'm breathing hard as I toss my keys and purse on the table and flop down on my couch. I close my eyes and concentrate on slowing the racing of my pulse.

Unbidden, I imagine Eli's hand around mine. *Try to take*

deep breaths rather than short ones, he'd said. Focusing on those words, I suck in as far as I can, then let the air out again, willing my throat to open back up. I close my eyes and slowly, my breathing grows steadier again, my heart beating a little less frantically. I lie there prone, wondering what set me over the edge.

I'd wanted so badly to say *yes*, but the words stuck in my mouth. All I could think is what my mother would say, the way she would look at me. How would I explain it to Hannah and Aisling? It's just too ludicrous.

Still, Leon's scent, the playful tilt of his mouth, sticks with me. In a different world, with different rules, I would have happily agreed.

But that's not who I am. That's not the world we live in. Right?

Chapter Five

After staying up all night obsessing over Leon and Jace, I barely get into the office on time the following day. I had bags under my eyes when I put on my makeup this morning, and I look like a wilted plant.

I curse under my breath when I come in and find a stack of papers already waiting on my desk. I have a lot to do today, and I can't have my thoughts wandering to what I might have missed last night by turning Leon down.

Of course, on the one day I don't have the extra braincells, the invoices I need to process aren't adding up when I compare them to the orders I placed a few weeks ago. I want to ask Mr. Bosley, but he hates when I interrupt him for anything but a call or a visitor.

After two hours of trying to solve the problem, though, I give up and decide I have no choice.

"Mr. Bosley?" I ask, tapping lightly on his door. He looks up from his desk and glares daggers at me.

"What is it, Ms. Dockett?"

I pull my shoulders tight around my neck and clasp my

papers to my chest. "The invoices you gave me aren't matching what we ordered. Are there any missing?"

If looks could kill, I'd be dead and underground.

"There's nothing missing unless you lost it," he says, returning to his work pointedly. "Figure it out."

Great. I'll need to think of some way to reconcile these on my own. I nod quickly and speed out of his office, back to my desk.

I'm deep in recalculating the numbers when I hear a light knock.

"Hello?"

The door is slightly ajar, and the woman with the slick bun from before is peering inside. She knocks again, and I realize my mind is a blank space.

"I'm so sorry," I say, getting out of my chair to let her in. But the woman steps inside on her own and flutters a hand at me.

"Stay put. I can open a door. I just didn't want to surprise you."

I nod in thanks. "Mr. Bosley's in his office."

The woman's about to stride right past my desk when she stops and tilts her head down to me.

"You look... unwell," she says, arching an eyebrow.

Is it really that bad? I force a smile onto my face. "I feel fine. I promise, I won't get you sick or anything."

"Not like that." Now the woman is studying me carefully. "Boyfriend problems?"

I blink. "Huh?" How could she possibly know? Not that either of them is my boyfriend, but she's a little too close to the truth for comfort.

"Well, you have a look on your face like someone's in the doghouse," she says, then gestures at my hand. "No wedding ring, though." She leans against my desk, and I hope Mr. Bosley doesn't come out and chastise me for chatting up one of his visitors. He hates it when they stop to talk to me. *It's not your job*, he always says.

But the woman doesn't seem to notice my discomfort. "What did this person do to end up on your bad side?" she asks.

I can't possibly tell a complete stranger what happened last night. The woman has a very stern face, too, that sends a chill up my spine.

"Um..." I wring my hands together. "It's complicated."

She sighs and checks her watch. "I have time."

Maybe I should make something up—but I have the sense this intense person would see through me like I'm a piece of glass.

"I went on a date with this guy," I finally say, my gaze flicking up to hers and then away again when I see how sharp her eyes are. "And it went really well. But then the next day..." I feel my face flaming already. I don't want to divulge this information to a complete stranger, but her eyes are burrowing into me like drills. "His brother said he wants to date me, too."

At this, I finally get a reaction. Both her eyebrows lift ever so slightly, and she uncrosses her stiff arms.

"At the same time?" she asks, still cool and collected.

I nod hurriedly. "I said 'no,' of course. It's too weird."

"Too weird for whom?" The skeptical look has returned to her face. "For you? Or for society?"

The question takes me by surprise, and I don't answer for a moment. If I really think about it, what terrifies me most is what my mother would say—how she'd judge me. I couldn't possibly show up at her house with two boyfriends in tow. She'd eat me alive with just her eyes.

"Society, I guess," I finally say.

She *hmms*. "And you're going to let a broken, dysfunctional culture like ours tell you what to do?"

"Well, I—"

"Be another pawn of the system if you want." She lets her arms drop and turns away. "But it seems stupid to me to deny yourself because others *might* disapprove."

Without waiting for my response, the woman strides off into Mr. Bosley's office, opening the door without even knocking and then shutting it firmly behind her.

I stare at the space where she was standing a moment ago, like an abrupt storm just passed over and left me soaking wet in its wake. Part of me wishes I'd just told her to mind her own business, but another part of me wonders if she's right. What was it that really upset me about Leon's suggestion? That people would look at me differently? That they might disapprove?

I worry my lip between my teeth, thinking. Of course I wanted to say *yes*. Leon's gorgeous and charming, if a little awkward. He smelled so damn good, and that lopsided grin of his was devilishly handsome. Not to mention those strange blue eyes.

I have to admit that she's gotten into my head. So what if people disapprove? So what if my mom couldn't stand the idea? She hates everything about me, anyway.

I pull out my phone and text Jace.

> Can you give Leon a message for me?

The answer comes almost immediately.

> He's here, what would you like me to say?

I swallow hard and glance around, as if someone could be spying on me, before typing my answer.

I'd like to take him up on his offer

There's a long pause before I see the three dots pop up.

He's excited. He'll text you

My heart does a somersault. I still can't believe Jace is fine with this. His next message is even more surprising.

Have a good time. Look forward to seeing you soon!

It makes me feel warm all over, from my throat down to my thighs. Not a few moments later, my phone chimes again, and it's a number I don't recognize.

I'm really happy to hear from you ☺

It must be Leon. He quickly sends another one.

Do you want to meet me at Lucky's tonight?

I don't hesitate this time before answering.

Sounds good

6:30 work for you?

A little bubble of excitement floats to the top of all my stress and anxiety. I hastily type out my answer.

See you then!

I'm putting my phone away, a pleased smile on my face,

when the door to the office flies open. Mr. Bosley storms out, rattling the very floor like a herd of elephants.

"Ms. Dockett," he says thinly, like he's doing everything in his power not to grind his teeth. "Please schedule another appointment for…" He glances at the woman in the bun as she emerges from his office. "Mrs. Smith."

I'm startled by the obviously fake name, but I pull up his schedule, anyway. While Mr. Bosley returns to his office, "Mrs. Smith" and I figure out a good time for her to return, and then she walks out, just as calm and frosty as when she came in.

During my drive home, I'm on autopilot as I think about what I should wear, what color eyeshadow would offset it nicely, how I could do my hair. The other night, I'd already been in my work clothes when Jace saw me, so I didn't have an opportunity to prep. This time, with Leon, I really want to put my best foot forward—especially after speeding away in my car last night.

I feel a little overdressed when I walk into Lucky's. Leon's already waiting at a table in the back, wearing slacks and a collared shirt. I guess we'll both stand out like sore thumbs. But wow, the button-up looks almost as good on him as his tight work shirt did. His neck is almost too thick for the collar.

Leon gets up when I approach and waits for me to sit down on my side of the booth before he returns to the seat opposite. It's incredible how his blue eyes stand out against his dark hair and tan skin. There's almost something supernatural about them.

"So," he begins, leaning forward at the table. "Jace told us a little bit about you, but I'd like to know more."

More? I feel like I spilled everything to his brother already. There's not much else to learn about me.

"Like what?" I ask.

Leon props his chin on his hands. "Tell me about your parents, maybe?"

It's such a deep-dive question for just starting out that I'm taken aback. I'm not sure how much to say. Should I really confess that I hate seeing my mom because she makes me feel awful about myself every time? I shouldn't shit-talk my own mother in front of someone I just met.

"Hey, it's okay." Leon reaches out and runs a hand over my forearm. It's such a casual and open touch, but I find I don't mind it. "Any answer you give is the right answer, as long as it's honest. I'm not going to judge you."

I swallow hard, because opening this door means opening the door about how I look, too. How as much as I try to tell myself that I'm worthy and deserving, I'm still shocked that Jace showed interest in me in the first place—not to mention Leon.

With a deep breath, I dive headfirst into it. As I talk about my dinners with Mom every week, Leon listens without interrupting.

"I'm happy in my own skin," I say. "I just hate how Mom insists I shouldn't be. That I don't deserve it." I tug on the dress I'm wearing mournfully. "My mom would say, 'this barely fits you!'"

Leon's eyes travel down from my face to the collar of my dress, then back up again.

"I think it fits perfectly," he says, his nostrils flaring. Those big blue eyes are focused on me, and suddenly I feel very exposed, even though I picked a neckline that would cover me. "I'm sorry your mom makes you feel that way. I know you don't need me to tell you how gorgeous you are, but I admire how you don't let it get to you. It's important to know yourself and own it."

Is this really the same guy who howled at me on the street? He's so sincere, he must have really thought it was a compliment. What an adorable, endearing weirdo.

"I guess so," I say. "Sometimes she does still get to me. She's my mother, after all."

"Have you ever told her how you feel?"

I could simply laugh. "No. I don't think she'd take it very well."

"Of course not." Leon huffs. "Then she'd have to acknowledge that she hurts you regularly. And people never want to admit it when their words and actions hurt." He smiles apologetically. "Sorry to rant. I say that as someone who hurt you pretty recently."

It seems like he's really trying to make up for it now, though, so I offer him a smile.

"Water under the bridge," I say. "But I still don't understand the whole... smelling thing." Perhaps that's not true. Even under the scent of shampoo and deodorant, I can still get a whiff of Leon's natural scent from across the table—and goddamn, it's good.

His expression tightens. "It's a very important sense to us."

Is he saying it's a genetic thing? I'm about to ask more questions when he interrupts me.

"What do you say we get out of here?" Leon asks. "There's an arcade around the corner, and Thursday is nickel night. A lot of good, clean fun for cheap!"

I stare at him. He wants to go out on a date for fourteen-year-olds?

"Come on." He holds out one arm. "It'll be fun, I promise."

I suppose I could use some fun after the day I had, so I take his arm and nod. "All right. But I don't have any nickels."

"Don't worry." He winks. "It's on me."

Chapter Six

THE ARCADE IS GLOWING WHEN WE ARRIVE, BRIGHT NEON LIGHTS flashing behind the windows. There aren't many other people around when we walk in the front doors except a group of teenagers and some kids running around yelling while their mom chases them.

Leon takes my hand and leads me over to a pair of motorcycles. We sit astride them, and he pops some nickels into the machine. I'm utterly clueless about what I'm doing as we select our bikes, so I just pick the one that looks meanest.

"Oh, the Honda," Leon says with an approving nod. "Good choice."

Let's just say that I probably shouldn't get a motorcycle license. If I'm a terror behind the wheel of a car, it's a thousand times worse on a motorcycle. I crash into every conceivable wall, and even take out Leon a few times. I come in very last place, barely finishing the course before time runs out. He's laughing so hard by the end that he slips getting off his motorcycle.

"All right, let's try a different game, huh?" He glances down at my feet and gives an approving nod when he finds I'm wearing a pair of simple black flats. "Dancing?"

I squint at him. "Dancing? We're at an arcade."

"I know." Again, he takes my hand in his, twining our fingers together. It reminds me of being one of those teenagers on a first date. "Come on. It'll be fun."

I work up a decent sweat trying to figure out the dancing game, where I have to step on the buttons on the dance pad in time with the screen. My feet have no idea what to do, and it's the second time I've looked like an idiot in front of Leon. He's barely winded from the long round we just did, where I frantically tried to step on the right arrows.

But when I glance at him from the side of my eye to see if he's laughing, he's just looking at me with that intense blue stare of his.

"Do I have something on my face?" I ask, rubbing my cheek surreptitiously.

"No." The side of his wide mouth turns up in a grin. "You're just really gorgeous."

He steps off the dance pad and then offers to help me down, and his earnest compliment has made my legs a little shaky, so I accept.

"Don't take this the wrong way," he says, his eyes crinkled with amusement, "but you're really bad at video games. It's adorable."

I wonder what other possible way I could take that. Leon's a little clueless sometimes, which I have to admit I find cute, too.

"I never got to play video games growing up," I say. "Mom said they 'weren't good for developing brains.' Some of my friends had them, but I only ever got to watch them play." Now that I think about it, that's probably why I thought coming to the arcade wouldn't be fun. I dealt with the fact I didn't get to have a Wii as a kid by convincing myself video games weren't cool.

"Huh." Leon cocks his head. "So she's always been kind of controlling?"

I guess I hadn't thought about it. "Mom thought I should spend my time doing homework instead." I can't help but laugh. "You can imagine how mad she was when I dropped out of college."

Leon shrugs. "I didn't go to college and I turned out okay." He leans thoughtfully on one of the claw machines, which is full to bursting with stuffed animals. "There are lots of different paths to take in life."

I like that outlook. It makes me feel like less of a failure, seeing as he runs his own successful business.

I'm surprised when Leon drops a hand to my thigh, and he runs his thumb over my jeans. "I'm glad we can come here and play games together, then. We'll train you up real quick." He jerks his thumb over his shoulder toward a different part of the arcade. "Let's try some Skee-Ball?"

The longer we play, the closer I find myself getting to Leon— or he's getting closer to me. Or perhaps we're gravitating toward each other like magnets, because that's what this feels like: getting pulled in until I don't want to leave again. Just being near him, my skin tingles, imagining his touch on me again.

It turns out I'm fantastic at Skee-Ball. I have just the flick of the wrist I need to sink the ball in the middle hole every time, and we win half a roll of tickets. Leon looks at me like I'm a brand-new woman as we head to the front counter to take a look at the prizes.

"It's that hand-eye coordination," he says, mostly to himself. "Dang. I bet you'd be killer at Frisbee."

The attendant looks bored when Leon approaches, all smiles.

"Teddy bear or Nerf gun?" he asks me, counting up the tickets. "Or you could buy a dozen of those ring pops."

"Ring pop," I answer instantly, and Leon snorts as he hands the tickets over.

"Get the lady every ring pop I can afford," he says in an imperious tone.

Once I've got a whole armful, Leon takes my free hand. He uses it to draw me closer to him, until we're almost touching, and leans down.

"Tiff." I've never thought my name sounded sexy until now, until Leon says it that way. He reaches under my chin and tilts it up, so I'm staring right into those bright blue eyes. His mouth is just inches away from mine now, and I think...

I think he wants to kiss me.

"Leon," I answer cheekily, and he laughs. I roll onto the balls of my feet, so we're even closer together, hoping that he's feeling the same thing I am, this warm electricity between us.

In response, he presses his lips against mine.

I'm surprised to find Leon's touch is tentative and uncertain. So I kiss him back harder, showing him what I want: more. His arm tightens around my waist and then, suddenly, his tongue is tracing the seam of my lips. I let him inside, and as he slips into my mouth, he grunts in approval. I get sucked up into the whirlwind of his kiss, floating in it as our tongues weave around each other. Every single thing vanishes in that moment—my mom, Mr. Bosley, all the ways in which I don't feel right for this world.

Damn, he's a good kisser.

"A-*hem*," says a voice, and we instantly pull apart. The clerk is tapping a finger on the counter in annoyance. He gestures at the kids playing a shooting game nearby, who are unabashedly staring at us.

"What would you like to do next?" Leon asks me, steering us into a dark booth meant for playing a zombie game. "Because we could stay here and have a milkshake, or get a drink and talk all night. Or..."

The muscles in my abdomen clench at that *or*.

"Or what?" I ask, my voice coming out a squeak.

He arches one eyebrow. "Or we could leave."

"And go where?" I don't know why I ask the question when I already know the answer by the goofy, eager look on Leon's face.

"What if we went to your place?" He smooths his thumb across the back of my hand. "Then it's on your turf. You can do whatever you want, and you can ask me to leave whenever you need."

I live in a small, one-bedroom apartment on the third floor that's nothing to look at. The paint is peeling, and the water pressure is garbage. But taking Leon back there, where we can be alone, is marvelously attractive.

"Okay," I say finally, and Leon lights up. "No judging, though. It's the cheapest rent I could find."

He guides me to the exit, his fingers finally sliding down to cup my ass as we head outside. "I'll be much too preoccupied to notice."

Out front, while I open my car door, Leon stops at a motorcycle parked two spaces over. "I'll follow you."

Why am I not surprised by the fact this incredibly hot guy also drives a motorcycle?

I get in my car and head back to my place, turning over in my mind what might happen next. What do I *want* to happen next?

My thrill at having Leon following me home, so we can be alone in my apartment together, begins to morph. What if once he gets me undressed, he doesn't like what he sees? My hands clench tighter around the wheel. What if I'm not good in bed, because it's been too long? I stopped trying to online date last year, and I'm probably out of practice.

What if, what if?

By the time we reach the parking lot, my breaths are coming faster and I wonder if this is really a good idea. Leon might be here for one thing, just like Chris, just like all those other assholes before him. I'm great for a one-night stand, for getting your fill of tits and ass. Maybe Leon showed me a good time and treated me like a princess only so he could get my clothes off, and then he doesn't intend to call again.

And Jace! I met Jace first. Now I'm standing outside my apartment with some other guy—his *brother*.

I head to the stairs that lead up to the third floor, while Leon hangs his helmet off the handlebars of his bike. Briefly, I consider texting Jace again. Does he know? What if he's disgusted when he hears I slept with Leon?

I must be showing what I'm feeling plain on my face, because Leon's expression falls as he approaches me.

"Having second thoughts?" he asks, rubbing a hand down my shoulder. "It's okay if you're not ready yet."

The words are so genuine that it makes my heart swell up.

Someone like Leon... I don't think he's going to one-and-done me. Not after tonight.

"I'm ready," I say, putting as much certainty into it as I can.

His grin is wide and exuberant. He curls his arm around my hip and pulls me into him, and I'm surprised to find a lump in his jeans press against my thigh.

"God. You smell so good." He lowers his head to my hair and brings in a deep whiff. "So fucking good."

His hands are wandering, and I want even more of them. When I look up, I find Leon staring at me with a feral intensity. He leans down, keeping his eyes on me, and pauses with his mouth an inch away from mine.

It's an invitation, and one I'll happily accept. I need to touch more of him, to feel his hands on my bare skin.

So I kiss him. I kiss him hard, because damn, I want him. I want to *let* myself want him, and be wanted back. His arms wind tighter around my waist as he kisses me, slow but firm, then his hand trails down to my ass. I gasp when he squeezes it, and his kiss deepens even more.

Then, suddenly, Leon pulls away. He gestures at the stairs.

"Lead the way," he says, his voice deeper than before.

I'm unsteady on my feet as I go up the stairs and put the key in the lock. It takes me a few tries, but then we're inside, and Leon already has me tangled up in his arms. He kicks the door closed, my keys still in the knob, and kisses me again. It's much wilder this time, his mouth taking my lips like a conqueror. His tongue darts out and sweeps across them, and without thinking twice, I greet it with mine. Leon grips me tight, his fingers digging into my thick flesh as he swallows me up. The way he invades my mouth, it makes me think of his cock doing the same thing elsewhere, and I squirm in his hands, my hips grinding against his.

"You like it when I kiss you that way?" he asks, giving me a knowing grin. "I can kiss you like that other places, too."

I tremble at the suggestion. I want that, more than anything. His talented mouth all over me? Yes, please. But I'm not even sure where to start with someone as absolutely magnificent as Leon.

He squeezes even more of me, roving over all my mounds and curves with eagerness.

"You're still tense, though." His lips travel from my lips to my cheek, then to my ear. "What's wrong?"

I shiver, not sure I can tell him what's truly on my mind. But I think about how he listened as I talked about my mom, how he didn't judge me for what I feel. Maybe it's okay to peel back my armor and let him see me.

"I don't want to disappoint you," I say at last. "What if I mess it up? What if I'm not any good?" I swallow hard as all of it spills out of me. "Usually I know what to do. I know how to get coffee and use QuickBooks. But this..." I wave a hand at him. "I've had such a great time tonight, and I don't want to ruin it."

He reacts with a thoughtful nod. "I think I understand." He smooths a comforting hand down my back. "But all you have to be with me is you. Your whole self." It's easy to submerge myself in him as he brings me in close and tucks my head under his chin. "Why don't you let me take a load off your shoulders for one night? I can guide you."

But the load is so heavy, and so closely bound to me, I can't imagine he could carry it. Yet all I want is to let go, to stop worrying about where this might end up, for someone else to take the reins.

"Trust me," Leon murmurs, looking down into my eyes, "and I won't lead you wrong. I promise, Tiff."

Something about the words loosens a tight wire inside me.

It would be nice to let it go, I think. To not worry every step of the way.

"Okay," I say at last. "Show me what to do."

I feel him smile against my cheek as I relax into his arms. "There we go." He sucks on my earlobe as his hand roams back up to the swell of my breast. "Now take off your clothes and let me worship you."

Chapter Seven

NOW TAKE OFF YOUR CLOTHES AND LET ME WORSHIP YOU.

The command sends a ripple of searing-hot need through me. My hands instantly obey, as if on puppet strings, and Leon's fingers join mine as I slide them under the hem of my shirt. He guides me, showing me how he wants me to pull it up and off over my head, then he tosses it to the floor without sparing it a second glance.

He explores me, caressing across all the folds in my skin created by my tight bra. Then he reaches around my back and unclasps it without much effort, and we separate long enough for me to toss it away.

"Fuck." Leon groans when he finally sees me, and I cover myself up, not sure what he's cursing about.

He takes my arm with surprising roughness and pulls it away, getting a full look at my tits. Then he grabs his crotch, where I can make out the outline of his cock under his jeans. He drags his hand across it, just staring at me.

I'm a little bolder this time as my fingers duck under the hem of his shirt, because I'm pretty sure he wants the same thing I do. Without pausing, Leon yanks it over his head, then chucks it so hard it hits the wall. I don't even get a chance to look at him before he's kissing me again. Greedily, his hands slide up under my breasts, taking on the weight of them, his fingers kneading my flesh. A groan builds up in his throat as he cups each one, rolling my nipples between his thumb and forefinger. My hands tangle in his soft, dark chest hair.

"Your tits are perfect, Tiff," Leon murmurs, his hips rubbing against mine so I can feel that thick object in his jeans acutely. Downward he roams, over the curve of my belly to the button at the top of my jeans. "These now. Take them off."

I do as I'm told, and it feels good—so good—to hand over control, to trust someone else with how this should go.

Now that I'm bared to him, Leon slides down onto his knees. He kisses my stomach, digging his hand into the roll at my waist. He buries his nose in my crotch, where I'm still wearing my panties, and inhales deeply.

"You smell so goddamned good," he groans, his big hands fisting each of my ass cheeks as he drags me in closer. "Fuck."

He takes a few more deep breaths, then kisses his back way back up my body until he's towering over me again. I've never had someone say that to me before. It's weird and fucking hot, all at the same time.

"Bedroom," he growls, and it's most definitely a *growl*.

I've heard that sound before—like a bear in a documentary. I nod and lead the way out of the living room, through the open door to my bedroom, where all my various stuffed animals are piled up around my pillows. Embarrassed that I'm a grown woman who collects stuffed animals, I shove them off the bed, but Leon takes both my wrists to stop me. He pushes me down on top of them, as if he couldn't care less where we are or what's around us.

He's only interested in one thing, and that's me. It's never felt so good to be wholly and completely at the center of some-one's attention.

Immediately his mouth is on me, tasting my neck, my collarbone, the valley of my sternum. Eagerly, he sucks one nipple, grabbing the rest of my breast with one big hand, and flicks his tongue back and forth until I'm twitching and gasp-ing. Then he switches to the other nipple, so he's gripping both my tits tight in his palms and teasing me with his teeth. Those teeth are sharper than I expected, but the light shock of pain melds with the pleasure, and I arch into him and whimper for more.

"Good girl." Leon licks each tip one last time. "You make such pretty little sounds."

No one's ever called me that, and my hands grow more confident as I explore his body, too, running them over the dense muscle of his back, his corded neck.

When he gets back up, Leon's hands fly to the zipper of his pants. I only have my panties on now, so I pull them off as he kicks away his jeans. Underneath them, he's practically an underwear model—with significantly thicker body hair. He has on a pair of boxer briefs that wonderfully display the hard-on he's sporting underneath.

I lick my lips just looking at it. He palms his shaft again, stroking up and down as his blue eyes keep me pinned to the bed.

"What do you want, Tiff?" He takes a predatory step toward me. There's a vast emptiness inside me, warm and pulsing, that only he can fill. "Tell me."

"You," I answer, my breath coming fast with how much I need him. "I want you. Inside me. Please, Leon."

He gives me an approving nod. "You've been such a good girl for me. You'll have it." Slipping his thumb into the band of his boxers, he pulls them down.

Oh, wow. The cock that springs out is as large as it is... strange. It's bigger than I expected, even for a guy of Leon's size. But the shape, I've never seen anything like it. There's a lump at the base that's much thicker than the rest of it, and just as swollen. What on earth?

Maybe I just haven't seen enough dicks.

Leon doesn't give me too long to examine him. He drops onto the bed on all fours, crouching over me and blocking out the cheap overhead light. He kisses me again as his hips grind against mine, shoving his cock down between us, so the dribble of pre-cum on its head rubs across my belly.

Instantly, any thought of it being alien vanishes from my mind. The scent of him is driving me wild. I don't care what he looks like down there, as long as he fucks me with it.

Leon grabs my thighs and pulls them wide. His eyes dart from my face to my pussy, and he licks his lips.

"Good thing I didn't have that milkshake earlier," he says, and I could swear he's drooling. "Now it's time for my dessert."

Before I can say or do anything, he shoves his face between my legs.

I cry out with surprise as his tongue glances over my clit. There's no teasing here. It's like gasoline has been poured over me, and then a match dropped on top. My hips snap up as he does it again, and again, until Leon is licking me frantically, his tongue ducking inside me only to return to his target. I've never gone so quickly from zero to sixty, but I'm moaning and my pleasure is arcing up and down my body. He rubs me with his finger, then slides it down, dipping inside me.

Holy shit. All he has to do is stroke once, then twice, that tongue going wild over my clit, and suddenly I'm climaxing.

"Oh, god," I moan. "Leon. Yes!"

My thighs instinctively squeeze around his head, and Leon bites into my flesh, sending me spiraling even higher.

But he's not finished with me, not while I lie there twitching and gasping and trying to come down from outer space. He kneels between my legs, that huge, strange cock resting across my mound, swollen and alert. He wears a sly smile, and his canines look longer than they should be. His hulking chest, with the thick, cut squares of pectoral, is rising and falling quickly with his breathing.

"Are you ready for me to fuck you?" Leon asks, sliding his hips back slightly so just the tip grazes over my sex.

"God, yes." I need nothing else. "Please. Please fuck me."

The wicked grin spreads, and he reaches down to spread my pussy open for him with his fingers.

"You're so wet," he murmurs, dragging the head of his cock up and down through my folds without once dipping inside. "What a good girl you are, getting ready for me."

When Leon fists his cock in his hand and pushes it in, the head slides through, as if drawn to where it's supposed to be. It pulls me wide, and I really didn't realize how big he was before now.

Fuck. Is the rest of that huge thing going to fit inside me?

"Your pussy tasted so good," Leon says, reeling back his hips before I can even get a solid feel for him. All I want is for that strange cock to fill me up, but he's holding back. "And it feels even better around my dick." He leans down so his mouth rests next to my ear. "You'd better be on the pill, because I'm going to fill up that sweet pussy. I'm going to drench it."

Oh, fuck. Nobody's ever made it sound so hot. I nod rapidly. "Yes. I am. Please."

"What a good girl you are, love." Then he kisses my lips, curls his big shoulders, and sinks into me.

I cry out as he delves in, not fast, but oh-so-deep. He glides in smooth, even as thick as he is, and it feels unbelievable.

Once he's seated firmly inside me, Leon settles there for a moment, releasing my lips so his blue eyes can stare into mine. A ghost of a smile quirks the side of his lip, revealing one of his canines, which looks shockingly sharp. Has it always been like that?

Then he withdraws, teasing my wet entrance before plunging back in again. Leon fills me up to the brim, and soon I'm spilling over, moaning as he thrusts as far as he can before yanking himself back out. He sits back on his knees and lifts up my thighs, his whole muscular shape exposed to me as he slams into me again. He's staring at where our bodies are joined, riveted to it, his mouth open in wonder.

"Your pussy is so beautiful," he says between pants. "Look at you. You're taking me so, so well."

The praise cascades over me, and I feel like a goddess underneath him, his hips plunging that thick cock into me in a perfect, hungry rhythm. He squeezes my tits and moans, unafraid of showing me just how good I feel around him.

Then something thick, something wider than his cock, starts nudging at my entrance where Leon already has me stretched tight. Whatever it is, it's trying to work its way into me, and I writhe as my pussy objects.

"Not yet," Leon murmurs to himself.

His thrusts grow shallower, like he's holding something back. But then he ratchets up his pace, and soon I'm lost to him, completely entranced, gripping my stuffed animals and my comforter hard as he fucks me. He licks his fingers and slows down his strokes so he can play with my clit, and I whine with pure bliss. Then he starts moving again as he watches my face. I try to hold his gaze, as feral as those blue eyes look right now, but soon I'm so overwhelmed that my eyes close and my head falls back.

I need more, and more, and more.

Soon I'm teetering on the edge, only inches away from the cliff where the track ends. Leon groans as he buries himself inside me, again and again, pushing me closer to my finish as the lip of his cockhead drags over that sensitive place inside me.

"You're so fucking tight," he grunts. "This pussy was made for me."

And I think that he's right, the way he fits there.

Leon drops onto his elbows, so I can feel his breath on my face as he picks up his speed, pumping his hips in a glorious rhythm. I wind my arms around his neck, my fingers tangling in his thick, dark hair as he swoops down and kisses me.

Now he's plucking at my lips with his sharp teeth, plunging his tongue into my mouth in time with his cock, and I'm perfectly, wonderfully helpless underneath him. He drags that fat cockhead along the inside of me over and over, and then I'm screaming, tipping over the side at last. Leon groans as I clamp down on him hard, showing those unnaturally sharp canines.

"I'm going to stuff you so full," he says as my orgasm consumes me. He wraps his arms around me tight and pounds harder, pushing me farther and farther into the abyss. Inside me, his cock swells, spreading me even wider. "You're going to carry my smell all over you."

These guys really are all about smell.

I cry and buck as he shoves himself in one last time and releases.

There's so much of his cum that it spurts out, and then suddenly, that wide lump at the base of his cock is trying to make its way inside me again. I thought I had reached the peak, but as it starts stretching me, I'm in the stratosphere. I scream his name and Leon stops abruptly, panting hard.

"Sorry," he says, cradling the back of my head. "I didn't mean to use that part."

I'm so dazed I barely register the words, and they tumble over me like water.

"Thass okay," I answer, my words coming out slurred.

Leon grins and, ever so gently, pulls out. Then he falls down on the bed, where he twines my legs with his and runs a hand down to curl around my ass. Just taking a big whiff of him covered in sweat is incredible. I shamelessly bury my face in his armpit, and he laughs, bringing me in closer.

Maybe I do know what he means about smelling great.

"You were so wonderful for me," he croons, rubbing his cheek over my head the way a cat might. "Such a good and obedient girl."

His words fill me up, twirling me around, covering everything with sparkles. I've never felt any happiness like this before, like I did just what I was supposed to do and did it well.

I nuzzle deeper into him, and Leon chuckles as he holds me tighter. "Maybe next time," he murmurs, "we can make it a group event."

My foggy brain imagines Jace here, too, in this bedroom—and I almost can't make sense of it. But my pussy twitches, even now.

"Okay," I say with a yawn, without thinking twice. "Maybe next time."

Chapter Eight

IT SUCKS THAT I STILL HAVE TO GO TO WORK THE NEXT MORNING, but Leon wakes me up early with a soft kiss on the crown of my head. I'm bundled up tight in his arms, his hand stroking my curls.

"I've got to get out to the site," he says into my ear, trailing his lips down my jaw to my throat. My lower body wakes up, and I'm turned on instantly, remembering how he felt last night. "But I hope you know this is just the beginning."

I don't have time to ask, *The beginning of what?* before he's sliding on his shirt and heading out the front door. But it sure sounds enticing. I knew Leon wasn't the type to leave and never call back.

After getting thoroughly fucked last night, I'm so tired I could simply roll over and fall asleep again with my head in the pillow where Leon slept—the one that still smells like him —but it's time to get going for me, too. I simply don't have it in me to go for a run, and I'm pretty sore, so I drag myself into the shower and stand under the hot water, remembering every-thing that happened.

A group event. He can't be serious, can he? My imagination returns to last night, when Leon was crouched over me, deep inside me, making me scream until I was hoarse. Now Jace is standing there, too, right in front of me, with his cock inches away from my mouth.

Whoa. I blink a few times, realizing the water's starting to go cold and my fingers are wrinkled like prunes. I think that deep-dicking last night scrambled my brains.

No, it was more than that. I'd felt so close to him, like what we were doing wasn't just *sex*. Leon had shown me his dominant side, sure, but he was taking care of me, too. He made me feel comfortable and safe when he took control and guided me. He paid such close attention to my pleasure, when most guys have only ever bothered to rub me a little before doing the deed.

Certainly nobody's ever eaten me out like I was the last cupcake left on planet Earth.

Finally, I get out of the shower, wondering how I'm going to focus on my job today when I can't think about anything but my two hot landscapers and what filthy things they might do to me.

Without my usual run, I'm early getting into the office, and my good mood buoys me even higher. Maybe I can escape Mr. Bosley's wrath by having everything ready before he even shows up. Now I don't have to speed from the Starbucks to the office to get coffee onto his desk in time.

When Mr. Bosley comes in, I'm sitting in my chair, focused on my computer and the paperwork in front of me. He stops in front of me and frowns.

"Did you bring my coffee in with you today?" he asks. No remark on my punctuality, but that's fine.

"Yes," I answer quickly, politely. "It's waiting in your office. I got here early today."

That frown of his deepens, and I wonder what I've done wrong now.

"So it's cold already, is what you're saying?" Mr. Bosley asks in a dangerous tone.

I didn't even think of that. That coffee's been sitting there for ten minutes now. It's not only cooled off, but likely all his whipped cream has melted, too, and I know how much he hates that.

"Oh." It's the only thing I can think of to say. "I'm sorry. I didn't think—"

"Of course you didn't." The words are cutting. "You never think."

My heart is racing as he stalks into his office, grabs the coffee, and returns with it. He sets it down firmly in front of me.

"M-Mr. Bosley?" I ask, trying to keep the waver out of my voice.

"Get me a new one. Hot this time."

"But you have an appointment in ten—" I begin.

"I ask for one thing in the morning," he interrupts. "One thing. A hot coffee. That's it. It's not that difficult. It *shouldn't* be." He levels his gaze on me. "I wonder if I should find another assistant. Someone a little more competent."

Dread pools in my belly. I need this job. I've been here for two years already, and only recently started earning vacation. Before, I was unemployed so long that I nearly maxed out my credit card. I was lucky to find Mr. Bosley when I did, and he hired me even though I had little in the way of qualifications.

I've looked for other jobs, but there's simply nothing out

there for someone like me, with no degree, that would pay well and offer healthcare. And now Mr. Bosley is thinking about replacing me. How would I pay my rent then?

"I'll get a new one right away," I say robotically, as a familiar, sharp sense of panic rises up in my belly, to my chest and throat. I pick up the cold coffee and dump it in the trash as my boss watches me head for the door. I keep it together just long enough to get to the other side, and then I sprint to the bathroom. There, I crumple against the sinks, trying to bring air into my lungs. I can barely breathe as sobs wrack my body.

Why can't I do *anything* right? I'm like a drunk gorilla stumbling around in the darkness, knocking everything over in my path.

I sniffle a few times, remembering what Eli said. I close my eyes and focus on my breathing, until at last, my shaking subsides. Then I pull my keys out and rush to the Starbucks. The woman at the drive-thru looks perplexed to see me a second time. I hastily order Mr. Bosley's drink, then zoom back to the office so I can get it to him before it gets cold again.

He says nothing when I come in with the replacement, not even looking up from the note he's scribbling.

"I need you to sign the stack of orders on your desk," he says, without stopping what he's doing. He ignores the coffee, too.

"But I never sign orders," I say without thinking. He's supposed to clear those, not me. The last thing I want is to make a mistake on an order and clear a purchase for fifty AC units when we only need five. I'd definitely lose my job then.

Mr. Bosley's pen slaps down hard on the desk, and he sighs with impatience.

"Can you not do this one thing, Ms. Dockett?" he says, shaking his head.

I back away, holding up my hands. All I need is to piss him off even more today. "Of course I can. I'll do it right now."

Still trembling from my harried rush in the car, I head back to my desk. Sure enough, a stack of orders waits for me.

I barely look at them as I sign, hoping I still have my job tomorrow.

The moment I finish the last order, I get a text from Jace. Thank god. I hurry to open it, desperate for a distraction.

How was last night?

My entire body blushes at once at his message. He and Leon must have discussed what happened—and my mind instantly jumps to Leon on top of me, inside me, calling me a *good girl.*

Can these guys really be so casual about this?

It was good

I'm not sure how honest I should be. I don't want to hype up Leon in front of Jace and make him jealous, or worse, inadequate.

Just good?

I read the message a few times, trying to understand his tone. I wish I could hear his voice.

Then another message appears.

Did Leon make you cum?

My face is practically on fire. Yes, he sure did, to the point where I thought I might pass out. I swallow as I type the answer.

> Yes.

I don't know how much I should say. Could I tell Jace that he did it not once, but multiple times? Could I tell him how Leon buried his face between my thighs and made me climax in a few short seconds, which had never happened in my life? It usually takes a lot to get there, and most guys don't have the patience, or even the inclination, to go down on me.

There's a moment before I get a response from Jace.

> Good, because I can't wait to make you cum
> even more

This time, the fire spreads straight down between my legs. Holy shit. Are these guys for real? I'm starting to breathe a little harder when I get a follow-up message.

> What are you doing tomorrow night?

I don't really make plans unless Aisling and Hannah invite me out, so I'm a little embarrassed when I type out my answer.

> Totally free

The response comes instantly.

> Would you like to grab a drink with me again?

I gape down at my phone. So Jace isn't perturbed in the least by the idea that I hooked up with his brother last night?

In fact, he seems... almost pleased by it. And he's still interested in me.

I feel strange about never having gotten that follow-up date with Jace before things turned to the wild side. I moved ahead with Leon in intimacy, when Jace is the one I met first.

Besides, I want to learn more about the funny, second-oldest brother, to get a better sense of who he is. And I need to suss out why Jace doesn't seem to mind sharing one woman with someone else. If I'm going to be comfortable with this arrangement, I have to understand better where they're coming from.

Finally, I text back.

I would love that

Jace gives me a time and place, and I agree to meet there. It's a bit of a ritzy bar, but I hardly spend any money going out, so I don't mind dropping twelve bucks on a cocktail if it means I get to see Jace again. I loved his big laugh, and all his cute, silly stories about his childhood with his brothers. He had a lightness to him that infected me in the best possible way.

Not to mention that he's a great kisser. I wonder what we might do after going out on another date.

For a second, I even wonder if his cock is as strange as Leon's was. As greedy as it makes me feel, I hope I get to find out.

When I go on my run the next morning, I'm surprised when the Lupine Landscaping truck is missing out front of the big white house on the corner. The yard is still dug up, and it looks like some hoses have been placed under the ground, but the landscapers are nowhere to be seen. I wonder if something happened and they won't be working on this property anymore.

I hope they're okay.

After that, my day is a drag, just counting the hours and minutes until I can go home and get ready for my date. At least Mr. Bosley doesn't hassle me, too busy arguing with someone about *expenses* and *don't tell me how to run my business*. I'm buzzing with excitement by the time I clock out and head to my car.

Since we're going somewhere more upscale, I decide to doll myself up a little. Yeah, I want to impress Jace. I want him to look at me and lick his lips like he's about to eat the perfect burger.

Does that make me the burger?

After taming my curls into ringlets and putting on a solid dose of mascara, I change into a black dress with a slim waist and flared hips. It accentuates my curves perfectly, but my tits are somewhat reined in. I make sure to wear my cutest lingerie, which I haven't worn in years. Just in case.

The bar is a hip little place with rock music playing and neat, high tables arranged outside. I'm waiting for Jace to arrive, shifting from one foot to the other, when the Lupine Landscaping truck pulls up.

"*Awoo!*" Quinn howls out the window.

Before Jace can escape the front passenger seat, Quinn throws the back door open, hops out, and jogs over to me. I don't even have a moment to react as he grabs my hands in both of his and squeezes them.

"I'm sorry about the other day, Tiff," he says. His hair is

longer than his brothers', and it falls into his face as he urgently tries to get his message across. "I really am. I didn't mean to come on so strong."

Quinn is hot to the touch, surprisingly so, and his hands are rugged and calloused around mine. His face is so earnest and regretful, I have to sigh. He reminds me of a cute puppy desperate for approval.

Besides, what do I have to lose? Jace and Leon are both such nice guys, their little brother can't be all that different. I feel like I should give him a break.

"It's okay," I say, offering him a smile. "I won't hold it against you."

Quinn grins with relief but doesn't release me. "The offer still stands," he says, winking. "I'd really love to take you out."

I'm so stunned by the proposition that I can't manage an answer right away. Jace plucks my hand out of Quinn's and wags a finger at his little brother.

"Don't overwhelm her," Jace says. "We talked about this."

Quinn rolls his eyes. "Fine. I just thought I'd shoot my shot."

He is cute, in a younger guy kind of way. I like how his hair curls, and the addition of the puka shells gives him a kind of surfer look. He has the same strong jaw, pronounced chin, and upswept nose as his brothers, but a much more carefree attitude.

I shake my head to clear it. I'm ridiculous. Of course I find him hot, since I also find his brothers hot, and they all look alike. That doesn't suddenly make him an option for me.

"Can I at least get your number?" Quinn asks, and Jace shoots him a deadly look. "What? It's innocent. If she's going to date you guys, I want to get to know her, at least."

Leon stands next to the hood of the truck, watching us with interest. The only one who hasn't emerged from the truck is Eli, the skinniest of the brothers. He's got his arms crossed, drumming his fingers on his biceps like he's waiting impatiently to leave.

I glance sideways at Jace, asking him with my eyes, *What should I say?*

He shrugs. "Go for it if you want, but don't let him pressure you." Jace shoots his little brother a chastising look, and Quinn shamelessly shrugs in return.

"Okay, okay," I say. "Give me your number."

Once I have his digits entered into my phone and he's got mine, Quinn hops back in the truck next to Eli, who's staring straight ahead with a dark look on his face. I wonder what that's about. He'd seemed so nice and friendly before.

But I don't have time to ponder it when the truck speeds off, leaving Jace and me alone on the sidewalk.

"Shall we?" He loops his arm through mine. I'm so happy to see him again that I feel myself grinning like an idiot, and my heart starts beating faster.

"We shall." With an imperious nod, Jace tucks me tight against his side and leads me into the bar.

Chapter Nine

ONCE WE'RE SEATED AT ONE OF THE HIGH TABLES OUT ON THE sidewalk, Jace flags down a waitress.

"Can I get all the appetizers?" He peers down at the menu. "And one of those... lavender whatevers for me."

"The lavender lemon fizz?" she asks, giving Jace a shy smile. He is a snack, and I don't blame her for getting an eyeful of him—but I bristle a little, too, because he's here with *me*.

Jace passes her his menu. "That's it! Thank you."

Reluctantly, the waitress glances at me. "And what'll you have?"

"Just a beer," I say, because Jace already ordered plenty of food for the both of us. "A plain lager."

When we're alone again, Jace tilts his head. "Tonight's on me, you know. You can get something fancy if you want."

I shrug. "I like a classic beer. I get wasted too fast if I drink cocktails. They all taste like candy, then I can't help myself and I have too many."

Jace barks a laugh. "That's fair. You have a sweet tooth?"

Oh, boy. "Is the sky blue?"

He glances upward, a grin spreading across his wide mouth. "I mean, it's kinda blue and kinda purple and a little orange right now," he says with a wink. "The sunset is pretty."

I can't help laughing. "The point is, don't get me near a bag of Sour Patch Kids."

"That's me and Junior Mints." Jace gives a sincere nod. "I feel you."

Then I remember jogging by the house on Work Street this morning.

"By the way, where were you guys today?" I ask. "I didn't see you on my run. Did something happen with that land-scaping job?"

"Oh, we were down at the coast. Decided to say 'fuck it' for a day and get out of town." Jace leans back in his chair and spreads his arms, the picture of relaxation. "Got in some swimming and played Frisbee on the beach. Fucking Leon, though. So tall. I hate when he's not on my team."

I quirk an eyebrow. "What about the job, though?"

"What about it? It'll still be there tomorrow." He swishes his drink and takes a big gulp. "I did have to harass my brothers to get me home in time for our date, though."

All I can do is gape. They just ditch work whenever they want? I can't imagine having that kind of freedom.

"Do you have a deadline for getting the job done?" I'm prying, but I can't help it. I want to know how they run their business—and maybe live vicariously through them. I haven't taken a vacation day all year because I'm afraid it'll get me fired.

Again, Jace looks mystified by my question. "It gets done when it gets done."

"What about your other clients?" I ask. "Don't you have other jobs lined up?"

He bats a hand in the air. "Oh, sure. We'll get to them eventually."

My head is spinning. They're so *laissez-faire* about their work, I can't even comprehend it.

"Besides, we're out of tubing right now," he adds. "Gotta wait for the wholesale order to come in before we can finish."

I can't imagine waiting until you're completely out of supplies before ordering more.

"You look like I ran over your cat," Jace says with a chuckle. "I bet you're the kind of person who has all their ducks in a row, huh, Tiff?"

"It's my job," I say, a little affronted because of how boring it makes me sound. But it's not just the job. Even at home, I can't help putting everything where it belongs. I arrange my stuffed animals by color, and make sure my shelves are all alphabetical. "My brain just... likes order, I guess. Keeping everything neat and tidy."

I don't know how to explain that I just need things to be *right*.

Jace leans forward on the table. "Organizing is your kink, huh?" He licks his lips. "I'll keep that in mind. It just takes some color-coding to turn you on."

Even though we're talking about filing systems, it makes me tingle a little between the legs. The last thing I want is to be boring and weird, so I change the subject to what it was like for Jace growing up with three brothers.

"Well, we had to share everything," he says with a nostalgic huff of air. "Clothes, toys, food. We fought over dumb stuff, like who got to play the Xbox, but for the most part we're happy to share." He gets a mischievous glint in his eye.

"Is that..." I swallow before I can continue. "Is that why you and Leon are, um, okay with it?"

"With what?" Jace asks, that playful grin spreading. He wants me to say it out loud.

"With, you know." I flutter my hands, blushing. "Both of you. Dating me. At the same time."

"Aw, just dating?" He looks disappointed. "Sounded like you and Leon did a little more than 'just date' the other night."

I still can't believe he can be so cavalier about this, but it's also kind of nice having someone who's in on it—who knows about the wild night I had with Leon, when I don't even think I could tell my friends.

Still, I have more serious questions.

"But what if something comes up?" I ask, more earnestly. "I don't want anyone to get jealous or anything. That's not what I'm interested in."

Jace doesn't appear pressed. "Well, if there's ever a conflict, Leon wins," he says with a shrug. "That's just how it works."

"What? Why?"

"He's not just the oldest," Jace explains. "He's... the leader, really. You have to have someone in charge when you have a pack of—" He cuts himself off.

"A pack of big, burly guys?" I supply, chuckling. He nods.

"Yeah, that." But Jace looks perturbed, and as our conversation goes on, he gets quieter and more thoughtful. I tell him all about Hannah and Aisling, and how we met during high school. They're my support network, but they're also both pretty busy with their lives, so we don't see each other as much as I'd like. Jace nods and listens, but it's clear his thoughts are elsewhere.

"What's wrong?" I finally ask, wondering if I'm being tedious.

"There are just some things I haven't told you yet." Jace turns a serious expression on me. "Some important things about us."

This doesn't surprise me in the least. There is obviously something very weird about the four brothers.

"Okay," I say, spreading my arms wide. "What can you say that's any weirder than 'please, go ahead and fuck my brother'?"

The corner of his mouth turns up in a tense smile. "I guess we have set a high bar."

"So what is it?" I ask. "What aren't you guys telling me?"

"Oh. It's just that we, uh..." he trails off, not quite looking at me. "We live kind of far out of town! That's it. And we all live together."

That's a bit weird, I guess, but it also seems perfectly fitting for them.

"Makes dating a little more complicated, huh?"

He nods rapidly. "Yes. Exactly. I just thought you should know." Abruptly he rises from his seat and offers me his hand. "Why don't we get out of here? There's a lot more I'd like to do with you tonight."

My face heats at the suggestion. "Like... what?" I ask, hesitant to assume he means what I'm hoping he means.

"What do you think?" Jace's big grin returns, and he arches one eyebrow suggestively. Then he leans across the table so only I can hear him. "Leon said your pussy was so tight, he had to hold out. I wonder if you'll squeeze my dick just as hard."

Instantly, my whole lower body shudders. They really do share everything, I realize. Even the most personal details possible.

Did Leon tell Quinn and Eli, too? I can't help but wonder if that was the reason for Eli hiding in the back of the truck, a black cloud over his head. Must be awkward.

Well, Jace has made it clear what he wants, and I know I want it, too. But thinking about taking off my clothes with him, *alone...* I feel a little bubble of uncertainty. What I did with

Leon was wild, but still intimate. We have a relationship of some kind, that much is clear. Now that I've slept with him, going home with Jace almost feels like cheating.

My anxiety must show on my face, because Jace's smile fades.

"We don't have to do anything," he clarifies. "If you don't want to move that fast. Or if you're not interested. I understand."

"No, no. Nothing like that. It's just..."

"It's about Leon, isn't it?"

The last thing I want is for Jace to think he's not enough, because he is. I want more than anything to get naked with him, but my heart doesn't know what to do after sharing something so personal with Leon.

"Would he be upset?" I ask finally. "If we... you know?"

Jace blinks, then understanding dawns on him. His grin grows quite wicked.

"Would it make you feel more comfortable if he was here?" he asks, taking out his phone. "I know he'd come in a heartbeat."

My mouth opens to respond, but I don't know what to say. I'd liked how Leon commanded me, how his voice guided me from one step to the next so I didn't have to think. It took all my fear and replaced it with confidence, because I knew I could trust him.

With Leon there, I think he would help me through how tentative I feel. But... both of them at the same time? It's like the fantasy I had in the shower. Can I let myself have something like this, something so debauched and alluring?

"Okay," I finally say, my breath hitching. "Please, call him."

With a nod, Jace taps the phone screen and holds it up to his ear. The person on the other end answers right away.

"Leon? I think Tiff wants you to come over and join us." He listens for a few seconds. "Yep, mm-hmm. Great." He glances up at me. "Your place?"

I don't know if my bed will be big enough, but just the thought makes me tingle all over.

"My place," I agree.

Jace repeats it into the phone and then says, "See you there, bro."

He winks at me as he gets out of his chair, and I follow. Before we can get very far, though, he steals a kiss.

Jace tastes like his stiff cocktail, and his lips are smooth and sturdy. It's a very different kiss than the ones I shared with Leon. Jace is less of a conqueror and more of a partner, matching my energy and my urgency with his. His hand winds around my back, pulling me in closer as the kiss deepens, and his tongue explores my mouth. It sends a shiver straight down my spine.

Eventually he pulls away. "We'd better go," he says in my ear as the waitress from earlier eyeballs us. "Are you ready?"

"Yes." I say it confidently, but I'm not sure if that's what I feel. I'm about to step into the wild unknown, and who knows what will happen to me there?

Jace hops in my car, and I drive us to my apartment building, my mind whirling. What on earth have I gotten myself into?

When we arrive, he nods at Leon's motorcycle, which is already parked on the street. "Looks like he beat us."

Outside my apartment, Leon is leaning on the railing of the stairs, giving both of us a rather knowing smirk. I realize how big he is standing next to Jace—maybe three inches taller, but not built quite as thick. He and Jace exchange fist bumps as a greeting, then Leon turns to me.

"Having a good time?" he asks, reaching out to tuck some of my hair behind my ear.

"I think so," I say uneasily, because all of this still feels strange. Should I downplay how I feel about Jace to make Leon more comfortable?

Jace gives me a betrayed look. "You *think* so?" he asks, clearly offended. Shit.

"I mean, yes. I'm... I'm having a great time." I'm so flustered now that my words are getting all tangled up. I'm just making an ass out of myself. "I just, um..."

Leon takes my hand and rubs it in a soothing motion. "Hey. It's all right." He raises my palm to his lips and kisses it, and somehow, that one light kiss is incredibly charged and erotic. "You can say what you think around us. I'm not going to be mad that you're enjoying your date." He glances at Jace, who gives an affirmative nod.

"Oh." I clear my throat. "I'm having an amazing time, actually. Your stories are so funny. And I love how I can just talk to you for hours and the time flies away."

A wide grin takes over Jace's sweet face, and Leon gently nudges me toward him. When I close the gap between us, Jace wraps his arms around my waist and pulls me in closer.

"You like talking to me?" he asks, stooping down low. Light dances in his eyes like he's saying something else. "You think I'm funny?"

I nod quickly. "Yes and yes. Very much so."

His grin grows even wider. When he kisses me, it's forceful and sudden, much more than before. He grabs onto my shirt as he pulls me against him, bending me backwards with that kiss. All my nerve endings light up, mesmerized by the places my body touches his. When I raise one hand to his chest, he's firm under my palm, his muscles solid and hard. I gasp when he nips at my lower lip, then soothes over it with his tongue. I feel like I might simply float away.

Finally, Jace stands up straight and releases me from his arms. When I look over my shoulder at Leon, there's a smirk tilting up the side of his mouth. I think he liked it.

"Maybe we should go inside," he says as another car pulls into the apartment parking lot.

I nod quickly and lead the way up the stairs, then unlock the door. Jace's hand glances over my hip as he passes by me into the living room, but Leon stops in the doorway. His fingers follow the line of my spine down my back to my hips, and then over my ass. I don't even realize I'm leaning into him until he chuckles, then brushes his lips over my hair. They travel down my temple, then he tugs on my earlobe with his teeth. A shiver rolls through my entire body.

"I've been thinking about kissing you again," he murmurs, just for my ears. "And taking your clothes off again. And being inside you again." I feel like I'm on fire as he plants his hands on my shoulders and turns me around, giving me a pat on the butt. "Now go see Jace."

The command immediately settles my nervous stomach, and I obey without question. Leon will guide me through whatever strange things might lie ahead, and I know he'll make sure I enjoy it.

We go into the living room, where Jace is propped against the back of the couch. His arms open for me, and I fall into them. He touches every part of me as he kisses me, and we're both panting by the time we separate.

"I need to take your clothes off," Jace murmurs, inhaling a deep breath like he's taking a drag of my scent. "Right now."

Leon already knows the way to my bedroom, and he doesn't waste a moment leading us to it, Jace and I following with our hands linked.

I can't believe that I have both of them here, about to get naked with me. I must be the luckiest girl alive.

Chapter Ten

I MADE AN EFFORT TO CLEAR OFF MY BED THIS TIME—NOT THAT it matters when we step inside the room and Jace descends on me like an animal.

He explores the shape of me with his eager hands, over the top of my clothes, biting his lip while he palms my breasts. Like Leon's, his canines are a little longer and sharper than a regular person's.

"This has to go," Jace says, plucking the fabric of my dress. I have to agree. I want his hands all over me again, without this *stuff* between us.

He grabs the dress by the skirt and yanks it up over my head, revealing me completely in one swift motion. When my tits pop out, he groans. "Fuck. You're gorgeous, Tiff."

I know by the look on his face, like a drooling dog in front of a bone, that he's not lying.

First, Jace kisses the top of each of my breasts, then travels down my belly, touching every inch of me he can on his way.

I sense Leon approach me from behind, where he unhooks

my bra and tosses it away. Then Jace is on his feet again, bringing my nipples into his mouth, grunting as he buries his hand in my generous flesh. He takes off his own shirt next, and I fumble with the button and zipper on his jeans until he kicks them off.

Damn. Jace looks just as good underneath as Leon did, with even denser muscles in his shorter frame. Behind me, Leon is taking off his clothes, too, until I suddenly have two extremely hot men naked in my room with me.

I'm pretty sure this is a dream.

Much like Leon, Jace has... a strange penis. It's hard and firm already, pointing straight at me, the slit at the tip shining. Most noticeable, though, is the rather large swell at the root. He notices where I'm looking and chuckles.

"Neat feature, huh?" Leon says over my shoulder as he approaches me from behind. He's spreading my ass cheeks apart so he can slide his own cock between my legs. Jace reaches down and takes himself in hand, drawing his palm along his shaft to the odd lump.

"I felt it," I say between gasps. "When you were..."

"Inside you?" Leon asks, his dick leaving moisture all along the insides of my thighs. I nod. "I'm sorry about that. You weren't ready." He leans forward and places a kiss on my neck. "But maybe you will be tonight."

At this, Jace's face lights up. "You think so?"

"She might have a tight pussy, but I think it'll fit if we make her come enough times." The way they're talking about me... my body goes taut, just imagining how they plan to accomplish this—and how that strange, bulbous part would feel inside me.

I reflexively grind against Leon's cock and he groans behind me, reaching around to grab a handful of my breast. Jace cups my cheek in his palm and leans down to kiss me, swallowing up all the little sounds falling from my lips while Leon fondles me. Jace ventures down, his fingers trailing over my sternum to my belly, then to the place between my legs. After Leon came over, I'd meant to shave, but I was so dazed in the shower thinking about what outfit I would wear tonight that I forgot.

"Ah," Jace says as my thighs part for him, and he dips his hand through. "She has such nice fur, Leon."

I'm ferociously embarrassed by this. *Fur?* But Leon grunts behind me and says, "It'll feel great against your face."

Jace tests me with his fingers, parting my folds to see what's inside. He gives a huff of approval when he finds my opening. "You're so wet already."

"What a good girl," Leon murmurs into my neck.

Suddenly, Jace steps back from me, then falls onto the bed. He pats his chest. "Come here, Tiff."

Leon takes my hand and guides me over to him. I'm not entirely sure what they want me to do.

"Get on his face," Leon commands, and it sends a ripple of anticipation through me. Why does Leon giving me orders turn me on so much?

I climb on top of Jace, trying not to feel humiliated as I navigate my heavy body up to his head. But he only has a hungry look on his face.

"Leon told me how good you taste," he says, voice low. "Even better than you smell." He grabs me around the hips and pulls me down, onto his mouth. I cry out when he latches onto my clit, as if drawn to it by a magnet. After he finishes sucking there, his tongue swipes down and dives inside me.

"Oh, god," I murmur as he fucks me with it, licking up as much of me as he can. Jace groans, and returns to lapping at my clit, which feels like liquid starlight.

The bed sinks under me as Leon climbs onto it. He crawls

until he's in front of me, then leans forward to tease one of my nipples with his mouth, running those sharp canines gently over it. With Jace devouring me at the same time, I hit my wave much sooner than I expected. I buckle forward, overcome by the power of it, and Leon catches me. He chuckles into my hair.

"One," he murmurs, kissing me while I shake and twitch. Then he lays me down on the bed, like he's placing a delicate doll, and turns to Jace. A look I don't understand passes between them.

Jace gives a firm nod and slides over the comforter, pulling my legs open wide. His cock is even harder than before, hot and red and swollen, and I know by that determined look on his face what he wants.

He's going to fuck me right here, in front of Leon. And by the look on Leon's face while he strokes himself, he's excited about it.

Leaning over me, Jace reaches down between us and takes his cock roughly in his hand, using it to brush over my clit. I'm still sensitive from my orgasm, so I gasp.

"Are you ready?" he asks, his face very serious as he drags the head of his cock through my folds, up and then down again, until I'm squirming and whining for more. "Do you want it, Tiff?"

Do I ever. I need him, right now.

"Yes," I squeak out as he rubs that head all over me. "Please, Jace!"

"Fuck her," Leon commands in a surprisingly deep, intimidating voice. Anyone in their right mind would obey it.

Jace nods solemnly. "I'm going to need your help, Leon," he says, his eyes riveted on the slit between my legs. "So I don't go off too soon."

I wonder what Leon could possibly do to accomplish this, but I'm too distracted to think much about it.

Jace's gaze jumps to mine, and he watches me intently as his fat cockhead slips between my swollen lower lips. I suck in my breath as it opens me, insisting I spread for it and allow it through, even though I'm still swollen from my orgasm. Jace hikes my thigh higher up on his hip to anchor me, his eyes darting from my face down to my pussy. He licks his lips.

It's not as much of a stretch to accept him as it was when I took Leon the first time, but still, he demands my body open for him as he slides in almost halfway on his first thrust. We moan together as our bodies wrap around each other. There Jace pauses, panting, and pulls back out. I whimper, wanting more, but he ignores me.

Jace continues taking me like this, only sinking partway inside, taunting me, teasing me.

"Please," I beg, lifting my hips to meet his, hoping he'll give me more. I reach toward him with a beseeching hand, and he takes it, squeezing my fingers with his. I'm aching, and only him fully seated inside me will sate it. "I need it. I need *you*."

"Not yet." Jace lowers his head, his lips curling into a wicked smile. "You're going to come for me first."

His hand reaches down between us, and his finger glances over my clit. My hips buck as a spasm races through me. Suddenly every movement of his cock feels like twice, three times as much, just buried partway inside me, the head dragging over a spot that completely lights me up. His hand teases my clit faster and faster, matching the tempo of his partial thrusts, until I'm keening and my back arches.

"God, Jace," I whimper. "I'm going to... I'm going to..."

Only halfway buried in me, he feels so good that the maddeningly blissful combination of his cock and his finger sends me sliding toward the edge. I can't control the words coming out of my mouth as I'm pulled underwater, surrounded on all sides. Each of my nerves is electrified.

Then Jace thrusts all the way in.

My orgasm suddenly bursts, all-consuming, and I cry out as every muscle in my body draws tight. My legs curl around his waist, squeezing him hard as I tremble and shiver. Jace grunts and tips forward, changing his angle deep in me, so I squirm and moan again.

"You weren't kidding, Leon," he says, hoarse. "She's squeezing my cock so hard I'm trying not to come right now."

"Not yet," Leon growls, still sliding his hand up and down his dick. "That was two. Now get on your hands and knees, Tiff."

Jace slips out of me, and I feel his absence acutely. Though I'm still weak from my climax, I manage to get up and turn over so my ass is in the air, then I spread my legs. I don't even have to look over my shoulder to know what Jace is going to do.

He doesn't enter me fast, like I expect. No, he only samples me, dipping the head of his cock into me and then withdrawing it again while Leon kneels in front of me on the bed. With a surprising softness, Leon tilts up my chin and kisses me. Once he's sufficiently tormented my lips, he rises so his cock is directly in front of my face. It's drooling for me, the head emerging from his foreskin, and that strange bulge at the base? After how hard it made me orgasm last time, I'm much more fascinated by it now.

I take Leon's cock in my hands while Jace continues to taunt me, dipping just an inch deep inside me, and I lean forward to wrap my tongue around Leon. His whole body rocks forward, and he lets out a rough groan.

"Take more of him," Jace whispers in my ear, crouched

over me so I can feel the weight of him against my back. I nod quickly and bring Leon's big, strange cock into my mouth. As soon as I have the head between my lips, tracing it with my tongue, Jace sinks deeper inside me—not quite giving me everything yet, but offering a delicious promise. I moan into the throbbing length stuffed in my mouth. I need more, more, more. I need to be filled so I can be whole again.

"Deeper," Jace murmurs to me. "Swallow him, and I'll finally fuck you the way you deserve."

In my desperation to have Jace, all of him, I bring as much of Leon into my throat as I can. He grunts, his hips jerking against me.

I'm rewarded. Jace buries himself inside me, groaning as he does, filling me to the breaking point. Now the dam has been breached and Jace thrusts, deep and hard, while I swallow Leon's cock. My hand wraps around that lump at the base, and—

Leon buckles forward as I squeeze.

"Oh fuck," he whimpers, and I worry I've hurt him. But when I pull my hand away, he grabs it in his own and brings it back down to that bulge, mimicking how he wants me to stroke it.

I repeat the motion as I bring him back into my mouth, then tease him with just my lips. It's so hard to focus, though, with Jace ravaging my pussy. He's well and truly fucking me, sinking deep and then yanking himself out, and I feel like my very skin is lighting on fire. Every single pump of his hips is sending a sharp ripple of pleasure through me, ratcheting up my cries as his cock slides over my most sensitive place again and again.

"One more?" Jace asks Leon, huffing with effort. "Before my knot will fit?"

Leon nods, running his hands through my hair while I suck on him, harder and harder.

"Touch yourself," he tells me in that tone that demands compliance, but quieter and more tender.

I automatically listen, keeping myself propped up on one arm and dropping my hand from his cock to the spot down between my legs. The second I touch my clit, every muscle in my body clenches tight, and Jace groans behind me.

"Fuck," he hisses. "I don't know if I can—"

"Hold it, Jace," Leon says in that deep, echoing voice. "Don't go off yet."

It's as if his body is tied to a string, the way Jace stiffens behind me and starts pumping even more furiously. With Leon's cock down my throat and my hand working hard on my clit, I'm vibrating with my unspent pleasure. I suck harder as my peak hits me like a wave boiling me against the rocks.

Jace moans, squeezing my ass in his hands, but he doesn't erupt like I expect. He slows down, letting me come off my orgasm, while I try my hardest to stay upright—but both my arms are shivering so much I might just fall over. I take Leon's cock even deeper into my throat, bobbing my head back and forth, and he pets my hair affectionately.

"Good girl," Leon croons. "You're sucking me so well. And you're taking Jace wonderfully." Then he barks at Jace, "Now. Put your knot inside her."

Jace grunts in acknowledgment. I wonder what they mean by *knot*, but I can't speak around Leon's cock. That's when I feel it—Jace's bulbous lump is starting to nudge its way inside me. I'm still tight from coming so hard, but somehow my pussy is softer and hungrier. When that bulge can't wedge into my passage, Jace thrusts again, moaning and panting.

"She's so tight, Leon," he groans as the lump presses

harder, and surely it's far too big. There's no way I can take something that size. "It won't fit."

"It will fit," Leon growls in reply. "Fuck her. Claim her."

Jace obeys, grunting as he speeds up his strokes, and reflexively, I pick up the pace as I suck Leon's cock. Electricity is spreading across my body, growing and growing as Jace slides in and out of me at a brutal speed, softening me more, urging me to open for him.

This time, when he tries to push that swell at the base of him inside me, I'm so slick that it starts to squeeze through. My pussy is stretching as wide as it can, and the pressure is sending mixed signals straight to my brain—discomfort and eye-popping pleasure, all at once. I'm helpless as I swallow Leon's cock and release it again, pouring the force of all my spiraling pleasure into sucking him.

Again, Jace withdraws and then pushes through, forcing even more of himself into me. His moans turn into growls as he goes deeper and deeper, and somehow, my pussy swallows even more of him. When it seems like my body can't possibly accommodate more...

Suddenly, it bursts through, and then Jace's strange cock is all the way inside me. Oh, god. I've never felt anything as good as this. I'm so full now that there's no give at all when I clench around him, desperate with my need to climax. My spit and Leon's cum both drip down my lips as Jace snarls behind me, a noise that's purely animal.

"She's taken my knot," he says breathlessly. "Leon, I'm g-g-going to..."

He trails off in a whine as he pulls the bulge free, then fucks it into my pussy a second time.

"Hold it, Jace," Leon commands. "Not until she comes again."

Tears are building behind my eyes at the sheer, blistering

volume of my pleasure. How does that strange thing feel so incredibly good? Every time Jace pushes it in, another powerful burst of sensation ricochets out from it.

As if on cue, Leon shoves his cock deep into my mouth. It twitches and spasms, swelling up even bigger, until I'm choking. He lets out a strangled sound as he unleashes a load of hot liquid, and it shoots out with such ferocity I can feel it strike the back of my throat. I try to swallow, but now Jace is moving faster, that fat swell filling me so full on each thrust that tears are running down my face. It's stimulating every single nerve ending, and soon I'm standing in the shadow of a tsunami.

Leon pulls himself free of my mouth, and his cum spills down my lips. A cry bursts out of me as Jace jams himself deep and forces that lump all the way in again.

"Ah, fuck!" Jace roars as his balls slap my clit. I drown in my pleasure, almost drunk on it. Whatever that thing is on his cock, it feels utterly magical. I'm sobbing when my climax finally obliterates me.

I try to cover my scream, but I can't. I fall to the bed, my hands no longer able to support me as my whole body clamps down tight, and the edges of my pussy wrap around Jace's whole cock—lump included.

Now Jace is trapped inside me, rocking back and forth while my orgasm consumes me. He whimpers as he swells up even more. How is that possible? My channel is shifting to accommodate, stretching to take him.

Jace grips the flesh of my ass as he jerks behind me, chanting, "Oh, god, Tiff. Yes. Your pussy is amazing. Fuck."

Something warm shoots inside me, filling me even fuller, and I wonder if my body might simply pop.

Jace collapses on top of me, barely holding himself up with one arm. I've clamped down so tight around his cock that my body won't let it go again. All of his come is trapped inside me, unable to escape, and I whimper.

"Shh," Leon says, lying down in front of me to push my hair back from my face. "You took his knot so well, love." Then he kisses me tenderly, and I relax against him.

"You were right, Leon," Jace manages, his hands softer now as he cups my ass, then draws them up my back. I shiver under his touch. "Three is the magic number. I doubt our Tiff's sweet cunt will ever let me go."

Even when my knees give out, Jace is still trapped inside me. He rolls us to the side and presses his hand to my belly, massaging my bountiful flesh. We lie there, panting, while Leon settles in front of me.

"What's happening?" I ask, confused as to why Jace's cock is still locked inside me. "What... what is that?"

"Don't worry," Leon says in a sweet voice, peppering kisses across my cheeks. "It keeps all of Jace's cum inside you. It will go down soon."

I've never heard of such a thing. I sure hope my pill works, but I might pick up a Plan B tomorrow anyway.

Soon, that lump recedes, and with a loud, wet *pop!* Jace's cock suddenly pulls free. A torrent of cum slides out of me, gushing down my thigh. I shudder all over, so overstimulated that just the sensation of it is almost too much.

Jace cradles my body close, his wet cock between my legs, while Leon pets and strokes my hair.

"Someday, you'll take mine," Leon says. "All of it."

From what I saw, Leon's "knot" is even bigger. I tremble with anticipation, even as my pussy tells me how used it is.

With these two big men surrounding me, I'm barely hanging onto consciousness. My eyes flutter closed, and the edges of dreams drift in.

"Are you going to show her?" Jace asks over my shoulder in a low whisper.

Leon's voice is serious. "We have to, if she's who we think she is."

"Show me what?" I ask, half-asleep.

Jace kisses my ear, then the back of my neck. "Something really special. A secret."

I fall asleep wondering what secret that could possibly be.

Chapter Eleven

WHEN I WAKE UP, I FIND JACE'S ARM SLUNG AROUND MY WAIST, his face buried in my neck. Leon rolled onto his back in the night, and my legs are tangled up with one of his. Quickly disengaging myself from them, I check the clock on my phone to make sure I haven't overslept.

Oops. I'll have just enough time to shower before work. Thank god it's Friday. Things should be quiet around the office, and with how groggy I am, I'll need it.

Leon wakes up first and rolls over to face me. He kisses the tip of my nose.

"We'd better go," he says, despite the fact his cock is already at half-mast and making itself known against my belly.

I hear a yawn behind me, and Jace's chin hooks over my shoulder.

"Damn." His voice is sleepy but pleased. "That was incredible, Tiff. I could spend all day inside that sweet pussy of yours."

Just the words electrify me, and I can already feel myself getting wet. But I have to get going, and so do they.

On their way out the door, Leon kisses me first, and it's a gentle one. Then Jace pulls me into his arms.

"Thank you," he says into my ear. "I hope I get to see you again soon."

When they're both gone, I drag myself into the shower and stand shakily under the hot water. That knot of Jace's felt great last night, but today I ache between the legs.

What a bizarre phenomenon. I've seen quite a few dicks in my life, but nothing like that. I can't deny how erotic and utterly heavenly it was, though. Weird and yet delicious.

By the time I get into work, I'm still more or less a zombie, though I manage to grab Mr. Bosley's coffee and slide into my desk chair at exactly nine. Tonight, all I want is to curl up on the couch with some popcorn to watch a mindless movie—and let my body recover from last night's marathon.

I order lunch in so I can keep working through my break, and I've only just finished the first project by two in the afternoon. But on the second one, the numbers aren't adding up right, and I don't like passing anything off to accounting until I've done at least the barest of due diligence.

I'm scratching my head when Mr. Bosley stomps into the office, soaking wet. I glance out the window and find it's pouring rain. Great. His gaze zeroes in on me, and I cringe, knowing he's about to unleash hell.

"Are you done with Dunmar yet?" He towers over my desk. "That should have been finished this morning."

"I know," I squeak out. "But some of these payments aren't, um..." The last thing I want to do is question Mr. Bosley's work.

"Aren't what?" he prompts.

"They aren't reconciling. That's all."

"Well, reconcile them." He pins me down with his gaze, narrowing his eyes to make his meaning clear. "Do whatever you need to do to get it done."

Then the door slams.

Do whatever you need to do? I gape at my computer screen, where the erroneous spreadsheet taunts me. I would have to invent quite a bit of product to justify how much money was spent last month.

Mr. Bosley can't be serious. What he's asking—without *exactly* asking—is a federal offense, I know that much.

I chew my fingernails, though I know I shouldn't. What's the right way out of this? If I don't do what Mr. Bosley asks, he'll only get worse. Next week, he'll find some new way to grind me down into dust, and I'll spend my day fighting off tears. Maybe he'll tell HR that I'm not doing my job and then they'll can me.

But if I do what he's suggesting, there's a chance someone will find out down the line... and it will be my name on the files. He didn't tell me in so many words what to do, either, so I couldn't really say I did it on his orders.

The last thing I need is to be here all night figuring this out, so against my better judgment, I decide to do what Mr. Bosley asked. My throat closes up as I start fixing the files, my heart beating faster and faster the more fake cells I add to the spreadsheet.

A text interrupts me.

Hey Tiff, it's Quinn!

I stare at the message for a moment, then I remember giving him my number last night. I'd almost forgotten after what transpired with Jace and Leon.

Hey

It's the only thing I can think of to say with my brain feeling like vanilla pudding.

Do you want to hang out tonight?

Just the idea of it makes me tired. Quinn is a sweet ball of energy, and I don't think I could handle that today on top of Mr. Bosley. So I decide to be perfectly honest.

I'm exhausted, and I have to stay late at work. I don't know if I have it in me, to be honest

The answer comes soon after.

That's okay. I hope you feel better

He follows it up with a heart. Before I can type anything else, though, he sends another message.

I could just come to your place and baby you a little. Make you dinner?

I think of my bedroom and how it still smelled like sex when I left for work. What would happen with yet another one of the brothers in my apartment? It seems like a bad idea to me. Though Quinn assured me that all he wanted was friendship, I know he likes me after trying to ask me out— twice.

I type out a hesitant reply.

I don't know...

The last thing I want is for Quinn to want something more, and then I'd be forced to reject him.

> I won't put the moves on you, I promise. Just
> let me cook for you and take care of you?

That sounds surprisingly pleasant. Nobody has "taken care" of me in who knows how long. I take care of myself, which means ordering takeout on days when I come home too tired to cook. Even when I lived at home with Mom, she was usually too busy going out with her friends to make home-cooked food.

Now I have someone who wants to make me dinner so I don't have to lift a finger. Sounds like a dream come true—which means it probably comes with a catch.

But then again, Quinn doesn't seem like the type to demand anything that isn't freely given, unless I've misunderstood his brothers immensely.

Fine. After the day I've had, and will still have for the next two hours, being pampered sounds lovely. So I type out a quick reply as Mr. Bosley comes out of his office to leave for the night.

> All right, see you tonight

Quinn replies instantly.

> I'll bring everything. You just put on your
> favorite pajamas and wait for me, okay?

I can't help grinning at this. Quinn may have youngest brother energy, but that's part of what makes him cute. Maybe we can at least be friends, and I'll spend some time getting to know someone who's important to both Leon and Jace.

It's seven thirty when I send off the last of the paperwork, even though the accountants won't get to processing it until late next week.

I shoot Quinn a text to let him know I'm finally on my way home and lock up the office behind me.

Out in the parking lot, it's pouring rain, and my car is one of only two left in the lot. I wonder who else stayed late on a Friday night? The windshield is tinted so dark it's practically black, and it's a pretty nice SUV. Must be an executive from another office.

When I pull out of the lot, though, the SUV also turns on. It follows me out onto the street, and I think it must just be a coincidence. But as I take another turn toward my apartment, and then another, the SUV continues following me.

Fuck. What's going on? Who would be interested enough in me to follow me?

I decide to keep going and take another right turn, then a left. Finally, the SUV turns to the right, and the headlights vanish from my rearview mirror.

I let out a breath of relief as I stop at the light. It was nothing. The stress of work is just making me paranoid.

When I get home, I do what Quinn said and put on my most comfortable sweats. I really am tired, and I don't know if I made a good decision by letting him come over tonight. Too late now.

Quinn arrives soon after with a gentle knock on the door. I'm on my couch, watching a dating show, and hurry to let him in.

Quinn stands there, soaking wet, carrying a grocery bag and a big frying pan. It's *huge*. He grins a wide, toothy grin when he sees me.

"May I?" he asks, and I step aside to let him inside. He sets his things on the table, then gazes around my apartment. He studies my bookshelf, where I've perfectly placed my favorite knickknacks in front of my books. Then he takes in the few small pictures I've collected of family and friends, and a few ugly paintings from Goodwill. "Cute digs, Tiff."

"It's nothing." I reach for the bag of groceries, but Quinn flaps his hands at me to shoo me away.

"No, no," he says, urging me back to the couch. "Go lie down. Watch your show."

I open my mouth to object, but he gives me a gentle push, so I obey and sit back down.

"Do you want something to drink?" Quinn asks, unloading his bag. "Club soda? Wine?"

He really is just an adorable puppy. And damn, he smells as good as Jace and Leon do. What is it about their body odor that turns me the fuck on?

"Start with club soda, then work up to wine?" I ask. I'm being too high-maintenance already, and he'll probably get bored of spoiling me quick. But Quinn just nods, wearing that goofy smile, and retreats to the kitchen to fetch me a glass.

He's surprisingly quiet while he cooks, only calling over from time to time to ask my preferences. He seems to have no trouble at all navigating the kitchen and finding what he needs. It's not long before I've settled in under a blanket, letting the scent of cooking garlic and onions lull me into real relaxation. Whatever he's making over there is going to be good. I'm a little embarrassed he caught me watching *Blind Date*, but he did say I should make myself comfortable, and I'm never more comfortable than sipping some wine while watching couples on television turning into total train wrecks.

Then an oven timer beeps, and in the kitchen, Quinn clinks plates together. After a few minutes he emerges, bringing me a tray I didn't even know I had, laden with food.

"Shrimp paella and ceviche with roasted carrots on the

side." Looking rather pleased with himself, Quinn places the tray on my lap, then refills my wine glass. At last, he brings his own plate over and sits on the couch next to my feet, keeping a careful distance between us. It's cute how much he's trying to respect my boundaries.

"Wow." I breathe in the scent of food and my stomach rumbles. "I can't wait for this. How'd you learn to make paella?"

"Watched a video." He spears one of his carrots with a fork. "Come on. Try it."

The food tastes even better than it smells. Eating this dinner is almost an orgasmic experience in and of itself. My toes curl as I take another huge bite.

"Quinn," I hum, "this is incredible."

He has the same long canines as his brothers when he grins. "See, I can be an idiot, but I earn my keep."

Before I know what I'm doing, I've inhaled the whole plate of food—and the wine, too. For a moment I imagine my mother sitting here, telling me to stop stuffing myself, and I quickly sit up and look for a napkin to wipe my face. Quinn's staring at me, and I can't believe I let him see me eat like that.

"Damn," he says. "You absolutely wrecked that. Amazing." He eats his own food faster. "Only Leon's ever out-eaten me before."

He devours his own meal, too, then snatches up both plates and the tray. I get to my feet to take them to the kitchen, but Quinn raises a hand to stop me.

"I'm going to clean up," I say. "You just did all the cooking."

"Nope." His tone brooks no argument. "Sit back down. I'll bring you more wine."

So, I acquiesce and sink back down into the couch. A few seconds later, Quinn returns with a refilled glass for me. I settle in, feeling uneasy that he's doing all this work—but he genuinely seems to enjoy it, and maybe it's okay to let him.

Chapter Twelve

I DON'T REALIZE I'VE FALLEN ASLEEP UNTIL I HEAR A WHISPER IN my ear. "I'm going to let myself out, okay?"

I sit up abruptly, and bump my head right into Quinn's face. He lets out a yelp and backs up.

"I'm so sorry!" I scramble off the couch, hoping I haven't broken anything. "You surprised me!"

"It's my fault," he says, rubbing his nose.

There's no blood, thankfully. I reach up to check him over anyway, and Quinn leans into my palm when it brushes his cheek.

"Mmm," he says, releasing a heavy breath. "I've wanted you to touch me all night."

The words are so gently spoken, I'm not sure if I heard him right or not.

"You have?" But he's done such a good job of keeping his hands to himself and hasn't made any overt gestures.

"Oh, god, yeah." He inhales deeply as he puts his big hand over mine, holding it in place. "You smell like fucking rainbows. Like sunshine and ice cream and pizza and—"

I get the sense he loves food.

"What is it with you guys?" I ask with a chuckle. "All of you and your *smelling*."

A look flashes across Quinn's face, something like uncertainty, but it goes away just as quickly.

"Good noses," he says. He still hasn't released my hand, and I find I don't mind. I love how warm he is against me.

"Thanks for coming over," I say at last, breaking the contact between us. "And for treating me like a princess."

"Like a *queen*," he corrects, leaning down toward me. "Because that's what you are. Our queen."

I blink at him. "'Our'?"

He claps a hand over his mouth. "Sheesh," he says. "I really do come on too strong. I mean, you're only my queen if you want to be. And a subject doesn't ask for anything in return." He gives me a charming grin. "Just that you treat us well."

Maybe I don't know much about Quinn yet, but it also feels like I've known him for ages. He makes me comfortable in a way that's effortless. I guess I don't mind him calling me his *queen*.

It's nice to be someone's queen.

"It's okay," I tell him, sitting back down. "I think you're just a romantic."

His eyes glitter. "That I am." He sits down next to me, keeping a polite distance away, but I can sense how he wants to be closer. "And I've been looking for my queen for a long time."

This gives me a start. That sounds much more serious than what I thought we were discussing. Balling up my hands in my lap, I have to look away from his earnest, dark eyes.

"Quinn..." I begin, and he flinches.

"Uh-oh," he says, trying to sound playful, but I can hear the anxiety underneath it.

"Did Jace and Leon tell you?" I ask quietly. "About last night?"

He tilts his head. "Huh? Yeah. Of course they did." A broad smile crosses his face. "Is that what you're worried about?"

The relief is welcome, and my fingers finally unclench. At least he's aware. But that doesn't change where we are now—that I'm already in not one, but two relationships, and clearly Quinn wants even more from me.

"I have to admit," he says, "that hearing my brothers talk about last night..."

Oh, no. Is he going to tell me he was jealous, and that's why he's here? Am I a piece of meat and they each want a bite of me?

"...I just thought you might need a little TLC," Quinn finishes. "Leon's got that alpha energy, and Jace is a strong personality."

That's not what I expected, and it makes me happy. "Thank you. I did need it." Having someone baby me has really helped me shed off the anxiety from my week like a bunch of dust.

Quinn shyly takes my hand in his, as if waiting for me to take it back. Like before, though, his skin is so warm that I don't want to let it go. "I'm not asking for anything," he says carefully. "Nothing you don't want to give. I can just sit and hold your hand forever, and I'll be happy."

The sick thing is that I *do* want more. I like Quinn, I have to admit. Something about him is comforting and cozy and right. He really did treat me like his queen tonight, and I know he meant everything he's said and done.

If there's one thing the landscapers have in common, it's their sincerity.

But it's all so much. I'm still sorting through the endorphin-driven feelings I have for Leon and Jace, and I don't know where Quinn fits, if he does.

"I'm not sure what I can give," I finally say, lowering my eyes to my lap. Quinn massages my hand as I talk, digging his thumb into the tense flesh of my palm. "I feel like I'm barely keeping my head above water at work, and I'm already in a relationship with two other people." I glance over at him quickly. "You should be seeing someone your own age, anyway. You're too serious for only being—"

"Twenty-three?" he supplies. "I'm not a kid or something, Tiff. I can make my own choices. And I know what I want, because I've wanted it for a long time." He brings my hand up to his lips and hovers just centimeters away from kissing my knuckles. "But I also don't want to cause you even more stress. I'm glad to go home now, and just be here when you need me."

It seems far too good to be true. It must be. I don't know what guy sits around waiting to dote on you hand and foot without expecting anything in return.

"I guess I can always use a free, home-cooked meal," I say, trying to sound lighthearted.

But Quinn doesn't answer. He simply watches me as he presses a gentle but bold kiss on the back of my hand. It sends a shockwave down my arm, straight to my nipples. God, why do these guys turn me on so much? It's more than just the fact they're all fit as fiddles and carved like David, or how they smell amazing, even when sweaty. They draw me to them on a level that feels deeper than that.

"I'll take care of you every day if you want," Quinn says in a low voice.

"Every day?" Geez.

"If you'll let me." He tilts my arm so he can kiss up my wrist, then the inside of my forearm. I allow it, like I'm hypnotized. Maybe I am, but he feels so good, I don't want to stop him.

"I don't know about every day," I say, my breath hitching

when he kisses up to my shoulder. Little sparks of electricity are spreading across my body from each point of contact.

Then he leans back, looking into my eyes, and I find so much more there than I was expecting. If anyone in the world means what they say, it's Quinn. His dark brown eyes, I realize, have equally long, dark lashes, and they're so full of affection for me that I have to resist kissing him right there.

"I want to kiss you," Quinn says. "And I can leave it at that, if you're ready for me to go home now."

Why does my heart fall at this last part? Of course I want him to go home. I need a night alone, don't I? Besides, this is all moving fast. Everything was different just yesterday, and now it's changing again. I'm collecting landscapers like Pokémon cards.

"I shouldn't," I say finally. That would be insane of me, completely and utterly deranged, to even consider anything more with Quinn. Because I know what kissing will turn into if my body has its way. It already knows it wants him, and that's something I can't give in to after last night.

I'm not that greedy. The last thing I want is to make them think I'm a slut.

I shiver at the thought. That's the kind of thing my mother would say.

"Tiff," Quinn says, drawing my attention back to him. "If you can't, you can't, and I understand." He lowers my hand back to my lap. "But if it's a 'should,' if you feel like you're not allowed to do it for some reason..." His gaze is firmly locked on mine. "Then I want to ask why? Why can't you have what you want?"

I open my mouth to answer, but I can't think of what I would say. The only other person here is Quinn. The only person who ever has to know is Quinn.

"I can just make you feel great and then get on my way." He surreptitiously licks his lips. Immediately I wonder what he means by *making me feel great*, and my imagination conjures up all sorts of possible activities.

No, Tiff. Down. The sensible part of me says that I don't deserve Quinn offering to pleasure me, no questions asked. No, I can't do this after the night I had with Leon and Jace.

But I want to say yes. I want to know what Quinn has in store for me. And maybe, just maybe, it's not about deserving, but about living.

So finally, I say, "All right."

With a grin, Quinn turns to face me. His arm curls around my back and he leans over me, urging me with his body to sink back into the throw pillow. When his face is inches away from mine, he presses a gentle kiss to my lips. Before I can return it, he slides down until he's breathing against my collarbone, where he licks my exposed throat. His mouth trails over my sweatshirt, and I didn't even put on a bra. Chastely, he kisses past my two pert nipples to my belly, which is poking out from under the top. He presses his lips to that, too, and then continues over my sweatpants.

"I'll keep all my clothes on," Quinn says, his voice thick. "But I'd really, really like to take off your pants."

He's offering to eat me out, with nothing else expected? I'd be suspicious, but Quinn did cook me this whole dinner tonight, and he genuinely seemed to enjoy it.

"Okay," I say uncertainly. "I'm a little, um..."

"Sore?"

How can Quinn be so casual about that? All I have to do is think of Jace's bulge fitting into me, filling me up, and I blush all over.

"Yeah, sore," I say meekly.

"Don't be ashamed." He rests his face on my belly, nuzzling it with his nose. "I heard you even took Jace's knot. I'm proud of you."

For a split second, I wonder if Quinn has one, too.

"Now these need to go," he says, rubbing the band of my sweatpants. I'm certain now, as certain as I can be, that nothing will happen that I don't want to happen. Quinn is safe. The only one I need to be afraid of is myself.

I grab my sweatpants and my underwear and pull them down at the same time, so he can't see the granny panties I wore underneath.

"Can you sit on the edge of the couch?" Quinn asks, getting up to deposit my clothes neatly on the coffee table.

Curious, I follow his instructions, and he tugs me forward on the cushions until I'm splayed out in front of him. Then he kneels in front of me, between my open legs, and his eyes close as he simply inhales.

"Oh, damn," he says, shaking his head.

His gaze looks less relaxed and much more intent when he stares down between my legs. He buries his face in my pussy all at once, like a dog that hasn't been fed. I can't help the abrupt moan that spills out of me as his tongue dances around my clit, rubbing it every which way, alternating fast strokes and languid ones as if he knows exactly what to do with me. He carefully avoids my slit, as if he knows it's tender.

Instead, he pulls me even farther forward. "Lie back for me," he says, his mouth shiny and wet, and I obey. Now I'm fully revealed to him, and he lets out a huff of pleasure. He licks his index finger thoroughly, then sweeps it down, past my pussy to the hole underneath it. "Will you let me in there?"

I've only done anal play once before, with a real freak of a guy I went out with a few times. He liked all kinds of unusual things, when I was much more sheltered and vanilla. But I remember that after I got used to it, it felt great.

"Okay," I say with the slightest edge.

"I'll go super slow." Quinn licks his finger, then runs over the small, puckered hole again. He returns to licking me, and I fall back down on the couch.

That finger circles, pressing in, testing and coaxing me to open. Slowly, he works it inside my ass, all while he feasts on me. The moment that foreign digit settles in and my body adjusts, it feels *amazing*. It takes only a few more seconds of his tongue feverishly working my clit and that finger pumping in and out for me to break. Quinn keeps licking and thrusting as I crumble into pieces, moaning and squirming on the couch as my sensitized body reacts. Finally he stops, then pulls back and wipes his face.

"Wow," he says. "Fucking delicious. The perfect dessert." Without attempting anything else, he smooths over my thighs with his hands, kneading my muscles until I'm turning into jelly.

How many times have I orgasmed in the last seventy-two hours? I can't count.

Quinn lowers my legs down onto the couch, and I liquefy into it. I don't even realize I've fallen asleep again until I sense someone carrying me.

It's Quinn, and after opening the door to my room, he pulls back my sheet to put me in bed. I think he's going to leave, and the part of me that's half awake doesn't want that. He was so good to me, so kind to me, so gentle and caring that all I want is to hug him and snuggle his cute face.

I extend my arms out toward him and whimper, craving the warmth of him in my cold bed, and Quinn responds with a light chuckle.

"Don't mind if I do," he whispers as he climbs into the bed next to me, all of his clothes still on, and brings me in close. I realize I'm still not wearing any pants, but I find that I don't care.

I drift back off like that, wrapped up in him.

Chapter Thirteen

I FELL ASLEEP NEXT TO QUINN, BREATHING IN HIS HEADY SMELL, surrounded by his big arms.

I don't expect to wake up next to a huge, brown, and extremely furry body.

At first, I think I'm still dreaming, so I don't cry out. I lie there and examine it, wondering if I've found myself sleeping with a faux fur blanket I didn't know I had.

But no. It's breathing, whatever it is. I can't see the face high above my head, but furry arms are wrapped around me. There's something stiff and wet pressed against my belly, and when my eyes trail down the muscular, furry chest in front of me, I find...

A gigantic cock, thick and pink, with a pair of massive bulbs around the base. A dribble of pre-cum has squeezed from the tip, making my belly slick.

The landscaper's cock. I'd recognize it anywhere, even if it's far, far bigger than the ones I've seen before.

"Quinn?" I say uneasily. Where did he go? This can't

possibly be him. I want to wriggle away, but I don't want to risk moving too abruptly and waking this animal sleeping next to me. It's big enough to do some real damage. "Quinn, is that you?"

"Hmm?" a raspy voice says, and I can hear it rumble in the creature's chest. "Tiff?"

When the big blanket pulls away from me, I can finally look up at its face—and a massive snout with a shiny black nose is right in my face, with white fangs tucked over a curled lip.

I let out a scream. The creature cringes and covers its pointed ears.

"Tiff! Wait!" That's definitely Quinn's voice, just pitched down and filled with gravel. "Stop, please! It's me. It's Quinn."

I slap a hand over my mouth, and quickly crab-crawl backwards across the bed to put as much distance between us as possible. Whatever Quinn is now, he's huge and covered in fur, with a mouth full of sharp, glistening teeth. He has a big, wolflike head, a man's body—if that man were scaled up with a computer by fifty percent—and big, thick haunches. A fluffy tail lashes back and forth behind him, and he looks like he could eat me whole.

Instead of lunging at me, though, the gigantic monster slides off the bed, hands held up in surrender. It's such an insecure human gesture that it makes him look, well, ridiculous.

"I'm sorry, Tiff. It's me." Quinn's big yellow eyes tilt with fear and shame. "I promise."

"What the fuck?" I take in the sight of him, with that massive cock front and center. "What are you?"

He tilts his head. "Is it not obvious?"

"No! I mean, yes! It is! But werewolves aren't real, and so I'm asking for, like, a different explanation?" I pace around in a circle, waving my hands. "Are you a furry and this is some sort of elaborate fur suit?"

A laugh booms out of him, and it's definitely Quinn's laugh. It shows off the dozens of fangs scattered inside his big, long mouth. I can't believe what I'm looking at.

"Sorry about this." Quinn gestures down at his waist, where he's hard as a rock. He gathers the sheet up off the blanket and covers himself with it, but it only makes that tent-pole cock look even more absurd. He nods to the bed, where his shirt and pants are shredded from when he clearly split them open during the night. "I might need to borrow some clothes."

I can't imagine what clothes I would have that would fit a creature this size.

"It's really you," I mutter. I can't stop staring at him. "Man, is this why you guys are all so *weird*?" The howling, the smelling, it all snaps into place. "All four of you are werewolves, aren't you?"

Quinn shrugs bashfully. "I'm sure Leon was going to tell you at some point." He swallows. "He's the alpha."

"The leader," I say, echoing Jace from before. "Right."

I definitely feel like this is the kind of information I should have learned before Leon and Jace fucked me. But looking at Quinn, his shoulders curled tight like he's waiting for me to lay my judgment on him... I'm not as mad as I ought to be.

Werewolves aren't real. I knew, until a moment ago, that they didn't exist. And I wouldn't believe it unless I was looking at one.

"I guess I understand why you wouldn't tell someone this," I say, surveying his massive body. "It's, uh..."

"Terrifying?" Quinn's thick, bushy tail lashes nervously behind him.

"Something like that." But I don't feel frightened of it. The longer I look at this monster, the more obvious it is that it's Quinn, with the shape of his eyes and the same mannerisms. That massive cock of his hasn't softened at all, either.

"I'm sorry," he says, shoving it down with his hand. "I just have to wait to, uh, stop being horny, and then I'll change back."

"That's what caused it?" He transformed because we were cuddled up next to each other as we slept?

"I don't have good control." Quinn sits down on the bed, far away from me. It's so human, the way he sits, so familiar, even despite the big haunches, that I sit down on the other side of the bed, too, hoping to make him feel a little more comfortable. "Not like my brothers—they can all change at will. But I never got the hang of it. I couldn't even have a girlfriend after the first time this happened. I had to make up a really wild story to get out of that one."

I give him a sympathetic smile. "I imagine waking up next to someone like this makes things complicated."

Quinn nods, then raises one eyebrow in a way that's distinctly human. Even his lopsided grin, with his long wolf lips drawing back, looks like him.

"But you're not running for the hills," he points out.

"I mean, like you said, it's not as if you have any control over this." I wave in the general direction of his huge body. "And it doesn't seem like you're going to attack me or anything. It's fascinating, too. I have all kinds of questions for you."

Quinn's smile spreads even wider. He lies down on the bed and leans back on his elbows in a way that is, again, distinctly human, though he has long black claws at the ends of his fingers as he taps them on the bed.

"Like what?" he asks. He gestures at his cock under the

114

bedsheet. "This is gonna take a while." He turns and reaches for his phone on the bedside table. "And I should probably tell Leon that I spilled the beans."

"Wait." I have Quinn here, the perfect specimen of his kind. I'm certain his brothers will be unhappy with him for accidentally changing, and it might start all sorts of drama. I want to understand what I'm dealing with while I have this moment. "Don't tell them yet."

He blinks up at me. "Why?"

"Just give me a few minutes. I want to understand better."

Setting the phone back down, Quinn watches me as I slide across the bed toward him. His tail stiffens.

"Can I touch you?" I ask.

He blinks. "Touch me? I mean, sure." He waggles his claws. "Aren't you grossed out, though?"

"No," I answer automatically. I'm fascinated more than anything. I wonder what Quinn looks like when he transforms. His skeleton is completely different like this. Does it hurt?

"Wild," I say, creeping closer. Quinn watches me carefully but doesn't move. I pick up his hand and examine the claws, running my fingers from the base to the tip. They aren't deadly sharp, but dulled at the edges, like a dog's.

"Wh-what do you think?" Quinn asks as I explore his hands, which are still humanlike, though gigantic, with bare skin on the palms and fingertips. The fur spreading across his body is much softer than I expected.

"It's cool." I run my fingers down his arm to his thick chest. How often does someone get to see a real werewolf, in real life? "Shocking, you know, to find out lycanthropy is real."

A rumbling laugh comes out of him. "It's not like all that, I promise."

"Nobody bit you?"

He shakes his head and grins affectionately. "Just my brothers when we were pups. My dad's a werewolf, my mom's human. It's hereditary."

The more I touch Quinn, though, the more curious I get about him. There's just one part of his body I can't see.

"Can I..." I glance down at the tent pole under the sheet. I can't believe I'm about to ask this. It feels like objectifying him, but my curiosity is getting the better of me. "Can I see what's under there?"

Quinn looks like he's been struck by a bolt of lightning. He pokes the shape of his dick under the sheet with a claw. "This?"

I nod. What exactly is a creature like him packing? I only got a glimpse of it earlier, and it entranced me.

Furrowing his brow, Quinn picks up the sheet and drags it down, revealing all of himself. While his balls are furry—goodness, they're huge, too—the cock that pokes out of his fur sheath is enormous and pink, with veins spreading across the surface down to the lumps at the root. It's wet all over, and reflexively my hand trails down toward it, over his belly. His muscles tense as I get closer, so I stop.

"Can I touch it?" I ask, my voice quieter. Maybe I shouldn't want this, but I do. He turned into this because of *me*. Does that mean his werewolf form has desires, too?

And I'm one of them?

"That will make it take longer to go down," Quinn says tentatively, but there's an eagerness in his voice, too. "I won't object if you want to."

"It's Saturday."

He laughs and curls one clawed hand around his cock, holding it up straight for me. God, it's huge. Not that I'm surprised given his size.

"Go ahead."

The head of his dick in this form has an odd shape, not mushroomed like a human one, but still angled for penetration. White leaks from a hole at the tip. Down at the bottom, coming out of the fur sheath, is that lump—the same thing Leon and Jace had, but even bigger and more swollen.

Tentatively, I wrap one hand around the middle of his length, and it's much too big for me to fit my fingers all the way around. I have to use both hands, and Quinn gasps.

"Oh, shit," he says, as I drag my fingers up and down, testing him out. My palms skate along on his wetness, and his body jerks with each light stroke.

"Is that why you have, uh," I run my palm over the big bulge at the bottom, and he lurches under me. "Is that why you guys have these? Because you're...?"

Quinn's mouth opens and his long, pink tongue rolls out. "Yup. It's a knot. All werewolves have them."

I remember Jace and Leon using this word, too. It felt intense yet great when Jace managed to get it inside me. As a werewolf, though, that "knot" is even bigger.

Would something like that even *fit*?

Somehow, just thinking about it is like fire racing up the branches of a tree, spreading from my hips to my arms and legs. I wonder what Quinn would feel like.

I can't believe I'm thinking of him this way—a literal monster—but he smells just like he did when he was human, and his fur is soft, and his sweet face looks so worried that I'm going to reject him.

I lean in closer, still stroking his cock with my hands, and my tongue flicks out just to taste the tip of him.

"Fuck," Quinn groans. "Are you serious?"

"Do you not want me to?" I pull away.

His eyes go huge. "No! No, not at all, please." He

awkwardly pats my head, trying to keep his claws away from my hair. "Please do whatever you want."

I resume stroking, examining him as I go. His balls are contracting as I lick the tip of his cock. I swirl it around in my mouth, then bring it in as far as I can, which is, admittedly, not very far before I can't take any more. Then I suck, drawing him out again, and Quinn growls. I don't think that's the bad kind of growl.

I work faster, gripping his shaft, running my palm over his knot the way Leon showed me. Quinn's body snaps up when I grip it, and he lets out a low, grumbling moan.

"That's so good," he says, panting. "I... Oh, god." He licks his chops with that long tongue as I speed up my hands and mouth, and drool spills from his fangs. "God, damn, I... I want..."

I pause licking him to ask, "What do you want, Quinn?"

For some reason, this huge, furry monster underneath me, placid and desperate for my mouth, is really turning me on. I feel powerful making him squirm and moan. He could probably tear me to pieces with those claws, but instead he's gripping the comforter with them like he might fly off it.

"I want to be inside you so bad, Tiff." The words just tumble out of his mouth. He covers it with one paw, and curses into his palm. "Sorry. No. Pretend I didn't say that. This was supposed to be—"

"It's okay," I say, slowing down my strokes.

He wants to have sex with me like this? In this massive, furry, werewolf form?

Now that it's set out in front of me, my pussy clenches, and Quinn stiffens under my hand. He sniffs the air, and his eyes get huge.

"D-do you want that?" he asks uneasily, like he doesn't dare hope.

I can't honestly believe myself as I think over my answer. But I want to know what it would be like. He's bizarre in this form but also beautiful. Terrifying and fearsome but strangely, being with him feels safe.

"Yes," I finally say, my breaths speeding up. "Yes, I want that."

Chapter Fourteen

"LEON'S GOING TO KILL ME," QUINN SAYS, SCRAMBLING UP TO HIS knees.

He doesn't even ask before he yanks my legs apart, tips forward, and buries his snout in me. That cold nose makes me gasp. Then his big tongue lances out and drags up my labia to my clit, and holy shit. I've never felt anything like that. It slides down again, and I didn't realize just how big that tongue of his is until it tries to fit inside me.

But after the way Jace took me the other night, it manages to slide in. With a groan of delight, Quinn twists his tongue around, fucking me hard, his huge jaws open and his teeth dripping saliva all over me. It feels unbelievable, exquisite, absolutely divine. He groans as he withdraws and then laves across my clit again, making all my muscles clench and shiver. I can feel his claws biting into the flesh of my thighs as he jams that amazing tongue inside me again and then swallows, as if scooping all my fluids out of me.

"Fuck," Quinn-the-werewolf grunts, his hot, panting

breaths against my pussy making me twitch. He licks my clit between words. "You... taste... incredible."

I'm flying higher and higher as he works my body, that huge tail of his wagging wildly behind him. Tremors travel through me, and I can't help but grip the soft fur of his head to root myself to the earth. When I reach his pointed, furry ears and dig my fingers in, Quinn lets out a hum of pleasure.

Then I can't stand it anymore. I combust, a pure rocket of sensation, and my hips jolt up into his jaws. The tips of his fangs press into my belly, never breaking the skin, and the wolf moans as I feel myself squirt. Fuck, that hasn't ever happened with someone else before. With a snarl, he laps it all up, and I jerk my sensitive pussy away.

Hurriedly Quinn gets up again, sitting back on his huge haunches. That strange cock of his, with its sloped head and bulging shaft, is even more swollen than before.

"I've never done this," he admits, palming himself with one paw. The entire bed bends under his weight as he shifts nervously.

"At all?" I ask, still shivering from my orgasm. That makes me nervous. Will it even fit?

"Not in this form." Quinn crawls up the bed on four legs until he's crouching over me, wet pre-cum dribbling onto my belly. "The, um, anatomy is different." He repositions his hips a few times with a frown, like he's trying to figure out the best way to bring our bodies together.

"No kidding," I say, to bring some levity to this, but his ears pin back in what looks like shame. Something about this huge, monstrous creature behaving so awkward and afraid is deeply endearing.

I run a hand up his furry cheek, and Quinn-the-werewolf leans into it. "I've never done this, either, if that helps," I say, grinning.

He snorts, and I like the way his wolfish smile peels back his lips. "I'm glad to hear that." He leans down closer so his wet nose touches my ear. "Then I get to be the first werewolf cock to taste you. And feel you. And fuck you."

The words send a bolt of lightning straight through me. This massive creature hovers over me, waiting for the word. I imagine that big cock of his trying to fit into me, and my pussy already knows what it wants.

"Then do it," I whisper, reaching down to squeeze his knot.

Quinn groans, burying his snout in my hair. Then, he pulls back, and his lips curl in a snarl. Kneeling on his huge haunches, he grabs my hips with both paws, clearly trying to keep his claws from damaging me. He yanks me up by my ass and positions himself over me, his odd build forcing me to keep my hips elevated and my legs spread wide. That monstrous cock is weeping, the slit pulsing as he breathes and even more pre-cum dribbles down. Quinn slides the thick head between my folds, searching for...

"Oh!" I cry out. He's already trying to push it in, and my body fights immediately.

"Damn," Quinn grunts. "It's not going to fit."

He breathes hard, then tries again. This time the head slides in a little deeper before he meets firm resistance. My entrance is trying to accommodate him, but he's so big. Too big.

Quinn yanks his cock away and, sliding his big paws underneath me, drops his head down to lick me furiously. He delves deep into me with his tongue, then flattens it, the strong edges spreading me open. I squirm and moan in a combination of pleasure and discomfort as he twists it around, convincing my entrance to widen. When I'm soaked and he's thoroughly spread me, he positions my hips in front of him and stares down raptly as he grips his cock, pushing it inside me.

More of him fits this time, just a little more. Quinn's lips peel back, revealing all of his teeth and his pink gums, and his ears are pinned down. An animal fire is coming over him, and he shoves in again, urging me open. I feel my skin pinch—but then my channel gives enough that the tip slides through.

"Ah, damn!" Quinn's neck curls and his shoulders bunch up, all the hair on his mane and back standing up on end. His voice is helpless. "Tiff, I can't hold back—"

With a sudden, animalistic grunt, Quinn pushes inside me. I cry out as he breaches me, forcing me wide for him. My whole body convulses as he suddenly stills himself.

"Oh, god, I'm so sorry," he says, withdrawing his cock. "I just can't control it."

"Hey." I raise a hand up to his furry muzzle. It felt just as incredible as it did uncomfortable, and I want more. I want to get used to him, so I can really, truly feel him. "Do it again."

"Again?" Quinn asks, dumbfounded. Then his canine eyebrows lower mischievously. "Oh, I can do it again."

This time, when that thick cock of his burrows in, he reaches farther. He groans as he sinks into me, one arm curling possessively around my back, holding me up off the bed. On his next thrust, though, he goes even deeper, and I cringe as it touches something supremely sensitive inside me.

"Aw, fuck," he says, pulling back out, his brows tilted in worry. "You're small. I forgot."

Panting, I pet the tip of his snout. "It's okay."

"I'll remember," he says, like a Boy Scout, and then that massive, pink, slippery cock fills me up again.

Despite the animal vigor taking over him, Quinn is careful, never bottoming out inside me. When I look down, I find that he's not even all the way sheathed in me, and that big, fat knot of his isn't even close to the spread lips of my pussy. There's no way that could ever fit.

A knowing grin lifts his mouth on one side.

"Someday," Quinn growls, his thrusts growing faster, "you'll take my knot."

Just the thought makes me moan. I wonder how many times I'd have to orgasm for that.

Quinn strokes in and out of me with care, his snout bunched up in a snarl as he focuses on where our bodies are linked. The strange shape of him is stimulating all sorts of new nerve endings, and stretched as far open as I am, my body responds to every single stroke.

"Jesus, they were right," Quinn groans, his claws squeezing my flesh. "I can't believe how well you fit me."

Some drool drips off his fangs, and he leans his head down close to mine, his breath tickling my face. I open my mouth as if to kiss him and he opens his, then his tongue snakes out, darting between my lips. I moan as it slides down my throat, filling up my mouth just as full as he's filling my pussy. He groans into me, his teeth gently prodding my forehead and my jaw as he thrusts faster and faster, sinking more and more of that cock into me with every pump of his haunches.

"Oh, Quinn," I moan into him, burying my fingers in his scruff. My legs wrap as far around his waist as they can, and he pulls his tongue out of me so he can sit further back. He drags my hips high up into the air as he fucks me, his big jaws open, his gaze riveted on my body.

"You're so fucking beautiful," he grits out, his lips curling up in a snarl. "The way your tits bounce every..." He drives his cock into me again. "Time... I..." Then again. "Fill you up."

He snatches up my legs in his arms, slinging them over his elbows so he can fit even more inside me. He's ravenous, mad with animal lust. He leans forward, his big tongue lolling out to wrap around one of my nipples. It makes my pussy clench around him even harder, and his eyes roll back in his head.

"God, babe, you're incredible."

And that's when it comes for me. It's like a train, how hard my climax hits me. I scream, full-throated, and Quinn plunges into me harder. His grip tightens, digging his claws in, as he makes beastly noises that must be sounds of pleasure. His big, yellow eyes look almost pained as he crests.

"I'm going to come," he moans, and then suddenly, there's even more of him inside me than before.

My pussy stretches, desperate to accommodate his swelling cock, and I writhe and cry out as it hurls me into another powerful orgasm. I can feel that thick lump at the root of his shaft nudging at my entrance, but it's far, far too big.

Quinn snarls and thrusts hard, and for the first time in my life, I can actually feel his hot ejaculate shoot against my walls with a shocking force. He whines as he pumps a few more times, and he empties so much of his cum inside me that I feel it stream down my ass in a river, onto my bedspread.

With a grunt, Quinn falls down onto the bed, barely holding himself up over me with one arm. His tongue lolls out as he pants, his hot breath covering my face.

"Fuck," he mutters. He suddenly licks me from chin to forehead, and it makes my pussy flutter and shiver. He groans, dropping his big snout to the comforter above my head. "God damn, I've never felt anything like that."

"Neither have I," I say breathlessly, reaching around behind his head to stroke his fur. He moans and rubs against me. "Not in my whole life."

We're both still panting as the storm clears. Slowly and gently, Quinn pulls himself out, but it can't be helped. I wince because this wasn't completely without a price. The skin around my entrance must have torn a little, but I was too overcome by agonizing pleasure to notice at the time.

"I'm sorry," Quinn says regretfully, and pulls my legs apart to see what damage he's done. His huge tongue darts out, sweeping up my sensitive pussy, lapping up all of himself and me until I'm completely clean. Then he smooths the soft heel of his paw over it, sighing. "Damn. He's going to be pissed."

"Who?" I ask, sitting up as much as my exhausted body will allow.

"Leon." When Quinn looks at me again, I find that he's changing. His snout is receding, his fur disappearing to reveal human skin again. Quinn's body shrinks, and it's not long before he's back to himself, his cock now quiet between his legs. "I shouldn't have done that."

I frown at him. "Why not? It's your body. I'm the one who said 'yes.'"

Quinn nods, acknowledging this. "You don't understand, though. He tells us what to do." He scratches the back of his head. "And this wasn't on the to-do list."

I shrug. "He can get over it." When I sit up, though, even more white fluid streams out of me, making me squint. "I think I need a shower after all that, though. Do you want one, too?"

Quinn sits up eagerly. "Yes, please."

Chapter Fifteen

AROUND NOON, QUINN FINALLY TAKES A SKIRT OF MINE THAT FITS over his hips and leaves with no shirt on, carrying his massive frying pan with him. I fall back on the couch, squinting when my sore lady parts make themselves known.

Totally worth it.

I check my phone and find a text message from Leon that's been there for the last two hours.

Are you holding my brother captive?

I don't even know what to tell him. That I just fucked yet another of his younger brothers? From the way Quinn made it sound, Leon will be much angrier to find out he revealed their secret to me by accident.

Shame settles like a stone in my belly. I can't believe I did that. Not only did I hook up with Quinn, but I did it while he was, well, a monster. A beast. A huge creature with an equally huge cock that he had to stuff inside me for it to fit.

My body shudders just thinking about it. I swallow hard when I finally respond.

> Um, no. He's on his way home now

Leon texts back quickly.

> Was he any good? Quinn's the baby of the family. Not much practice

So Leon has guessed and doesn't seem upset. That's a good start. But should I be honest with him?

> It was wonderful

That's the truth, and I can't deny it. My hips in the air, Quinn's furry haunches driving into me, his drool leaking down my face... I feel like a bit of a harlot, but I fucking loved it. That thick, pointed cock of his is forever burned into my memory.

> Good ☺

Leon even includes a smiley face, but it's the default one, which looks a little bit creepy. Why does he text like he's fifty?

I massage the bridge of my nose, because I have to tell him the truth. I hope I don't get Quinn into terrible trouble, but I also can't pretend I'm not aware of what the guys have been trying to hide from me.

Biting my lip, I type out my next message, hoping I don't ruin everything by asking for some answers.

> I know now. About your secret. When were you going to tell me?

There's no response for a long time—not even the three dots to tell me Leon's typing. After waiting and waiting, my heart falls into my stomach.

Fuck. I screwed up by not letting Quinn handle this himself. I shouldn't have butted in. What if the landscapers never talk to me again?

My anxiety spikes just thinking about what a fuckup I am, so I decide to do some chores to distract myself. I drag my laundry basket downstairs and load some dirty clothes into the machine. Maybe Leon's just busy—though hopefully not busy chewing out Quinn.

I sit and stare through the little round window as the machine fills with suds and tosses my clothes around. Did I cross a line by sleeping with Quinn in his werewolf form? What if that's taboo in werewolf culture? Or perhaps they think I'm an awful person for corrupting him.

Once the machine finishes, I switch my wet clothes over to the dryer, and check my phone again. Still no answer.

Just great. We had a good thing going on. I almost felt like I fit with Leon and Jace and Quinn, like they understood me in a way I've never been understood. But it was foolish to hope. Of course I don't belong with three beautiful, kind, attentive men.

When my load of laundry is done, I trudge back up the basement stairwell to my apartment. I'm surprised to find Leon sitting outside my door, and my heart leaps up into my throat. Why is he here?

He stands up when he sees me and gives me a sheepish wave.

"Sorry to surprise you," he says as I approach, the laundry basket on my hip. "I just thought I should try to explain myself in person."

A little flame of hope sparks inside me when Leon doesn't

sound upset. I open the door to my apartment and step inside, wondering why he's come here to talk to me directly.

Will he try to threaten me to keep quiet? That doesn't seem like something he would do, but he also has a family, and a secret, to protect.

Leon hovers in the entryway to my apartment, wringing his hands together.

"Is this one of those vampire things where I have to invite you inside?" I ask in a joking tone, hoping to ease the tension.

He responds with a grateful smile. "No. Just being polite, in case you're angry."

I set down the laundry basket on the coffee table. "You can come in."

I've been so busy feeling anxious that I don't know if I'm angry or not. They hid something rather important from me. I vaguely remember the night I fell asleep in Jace's arms, and I heard them discussing a *secret* they wanted to share with me.

They probably thought I'd run for the hills the moment I found out. Still, I wish I'd known before embarking on this journey, whatever it is. Now I'm knee-deep with three werewolves.

Leon steps over the threshold into my apartment and closes the door softly behind him. If he weren't six feet tall and pure muscle, he would look like a little boy the way he's shamefully standing by my coat closet.

"Tiff," he begins, staring down at his feet, "I'm really sorry that I didn't tell you sooner—"

"You don't have to apologize." I usher him into the living room. "You did it for a good reason."

"I didn't want to scare you away too soon." Leon scratches the back of his head. "You're taking it a lot better than I thought you would."

I took it in more ways than one. My whole body shivers just remembering Quinn's enormous werewolf cock inside me. Leon's nostrils flare, and his pupils dilate, taking up his whole iris.

"How did it feel?" he asks, taking a step closer to me. "Riding a werewolf?"

My face is so hot that I wonder if my ears are about to light on fire.

"Amazing," I finally whisper. I can't deny it. I loved how Quinn was an animal, ferociously licking me and kissing me— if that's what it can be called—while he filled me fuller than I've ever been. His fur was so soft under my hands, and perfect for grabbing onto. And his huge body over mine, claiming me...

Leon smiles a big, toothy smile, as if he knows exactly what I'm thinking.

"You smell so good," he says with a heavy inhale, like the scent calms him. When I glance down, I find a little tent in his jeans. "Especially when you're turned on." He takes a step closer to me, then shakes his head like he's clearing away fog. "I really am sorry for not coming clean, Tiff. If I'd known you were so, uh, open to it... I wouldn't have waited until Quinn spilled the beans."

"Now I understand the whole howling thing, at least," I joke.

Leon's eyebrows lower, and his lips purse. "Yeah. I knew the moment I smelled you that you're our—" He balls his hands into fists.

I quirk my brow. What was it he was going to say?

"I'm your what?" I ask, pressing.

Leon swallows hard. "I just knew you were right for us."

I blink. "By how I smelled?"

"Yes." He nods rapidly. "And our bodies responded to it right away."

A chill seeps into my skin. "What do you mean, 'responded'?" My eyes travel down again to the clear boner Leon's sporting. "You knew you wanted to have sex with me? Just by smelling me?"

I can't help but wonder if that's all this is between us. That I *smell good*, and it makes their inner werewolf want me.

"Well, yes," Leon says hastily, "but it's not just about sex, Tiff."

"It's not?" My tone is getting defensive. I won't forget Leon's ravenous expression the first time we stumbled into my bed together, like he'd just walked into a sushi buffet. "That's all this is, isn't it?" My voice is getting higher and higher in pitch as my heart beats faster. "How all three of you just want to, you know." I mime sticking a finger in a hole. Once again, they just want me for big tits, big ass, and apparently, a tight pussy.

Leon groans and drags a hand down his face. "That's not what I'm after," he says with a helpless look. "I promise. I like you, Tiff. I like you a lot."

"But that's a big part of it, isn't it?" My chest feels tight, and my breathing is getting shallower by the moment. I fold the laundry, needing to keep myself occupied so I don't get emotional.

It's not really about me or who I am as a person. It's just about instinct, and need, and whatever else drives werewolves to fuck. A tale as old as time.

Leon frowns and sits down on the couch next to me. "Tiff, please."

He takes the shirt I'm folding and drops it into the laundry basket, then he places his hands on my shoulders and turns me to face him. When I don't look up, he stoops low and peers into my eyes.

"You're smart, funny, and beautiful." I like the way his dimples deepen when he says this. "You work hard and you're always kind. I really admire you. I would never have gone home with you that night if I didn't actually *like* you. Smelling wonderful isn't enough to make me want intimacy with someone." He shrugs. "All it did was show me where to look to find my..."

He pauses, his expression tightening like he's not sure how much to say.

"What?" I ask. "That's the second time now. Your what?"

"My person," he says finally, lowering his eyes. "My mate."

I freeze, catching on this last word. "*Mate*? Like an animal?"

Leon's sigh is deep as he rubs his temples. "There's a reason that you're so attractive to us. Our noses know things our minds don't yet." Those blue eyes of his lock with mine, begging me to understand. "I'm meant for you. So is Jace, and Quinn, and..." He trails off. "You smell incredible to us because our bodies know you're perfect—mind, body, and soul."

I'm meant for you. That's a pretty big statement, and I'm afraid of how much weight it holds. We've only slept together twice. It's a little premature to be thinking about more than casual dating.

My shoulders tense up. "And what does me being your 'mate' mean, exactly?"

Leon is clearly unsure of how he should answer. "It means someone you would give your life for," he says eventually. "Someone who's your whole world. Someone you want to care for, and make pups with, and—" He abruptly stops like he's just realized he let his mouth take over.

All I can do is stare at him. "*Pups*? You mean babies? You want to have *kids* with me?"

This is insane. Having children has always been a far-off idea for me, something I didn't really consider because I'd never come close to finding someone I wanted to have them with.

Leon drops his head into his hands. "I know. Sounds crazy, but I can't help it. None of us can. It's just what our bodies are begging us for." Now he won't look at me as he continues. "I understand if you want nothing to do with that. And all of us, too?" He chuckles darkly as he raises his eyes. "We picked up the smell at the same time and knew who you were then."

"Is it as rare in the werewolf world as it is in the human world for three guys to all want the same woman?" I ask, half-sarcastic.

He just taps his chin. "No, I guess it's not that surprising. We've always shared everything. And we're a pack—it's not out of the ordinary for packs to all imprint on one person." He keeps saying this word, *all*.

"But it's not 'all' of you," I point out.

Confusion settles on Leon's face. "Huh?"

Eli, the most polite and most reserved of the brothers, seems to be the only one with any rational sense. He must not be affected by whatever weird madness has come over the others.

"Eli's not interested like you are. So only the three of you 'imprinted' on me."

Leon frowns. "I didn't realize you liked him."

"I don't!" I kick the basket of laundry away. "I don't know him at all. Just like I don't really know *you* at all. It's a lot." He's basically telling me all three of them want to marry me. Have kids with me. That's too much weight to put on a girl.

"I'm sorry, Tiff." Leon's brows pinch together. "I didn't mean to dump so much on you at once."

"Yeah, it's a lot of pressure," I admit. "I'm dating three guys, and I just found out they're all werewolves hiding in broad daylight. I don't know if I'm ready for all that other stuff yet. We've been on a total of what, one date?"

I hardly know them at all, and they expect all this from me? I shake my head as I fold a shirt, placing it on the ottoman.

Leon nods solemnly, but I can tell he's hurt. "I understand. It's probably a little overwhelming."

That's one word for it. It's an unexpected avalanche of expectations. I haven't had a real boyfriend in years, and now I have three—who apparently all think I'm their... *mate.*

"It is," I agree. "And I'm not sure I'm ready for it."

Leon can't hide how my words take him down a few notches.

"We're happy to give you time," he says slowly. "We don't expect anything from you, and we're all here for the long haul. Whatever space you need."

Space. It's probably a good idea. I don't want to lead them on, when I don't know at all what I want.

"That would be good, I think." My voice comes out small.

"All right," Leon says, rising to his feet. Clearly he doesn't like it, but he's not going to argue his case anymore.

I look down at my hands. "I'm sorry. I just don't know what to think right now." My chest is tight and my heart is racing as I try to process it all. "This is a lot for one day."

"I understand, Tiff." With a sad smile, Leon heads for the door. "Let me know when you're ready. *If* you're ever ready."

The way he says it makes my throat close, but before I can answer, he shuts the front door behind him.

Chapter Sixteen

I SPEND ALL OF SUNDAY AT HOME, MOSTLY MOPING. WHY DIDN'T I see this coming? All the signs were there. If I'd been paying attention with my brain instead of my vagina, maybe I would have seen it.

The howling. The smelling. The secrets.

Maybe they think they want commitment, but that's just their hormones talking, whatever hormones werewolves have.

After obsessively cleaning my apartment all day, then ordering Chinese takeout, I stumble into bed thinking about Leon's downtrodden face as he left my apartment. He might believe that I'm his "mate," whatever that means, but I have no such certainty.

I don't know if I can give him what he wants.

Going into work on Monday feels like walking to the gallows. The moment I sit down at my desk, I start obsessing over the numbers I had fudged so Mr. Bosley would get off my back. I bite my nails all day, thinking that surely someone from accounting is going to give me an earful, but it doesn't happen. Clients and partners come and go, keeping both me and Mr. Bosley busy, and for once, I'm grateful for the distraction.

Around two in the afternoon, a familiar woman walks in the door. She's dressed to kill, and honestly, her eyes could probably murder someone, too. But she stops when she sees me and the side of her mouth twitches in a smile.

"How's it going with the two boyfriends?" she asks, pausing at my desk.

"Um..." I flounder for an answer. I'm not sure anymore after yesterday. "It's not, I guess."

She quirks an eyebrow. "Already?" With a shrug she adds, "Too bad." Then she strides into Mr. Bosley's office and closes the door.

Briefly I wonder if they're having an affair. Mr. Bosley's married to an uptight woman who drives a Range Rover, and they don't seem to like each other much. But I have a hard time believing Mrs. Smith would stoop that low.

Soon I can hear Mr. Bosley's raised voice behind the door. Whatever she has to say, it upsets him. Just great. He'll probably take it out on me later. But after Mrs. Smith leaves, he doesn't emerge for the rest of the day.

Unfortunately, I have dinner with my mom scheduled for tonight. I definitely can't tell her about Leon, Jace and Quinn. Not that it will matter, or last long enough to be necessary.

Something about that thought makes my heart sink. While it's difficult to imagine a future where I share my life with not one, not two, but *three* people, I also don't want to imagine one without them. I want to get to know them better, understand them better, maybe see if I can feel that deep connection they clearly feel with me.

At the end of the day, I find the black SUV in the parking

lot again. I watch it carefully as I pull out onto the street, but this time, it remains where it is.

Nobody's following me. It's just my anxiety acting up, like always.

Back at my apartment, I pick out one of my "mom-appropriate" outfits: a flowy top that hides my belly and a pair of tummy-control slacks. I hate how I look in it, but it will give Mom fewer things to gripe about.

Dinner starts with the usual interrogation. Usually her niggling comments wash over me like water because I've grown so used to them. Tonight, though, it's tugging at a deeper part of me. I remember Leon's question: *Have you ever told her how you feel?*

The idea of actually letting my mother know how her words hurt me has always been far, far out of the question. All it would do is set her even more staunchly in her ways. My mom has always believed she's without flaw, and pointing one out wouldn't go well, I'm sure of it. She's obsessed with how she appears to others, and suggesting that maybe she isn't as good of a mother as she thinks she is would challenge everything she believes about herself.

And yet, I'm stewing under the surface as Mom starts in on how one of her friends has a son who's gainfully employed, and just got out of a bad relationship. Mom even knows his salary, which she counts off to me with her fingers.

"It might be a good match for you," she says, tut-tutting. "We already know he comes from a good family, and I don't think he's terrible to look at."

What a high bar for a partner. I roll my eyes.

Mom has tried to set me up before, and only once have I ever accepted. It was one of the worst dates of my life, and like every guy I've met before, all he wanted was a fling. We hooked up, and then he never called again.

I need some way to set my mother off course, because turning down her proposal will make her unbearable for the rest of the night. The next thing that comes out of my lips is not something I anticipated saying, but it's the only thing that will shut her up.

"I have a boyfriend already."

I cover my mouth as if I can pull the words back in. Shit. Now she's going to want to know everything about him, and I'll have to lie. I'm not a great liar.

Mom's eyebrows fly high on her forehead. "What? You have a boyfriend?" She huffs with annoyance. "Why didn't you tell me sooner? You could have called me! That's a big deal, Tiffany."

I fumble for an excuse. "I didn't know if it was serious yet." Though Leon made it pretty clear last night just how serious he is about me. How serious all three of them are about me.

"You should have told me when you had a date." Mom looks deeply offended. "I could have helped you pick something out."

I sigh. Like usual, she wants to control me, all the way down to what I wear on a date.

"Why would I have asked you?" I suddenly feel bold. "You would have just told me everything I own looks bad, or that I should tuck my tummy in."

Mom's eyes go wide and her mouth drops open. "That's not true! How could you say that?"

I want to tell her everything: how her words chew away at me one piece at a time, each of her comments burying themselves in my flesh like tiny daggers, but I don't know if she could possibly hear me above the noise of her own ego.

"Whatever," I finally say as our food arrives. "Doesn't matter now. He liked me enough to ask me to be his girlfriend, so I must have done an okay job of dressing myself."

Mom doesn't answer as she starts eating. The meal passes mostly in silence, which is odd, because usually she's spouting off about the latest work drama by now, her food lying untouched. Her silence is deafening.

Have I actually hurt her feelings?

"Well, tell me about him," Mom says eventually, putting down her fork. "What does he do for work?"

Of course, the thing she's most interested in is what kind of job this hypothetical boyfriend has. I think for a moment about making something up, something she would approve of. But why should I have to lie? The guys clearly love their work. They're happy doing it, and they live a good lifestyle.

"He's a landscaper," I say.

It's hard to read the look on her face. "Hmm. So he works outside all day?"

I nod uneasily. "Five days a week."

"Not exactly a high-paying job," she says, and I groan. Of course. "What?" she snaps. "It's not!"

I want to slap my past self across the face for even mentioning it.

"So what if it isn't a six-figure job?" I ask, my tone pinched. "They're happy, and that's what matters."

I don't realize what I've said until my mom's food spills off her fork.

"They?" she asks, arching one eyebrow.

"I mean, *he's* happy." I hastily try to come up with a correction that'll get her off my back. "He has three brothers, too. They own a company together."

Her eyes brighten at this. "Oh, he owns his own landscaping *company*? Well, that's different then, isn't it?" I don't like how wide and bright her smile has become. "How'd you score that, Tiffany?"

The way she says it, as if I should be so lucky, makes me grind my teeth together.

"I met him when I was out jogging." There. That's close enough to the truth that she should leave me alone.

"You met him in your workout clothes?" she asks, a tinge of horror in her voice.

I don't know if I can take it anymore.

"Yes. I did." Something in me sparks to life after already telling her one truth tonight. "He thought I was hot, so he called me over and asked me out."

That's one way to spin the guys howling at me from across the street.

Mom gapes at me like she can't even conceive of it. "And you said yes? To some strange guy?"

"Yep." I plaster on a big smile. "He's a good man, and no, you can't meet him."

"You're so defensive tonight," Mom grumbles. "Is this all because of this *boyfriend*? He's turning you against me?"

It's just like her to assume that we're on opposite sides of a war. But I don't want to fight this fight tonight, so I decide to back off and live to pick up the torch another day.

"No. I'm tired, Mom, that's all." I push away my empty plate of food and stand up. "I should get going so I can get some sleep tonight."

She squints in a way I can only interpret as mischievous. "Is he keeping you up late?"

It sets me off-balance. Is she honestly joking with me? About my sex life?

I feel my whole face get hot, and Mom laughs when I don't respond right away.

"Question answered," she says, and I'm stunned by her playful jab. "Well, I won't keep you out, then. But I hope you'll

141

introduce him to me." Then, of course, she adds, "If it works out that long."

And I had such high hopes for her.

That night, I don't hear from Leon, Jace, or Quinn.

I'm not sure why I expected to after Leon agreed to give me space. They're all just doing what I wanted. And this is what I want, right? To have some time to think, and decide if I'm up for being someone's *mate*?

Or the mate of three someones. Whatever that word means.

I'm surprised when my phone lets out a little *ping!* and a new text message arrives. I don't recognize the number, but it's local.

> Hey, Tiff, it's Eli. Leon gave me your number.

I gape down at my phone screen. Eli, of all people? The sweet brother who helped me during my anxiety attack? Who then sat in the back of the truck and moped without even saying hello?

> Oh, hi

I don't know what else to say.

> I know you're overwhelmed right now. Please don't think that because you haven't heard from my brothers that they don't care about you.

My brow furrows. He's reaching out on Leon, Jace and Quinn's behalf? Is he going to interfere and argue their case?

Another message appears.

> Remember to take deep breaths. Everything will be okay.

I don't know what to say, but I can hear the words spoken in Eli's soft voice, and that steadies my nerves. I quickly type a message back.

> Thanks for reaching out. I'm not sure what I want yet.

The answer comes immediately.

> That's all right. They'll wait for you. Take your time to sort out your feelings.

But for how long? And do I *want* them to wait?

I read over the messages again, remembering how he told me to breathe, how he held my hand. That he reached out now, at my most uncertain—I feel like Eli understands me.

> I appreciate it, Eli

He hearts my message and doesn't reply. The other brothers are all so open and stumbling over themselves to tell me how they feel, but Eli is a mystery to me.

I avoid jogging by the landscaping site the next morning. It would be too awkward. Instead, I take a different route to the park, which unfortunately makes my jog longer. I'm almost late to work, but when I get in, Mr. Bosley isn't even there.

I find a message on my phone. "I'll be out all morning looking at some, um, project locations," Mr. Bosley tells the answering machine. I shiver at the uneasy tone of his voice. "Cancel my morning meetings."

It's a pain, but I'm able to move everyone to later in the week. Still, when afternoon comes, there's no Mr. Bosley. It's actually a rather lovely day, and I start wishing I had a date with one of the guys to look forward to.

And I always have my friends. Maybe if I can come at least somewhat clean with them about the landscapers, they can help me figure out what to do.

Chapter Seventeen

"I'm sorry. I want to make sure I understand right. You're complaining about a guy being *too* committed?" Aisling swirls her wine around.

We're all sitting on the floor at a low coffee table in Hannah's apartment, two boxes of pizza mostly empty between us. Her expression is extremely judgy.

"We just found out you had a boyfriend three seconds ago," Hannah says, annoyed. "You didn't even text us. And now you're saying he's looking for marriage and you're running away scared?"

I slide over my empty glass with a pout on my lips. Aisling rolls her eyes as she refills it with wine.

"It's just a lot, you know?" I sound pathetic to my own ears. "We've only been out once." And with Quinn, we haven't even had a first date. But my friends don't need to know about all that yet. I'm especially not going to tell them that all *three* of my boyfriends are, apparently, werewolves. I don't think they'd believe me for a second, and it's not my secret to tell.

"But you hooked up," Aisling says, eyebrow raised. "Twice. How was it?"

How do I even put it into words? I think about the first time Leon came home with me, how he bossed me around, how he told me I was beautiful, how he praised me until I was floating on a cloud as he fucked me into a shivering puddle. How I came so many times with Leon and Jace together that I thought my body might implode.

"It was amazing," I say quietly into my glass of wine. "Best sex I've ever had in my life. And he really liked being in charge."

"Oooh," hums Hannah. "So he's a dom?"

I guess that's one way to put it. "Yeah. And it felt fantastic. He just told me what to do and I did it." I feel blood racing up into my cheeks. "It was so comfortable. Like I could trust him to lead."

Aisling and Hannah exchange a look I can't decipher.

"A guy you just met, you say?" Aisling leans forward, chin on her hand. "And you trust him enough to boss you around in bed your first time doing it?"

I pull my shoulders protectively up around my neck. "Yes? He hasn't given me a reason not to. He's a really good guy. A little dense sometimes, but a great guy."

"Tell me again why you're so afraid of him wanting commitment?" Hannah asks. "You've got a man who's an awesome lay, has a good personality, and he's seriously interested in you. I'm not understanding the problem."

I wish I could explain that it's not just Leon, but all three of them. That's a lot to ask of a girl on the same day she found out she's fucking three *werewolves*.

"He kept a secret from me, though," I finally say.

Aisling raises an eyebrow. "What kind of secret?"

"Just about who he is. His past, where he comes from."

Hannah refills her wine, then turns a serious look on me. "Is it a big enough secret to be a deal-breaker?"

"Maybe there was a reason he didn't tell you," Aisling says.

She's right, of course. If Leon had told me at the beginning he was a huge, furry monster, would I have even considered a relationship with him? Maybe he wanted to get to know me first, too, before trusting me with the truth.

And after Quinn showed me what his werewolf form can do in bed, it's definitely not a deal-breaker.

"Yeah," I say. "He did have a good reason, I think."

"I know you don't like surprises." Hannah puts a hand on my arm. "It triggers your flight-or-fight response. But maybe it's worth asking yourself why you're running. Are you afraid because it could actually work out?"

Her question stuns me into silence. Is that it? Am I scared of what might happen if I lean in to what Leon, Jace, and Quinn are offering me? Being the one and only for three whole super-hot guys—who also happen to be giant wolves—is a lot to take on, sure.

But it could be supremely lovely, too.

I sigh and guzzle down some more wine. "Maybe. I've never dated anyone who wanted commitment. I don't know what it feels like."

Aisling props her chin up on her hand, studying me. "Tiff. Do you feel like you don't deserve it?"

I pause. It's the kind of question only someone who knows me well would ask, and it stings that she's right to ask it.

Is that it? That I don't understand what these three men see in me?

"I'm afraid they're—I mean, I'm afraid that *he's* going to change his mind. That he'll see I'm nothing exciting." I squeeze my glass tighter. "I don't want to invest in someone who will leave me."

"So you want it?" Hannah asks eagerly. "Let's say he's telling the truth. Let's say he really sees you for what you are, which is a smart, fun, sweet woman with lots of love to give, and that's really what he wants. Do you want him, too?"

It's easy to dismiss what Hannah's saying about me, because she's my friend and she's biased. But in her hypothetical universe...

"Yes," I say. "I do."

My friends grin at me.

"Then let yourself have it," Aisling says. "Explore it. Maybe it won't lead to happily ever after this time, but you won't know unless you try. And it very well could. He sounds like a good dude, Tiff."

I nod in agreement. They're all great guys, each of them with their own wonderful qualities. Maybe they really could be the thing I've been looking for.

Hannah squints at me. "You didn't tell us how you met."

"Oh." I swallow another big sip of wine. "Well, uh... Remember those landscapers?"

"What?" Aisling gawps. "The ones who howled at you from the side of the road?"

I nod slowly.

"Oh my god." Hannah starts laughing. "No way. You went out with one of them?"

"I ran into him at the bar. He was a lot nicer of a guy than I expected."

Soon, both of them are cracking up.

"What a meet-cute!" Aisling almost spills her glass. "From 'random dude howling at you' to 'serious, long-term boyfriend.' I wouldn't have guessed."

"That will make a fun story to tell at your wedding," says Hannah, smirking. "I'm happy for you, Tiff. Just don't let the anxiety get the better of you."

I ponder these words for the rest of the night as we drink far too much wine.

Maybe I do deserve to be happy. Maybe when Leon says I'm what they really want, I should believe him. And, maybe, the three of them are worth the risk.

As I walk home, I take out my phone and text Leon.

> I'm really sorry I flipped out

I hesitate before typing out another message. Maybe it's just the wine talking, but it's the truth.

> I miss you. All of you

The three dots appear that say he's typing an answer, and my breath comes short. What if they've changed their mind about me already?

> We've missed you, too. And I understand
> why you said what you said. I didn't mean to
> come on so strong, but I can't lie to you
> about what we want, either

My heart swells, and I type out the message so fast it has a few typos in it.

> I thimk I want to try it. Being with you

The response comes as I reach my apartment building.

> I would love that, and so would Jace and
> Quinn. You said you wanted to get to know
> us better, so what do you think of a date?

I quirk an eyebrow.

A date? With all 3 of you?

Yeah. We'll take you somewhere fun!

Smiling to myself, I open my front door and stumble inside. I fall back against it as I hastily write my answer.

I'd love that

Getting Jace, Quinn, and Leon all to myself for a few hours? Sounds like a dream.

But I wonder what Eli would be doing while his brothers go out with me—and if it's as awkward as I'm imagining it is. Do they usually do everything together? Does Eli have his own life, or his own girlfriend? I realize that I have no idea.

But I also loved hearing from him when I was uncertain. I loved that he was watching out for me, asking his brothers to give me room to breathe while I sorted out my feelings.

So I type out another message.

Would Eli like to come?

Maybe I'm overreaching, but the wine is working its magic on me, and I feel bolder than usual. I think about Eli's kind text messages and find myself wanting to see the version of him that held my hand that day and talked me down from my anxiety attack.

There's a long pause before Leon starts typing his answer.

He would love to

I grin and hug my phone to my chest as I stumble into bed, still wearing my makeup. I fall asleep wondering what I did to deserve them—and for once thinking that maybe I just do.

Mini-golf.

That's the big "date" that the landscapers have planned for me. *Mini-golf.*

Jace is the one who started the group chat with all five of us.

> It's the perfect place. Big, long shafts and lots of balls 😏

Quinn seems the most excited about it.

> And all the cute little courses! I love the moving obstacles!

> Besides, Tiff, then we all get to see you bend over

Leon, I've discovered, is the filthiest one. He has an endlessly dirty mind and isn't afraid of making it known how hungry he is for me.

> You're disgusting, Leon.

Eli, as I expected, is the gentleman.

"What are you doing on your phone?" snaps Mr. Bosley. Shit. I didn't even hear his door open. These guys are so distracting.

"Sorry." I slip the phone into my pocket. He narrows his eyes but doesn't say anything else as he strides out of the office for his lunch meeting. I quickly sneak out to get some drive-thru food, then bring it back so I'm eating at my desk when my boss returns, completely red in the face.

"Ms. Dockett!" He comes to a halt in front of me. "When you're done getting ketchup all over your keyboard, I need you to sign off on this inventory manifest."

I stare at him. Why would he want me to do that? I wasn't there when inventory was taken—it's usually the warehouse manager who signs off on what equipment we have in stock.

"I'm not authorized to sign off on these—"

"You have one job," he says with a withering scowl. "It's to do what small things I ask of you. Do I need to go out and find another assistant?"

Fuck. I can't get fired. Maybe he forgot to have the manager do it. Mr. Bosley would never, ever admit when he was wrong or made a mistake, and I don't want to make him even madder. He might really just fire me in a fit.

Instead, I say, "Oh, o-okay. I'll handle it."

With a huff, Mr. Bosley drops the papers in front of me and returns to his office.

"This is a lot of AC units," I mutter to myself as I sign on the line for almost a hundred of them, ten times as many as we usually have. Must be that time of year.

Then I file it along with everything else.

Chapter Eighteen

When I finally get home, I'm buzzing. I put on some comfy shoes for our date so I can enjoy myself while we're trawling around the mini-golf course.

I'm a combination of anxious nerves and anxious excitement when I arrive. The whole place is fairy tale themed, which is cute but childish, and there's a bumper car course next door. Given the way I drive, we should probably stay away from it.

I find the Lupine Landscaping truck parked in the lot with Leon, Jace, Quinn and Eli leaned against the bed chatting. When I park next to them, they all stand up straight and wave in unison.

Leon hugs me first, lifting me up off my feet and kissing me squarely on the lips. He grins as he puts me down, and then it's Jace's turn. This kiss is more tender but more charged, making me think of what he might do to me later. Quinn pecks my lips, then my nose and cheeks.

"You look cute," he says, surveying my outfit of a short dress and brightly colored jewelry. "Scrumptious."

Jace arches an eyebrow. "Scrumptious?"

"Isn't she?" Quinn takes my hand as we head toward the entrance. "Like you could just eat her up in one mouthful."

Leon laughs, but Jace just shakes his head.

"I promise you're not a bonbon to me," Jace whispers in my ear, and I giggle. There's nothing like three devastatingly hot men lavishing attention on you like you're the center of their world.

Eli is the only one who doesn't speak. He gives me a cursory nod of greeting, and then as we head into the course, falls into step behind us.

"How are you?" I ask him, letting the other three go on ahead so I can walk alongside him. "I haven't seen you in a while."

He offers a half smile. "Yeah. You've had a lot going on, haven't you?"

I feel the flush before it even shows on my face. That's one way to put it. "I guess so. I haven't even gone on a good run in a while."

He nods, like he knows already. "Yeah. I haven't seen you at the site recently."

That must be why he's quiet today. We haven't had the same chance to get to know each other, and I haven't really put the effort into trying. I've been too busy *getting to know* his three brothers instead.

While Quinn, Leon, and Jace walk on ahead, all laughing and jabbing each other with elbows, I take a good look at him. I love Eli's dark hair, and how his eyelashes are longer than his brothers'. He's a little more slender, but his muscle is packed in tight. What does his werewolf form look like? He must have one of those knots, too.

Woof. I really let my imagination get away with me, and now I'm thinking about him in a completely inappropriate way. Eli turns to me and blinks, and I quickly look forward again. Fuck. Can he tell what I'm thinking?

After checking out balls and clubs from the front desk, the five of us head to the starting hole. Quinn urges me to go first, which makes me deeply self-conscious about how badly I'm going to fumble this. Sure enough, my ball goes flying across the small green, completely missing the gate for the castle.

But none of the guys remark on my abject failure as Jace goes next, knocking his ball right under the open portcullis. Leon's ball gets close to going in, but Quinn's ends up somewhere near mine, on the other side of the course.

Eli gives a firm hit, and his ball sails past all of us. It rolls perfectly under the portcullis, then bounces off the edge of the green and flies directly into the hole at the end.

"Hole in one!" I exclaim. "Good job, Eli!"

He gives me a shy nod, then slings his golf club over his shoulder before moving on ahead. It might take some time to coax him out, but I'm intent on doing it today.

"Have you played before?" I ask him as we head to the next hole. "You're pretty good."

"Quinn makes me go to the range sometimes," Eli says. "He just likes to hit balls as hard as he can, but I've been working on my putts and my accuracy."

I like how the brothers all do activities together.

"Having siblings must be fun," I say wistfully. "Built-in friends." I wish I'd had some growing up, even if it was just so I'd have someone else in the trenches with me managing Mom.

Eli shrugs. "We weren't always friends. Kids have rivalries. Since I'm younger, sometimes Jace and Leon pushed me into things I wasn't ready for."

I squint, because it sounds like he's saying something without saying it, but I don't know what it is.

At the next hole, I go first again, and try to position myself for a better hit. Leon walks up behind me and puts his hands on my hips, then he leans down low.

"Do you want to get in through the gate this time?" he asks into my ear, making the hair at the nape of my neck stand on end.

"Yes." My breath comes a little bit short at how good he smells this close to me. "What do I need to do?"

I stand up straighter and try to hold the club a little more level, but Leon just chuckles.

"Your form isn't quite right." He adjusts my stance with his fingers on my waist. I let him do it, because damn, I like him showing me what to do. His fingers trail down my arms to where I'm gripping the club, and he wraps his hands around mine. "Now try again."

I stay in the position he's shown me as I tap the ball with the flat end of my club. Obediently, it rolls in through the gate to the other side of the castle wall, and I whoop. Quinn claps his hands, and Leon gives me a wink. I still hit three over par by the end of the hole, but that's better than the previous one, so I don't mind.

As Leon, Eli and Jace head on past the scary gothic castle course, Quinn comes up beside me and grabs my hand, twining our fingers together.

"Hey," he says conspiratorially. "It's pretty quiet here today, isn't it? Not many people around."

I quirk an eyebrow at him. "That's true."

We've only seen one or two other groups. When we pass the castle, Quinn tugs me toward the green, and steps onto it.

"You're not supposed to walk on the courses," I hiss at him, but he just laughs.

"Come on. I just want a little time alone with you."

I think I understand. It's fun to do something as a group,

but I feel like I'm not getting any one-on-one with any of them. So I nod and follow along as Quinn crosses the green, still holding my hand. There's a door on the other side of the castle that must be meant for staff. Quinn tries the knob, and it opens for him. With a wicked grin, he tugs me inside.

"Won't the others miss us?" I glance around for his brothers, but they've all gone on.

"Maybe." Quinn takes my other hand and gently pushes me toward the wall. Then he draws my arms up over my head so he's caging me in. "But once they realize we're gone, they'll just wait up."

I enjoy the mischief in Quinn's voice, like he has a plan for me. He leans down, and I realize just how much taller he is, even in human form. His mouth stops just centimeters away from mine.

"I'm excited to kiss you like this," he says. Then presses his lips to mine.

He's a much less experienced kisser than his brothers but has plenty of enthusiasm to make up for it. He ravages my mouth as his hands trail down my sides to the hem of my skirt.

"Tiff?" he asks, hovering there. "Will you ride my cock inside the princess's castle?"

My whole face flames. I've never had sex in public before, but I love what Quinn's offering. A pick-me-up in the staff entrance? It already feels like it's been too long, even though only a couple days have gone by since last time.

"Yes," I say breathlessly. He flips up the skirt of my dress. "Won't you transform, though?"

Quinn rapidly shakes his head. "I can keep it together. I think."

I glance up at the ceiling, and hope if that happens, he won't just burst through it.

His jeans go next until they're in a puddle on the floor and his thick cock is sticking out straight toward me. Then he shoves me up against the wall, lifting one of my thighs to fully expose me. He's panting, his eyes trained on where he's lining up with my pussy. He dips the head inside of me, and his shoulders bunch up around his neck as he tests me a few times. I gasp at the slight stretch. Not nearly as much as when he was in werewolf form, but enough that I'm already hungry for more.

When Quinn plunges in deeper, he lets out a ragged moan. "Babe, you feel so good."

That amazing cock of his pulls out, then slides in again, reaching even farther. I'm surprisingly wet for almost no prep, and he glides easily until his knot stops him. I cover my mouth as a whimper comes out of me, and I know I need to keep quiet.

"Too bad I can't make you scream," he says with a self-satisfied smirk, then pulls out again before burying himself inside me as far as he can. His knot pushes against my entrance, and he gasps before reeling his hips back. "Might not be able to get it inside you this time—" Quinn thrusts in again, and I bite my palm. "But soon I will."

Keeping me pinned against the wall, he moves his body faster, slicking in and out of me in a punishing rhythm.

"Touch yourself," Quinn growls, fur sprouting all over his skin. I nod hastily and reach down between us to rub my clit, and he grunts as I tighten up around him. "There we are. Come for me, and then I'm going to fill you up. Completely. So my smell is all over you."

I moan as my orgasm creeps up on me, and Quinn fucks me harder and harder. Some of his knot starts to fit into me, and his face falls against my shoulder as he stuffs me full again.

"Tiff?" Eli's voice calls. "Quinn?"

Footsteps get closer, and my heart leaps into my throat. Fuck.

Quinn smirks at me. "Afraid?" he asks quietly. "Of Eli seeing us?"

I am, but not because I'm ashamed. I just don't know him well enough yet, and the thought of him seeing me naked, like this, with Quinn... Are either of us ready for that?

The door opens, and Quinn slams into me once more, unleashing everything. I can't help it when my climax washes over me, and I cry out as light spills in.

"Oh." I look up to find Eli standing there, silhouetted by the bright sun outside. His eyebrows are high, his dark eyes wide. He looks us up and down.

"Hi," I manage out, as Quinn lowers me to the ground. His cock slides out of me, and cum slips down my thigh. I try to wipe it away with the hem of my skirt.

"Come in, Eli," Quinn says. "Close the door."

Obediently he does, but now his brow is furrowed.

"She's nice and wet now," says Quinn in that mischievous voice. "Tiff. You want Eli, too, don't you?"

My mouth falls open at being put on the spot like this. I don't know what to say. I barely know Eli, and we've never even kissed.

"You don't have to answer," says Eli, his lips pressing into a thin line. "Quinn, you know I need more time."

Quinn frowns. "We had this whole nice date today, though, and—"

"I'm not like you." Eli shakes his head in irritation. Then he turns an apologetic look on me. "Sorry, Tiff. I think... I think I should go now."

"What?" I push my dress back down. I don't like how this is going. "You're leaving?"

"I'm just not—" Eli cuts himself off, then turns away from

us as Quinn pulls up his zipper. "Maybe we can talk another time, Tiff. It's just more than I can handle right now."

With that, he opens the staff door and leaves, letting it fall closed behind him. I want to go after him and tell him he should stay, that I want to spend more time with him, but he made it clear this situation has become too overwhelming.

I wonder if he understands me so well for a reason.

Quinn rubs the back of his head. "Well, that's Eli for ya. Try not to worry, though. It's not you—it's him." He takes my hand and kisses the back of it. "Thank you for the moment of your time."

I want to enjoy the post-sex buzz, but as we step back out into the afternoon sun, all I can think is that I wish Eli would have stayed. I wanted to get to know him even better. I wanted to make him feel comfortable with me, and maybe even be his friend, if he'll have me.

There's so much to learn about him, but I think I fucked it all up.

Chapter Nineteen

LEON AND JACE EXCHANGE A LOOK WHEN QUINN AND I RETURN, and if the big sniff Jace takes of me is any indication, we both must still reek of sex.

"Eli took off," Quinn says when we pick up our clubs.

"Thought he might." Jace takes his shot, then sips some water he brought along. He passes it to me and nudges my arm with his elbow. "It's nothing personal, Tiff. He's just a tough nut to crack."

I guess I can be content with that answer if it's coming from Eli's own brother, but I still feel like I missed a golden opportunity to get inside his shell. We scared him away, and that tugs on my heart more than I expected.

As much as Leon tries to help me with my putting form, I'm still seven points over par when we reach the last hole. Quinn and Jace have been ribbing each other, but I notice they don't give Leon a hard time. He's certainly the one in charge.

Quinn isn't too far behind me with six points over par, and he snaps his fingers. "Next time, we'll kick their asses," he promises.

"Should we go to the bumper car place?" asks Jace. "To drive around and hit each other?"

Quinn is practically vibrating. "Oh my god, *please*, Tiff? Those cars can go surprisingly fast."

"Sure." Maybe I didn't manage to save the princess at the end of the golf course, but I'll have my own happy ending—I hope. "But don't go crying to your mom when I win."

Leon hoots. "Confidence!" His hand trails over my hip and the curve of my ass. "Hot."

I can't help but notice when the dad playing the course with his two kids behind us gives me an odd look. I've been so caught up in having fun with the guys that I didn't think how we must appear, with each of them finding excuses to touch me and competing for who can sneak in a kiss.

Maybe I should play it cool. I hadn't really considered what people might think of us out in public, and my stomach feels a little sour as we head for the bumper cars.

Jace makes sure my helmet is on tight before we hop into our vehicles. Quinn takes off first, but I'm close behind him, and I slam into him from behind. Little does he know I have experience racing to and from the coffee shop every morning. Quinn glances over his shoulder with wide eyes.

"So aggressive!" He grins wickedly and veers toward me as I try to sneak by, which tosses me into the wall. My car bounces off again, though, and then I'm zooming away. Jace tries to catch up, but I block him from passing.

I finish the course in first place after ruthlessly bumping and slamming into the others. When we park at the end and take off our helmets, Jace is gazing at me in awe.

"You're a terrifying driver," he says, stooping down to push some of my curls away from my face and peck me on the cheek. "My life flashed before my eyes."

When we head out, Leon takes my left hand in his, and

Quinn scoops up my right. I feel warm all over, as if for once, I fit right where I belong.

By the time we get to the restaurant for dinner—an event which I hadn't realized was in the plan, but the guys insisted they "take me out somewhere nice, since it's a date and all"— my stomach is demanding to be fed.

"I didn't realize mini-golf used so much energy," I say as Leon pulls out my chair at the table for me, and I'm surprised at the place they picked. It's upscale, with things like clams on the menu. I feel a little out of place.

"It's all that focus!" Jace says. "You have to keep your eye on the prize."

We order a few different dishes to share, and it feels good and right to watch Jace and Quinn bicker over who gets the one piece of garlic bread that came with our mussels. They end up playing rock-paper-scissors to pick the winner. As we sit and talk, Leon's arm curls around my back, his fingers slipping under my hair at the base of my neck, and it electrifies my skin. On the other side of me, Jace runs his hand down my thigh, his grin as playful as it is enticing.

"Maybe tonight," he says into my ear, "I can take you in my wolf form, too."

It's like hot water pouring down between my legs, and my thighs clench together. I have to admit I've been wondering how tonight will go, and I think Jace just cleared up one question for me. He breathes in deep, and then chuckles.

"What are you saying to her?" Quinn arches his eyebrow, leaning toward us from across the table. "I just got a good whiff of Tiff, and it was delectable."

My face instantly heats, and Leon lets out a big laugh.

"Do you want us?" he asks, lowering his voice as he leans closer to me. "Think you can take Jace's big werewolf cock tonight, love?"

Holy shit. That spark bursts into a flame, and I glance up as Jace squeezes my thigh harder. I wonder what he looks like in his transformed state. I suppose I'll find out.

"It's amazing you guys can smell that much," I say, changing the subject. "Even when you're in human form?"

Jace grins. "I can smell what you ate for breakfast. I can smell that you stepped in bubblegum at the golf course. And I can smell the second your pussy gets wet for us."

The three of them are grinning at each other like idiots, clearly pleased they managed to get me riled up at the dinner table in a nice restaurant. But I'm thinking about how Eli left, and how much I wish he was here enjoying this with us instead. Maybe it would be too awkward, though, with the way the guys are acting.

Jace leans toward me and whispers in my ear while we eat. "You all right, Tiff?"

I don't want them to think I'm not having a great time, so I plaster on a smile. "I'm fine."

All three of them exchange a knowing look.

"Don't worry about Eli," Leon says, rubbing soothing circles on my back. "He's always been like this."

"You mean moody?" Quinn says.

"Thoughtful," Jace corrects him sternly. I'm surprised to see Jace has a sharper side. "Reserved, maybe."

I think about this as we finish eating. When the guys have wolfed down every piece of food in sight, Leon whips out a card.

"Where would you like to go after this, Tiff?" he asks, sliding it to the waiter. "Think we could all fit on your bed?"

My eyes must go huge because the three of them laugh.

Leon tangles a finger in my curls and tugs my face toward his, then plants a rather charged kiss on my lips. When he's done, I lean back against my seat, a little stunned. Then Jace tugs on my hand.

"Me, next," he whispers in a sultry voice. When I turn toward him, he strokes my cheek, then leans in for a much more tender one. All I have to do is think about how he and Leon took me in their human forms, and what it might be like with them in his changed one, and Jace groans against me.

"We should get out of here," he murmurs in my ear. "I can't stand how good you smell."

That's when I hear a familiar raised voice somewhere in the restaurant behind me.

"I can't keep doing this!"

I spin around so suddenly that I bonk Jace in the nose with my head. It can't really be him? *Here?*

"What is it, Tiff?" Jace asks, rubbing his face.

"I'm sorry," I whisper hastily, searching the faces of the other people in the restaurant. That's when I spot Mr. Bosley sitting at a table on the other side of a low wall, right across from "Mrs. Smith."

Maybe they are having an affair. I can't make out anything that she's saying.

"Someone's going to catch on, Beatrice," Mr. Bosley says, a little quieter now. "I have to stay low for a while."

Once more, I can't make out her answer, but he groans in frustration. "I know, I know. But it doesn't help either of us if I get caught."

Fuck. I have to get out of here before he sees me. I grab Leon's hand in mine.

"We're done, right?" I ask quietly. "We can go now?"

He frowns. "Yeah, just got the receipt." His eyes follow

mine to the other table, where Mr. Bosley sits with a face as red as a ripe tomato. "Who is that?"

"Someone we need to avoid," I say, but it's already too late.

"Beatrice" is standing up, sliding her purse on over her shoulder, lips pressed into a thin, angry line. As she passes by our table on the way out of the restaurant, she notices me sitting there with Leon's arm around me, Jace's hand on my thigh. She quirks an eyebrow.

"I'm glad it's working out with the *boyfriends* again. But, Ms. Dockett, I advise you to seek other employment."

With that, she strides past and out the door, letting it fall closed behind her. Mr. Bosley jumps to his feet to chase after her, and all I want is to hide underneath the table. I push away Leon and Jace, but it's too late.

"Ms. Dockett." He arches an eyebrow at me. "You've been enjoying yourself tonight, have you?" His gaze travels around the table at Leon, then Quinn, then Jace.

"S-sure," I say tentatively. "It's a nice place, and the food is good."

"You certainly have some interesting company." A cruel grin is slowly spreading across his face, like a hawk staring down a rat. He laughs. "I'm honestly surprised to find you're that greedy. No wonder you're so sloppy at work."

My breath is coming shorter and faster, but I can't seem to compel my mouth to open. I'm frozen as Mr. Bosley cocks his head to the side. The pleasure he's getting out of my shame is clearly monumental.

"Who knew my shy little assistant had such an active *social life*?"

I could simply keel over right here and that would be better. My throat tightens, and my cheeks ache from where a heavy stream of tears is building up behind my eyes.

"Who the fuck are you?" Leon says, rising from his chair.

Mr. Bosley shrinks back as Leon reaches his full height. I forget sometimes just how tall they are, how broad and, in the wrong light, menacing.

"I'm Ms. Dockett's employer," my boss says firmly, though his body language is anything but confident in the face of someone Leon's size. Jace's eyes widen, and his eyes snap over to me. I'm struggling to breathe just sitting here. Jace snakes his hand into mine and squeezes it.

"Well, it's nice to meet you, *employer*." Jace can barely disguise the distaste in his voice.

Leon takes a step toward Mr. Bosley, who responds by taking one backward.

"I'm going to politely ask you to leave now," Leon says, anything but polite, "and if I don't see your backside in three, two..."

Mr. Bosley nods rapidly, his eyes flicking from Leon to me, as if I'll step in and save him. But Jace's hand in mine steadies me. Quinn's on his feet now, too, and walking around the table so Mr. Bosley is now standing off against both of them.

"This is the fucker?" Quinn says, curling one hand into a fist. "This is the guy you've been complaining about?" I reach out and grab his arm.

"Don't," I whisper. "Please."

Quinn's hand loosens in mine, but he doesn't take his eyes off my boss.

"I'll be going, then." Mr. Bosley's eyes are huge as all three of them bear down on him. He shoots me a quick scowl. "See you at work, *Ms. Dockett*."

Then he turns around and scurries out the door.

As hard as I've tried to hold them back, the tears break free the moment he's gone, and I stumble into my chair at the table as they pour down my face. Leon, Jace, and Quinn all rush to my side. Quinn leans in to wipe some tears from my face, but I jerk back at his touch. Everyone in this restaurant must be staring at me, thinking the same thing as Mr. Bosley.

I suddenly get up from my chair. I shouldn't be here. This is all too much.

"Tiff?" Leon asks. More and more people are staring at us as I cry harder, my breaths coming so fast that my head is starting to feel light and heavy at the same time. Leon grabs my hand in his and pulls me toward the exit. "Tiff. Come with me." His voice drops to that familiar, commanding tone. "Right now."

I have nothing to hold on to except him, except those confident words, so I cling onto them and him as he guides me out of the restaurant and into the cool night air. I'm gasping, struggling just to get air into my lungs. I stumble, but Leon's holding me up.

"Please, love. Try to take longer breaths." He imitates what he wants, inhaling deep and then waiting to exhale again. "I'm right here. Quinn and Jace are right here."

But that only makes the tears run faster. It's humiliating, all of it, in every possible way. Mr. Bosley surely thinks I'm a slut, and for fuck's sake, is he wrong? After what Eli caught Quinn and me doing, just a few hours ago?

That's why I scared off Eli. I'm sure of it. He hates me now, for the same reason Mr. Bosley does.

"Tiff." Leon brings me into the soft curve of his arm. "It's all right. Nobody's watching."

I close my eyes and let Leon's voice seep into me. I imitate his slow breathing, trying desperately to get my throat to open again. His hand runs in soothing circles up and down my back, and the intoxicating smell of him is so close, I finally feel my contracting diaphragm start to release.

"There we are." He draws me in to his chest, still stroking me.

Quinn gently pats my hair. "Fuck," he mutters. "That asshole."

Now that I can almost bring oxygen into my body, all I want is to lie down and cry some more about what tomorrow at the office will be like, now that Mr. Bosley's caught me.

I'll never, ever live this down.

I sag into Leon's arms, but he easily holds me up. He leads me to the truck and Quinn opens the door, setting me in the passenger seat while Jace gets in on the driver's side.

"My car," I whimper, because I don't want to have to come back for it in the morning.

"Leave it," Leon says. "One of us will get it."

Quinn buckles my seatbelt and hops into the back of the truck. Soon Leon returns and gets in on the other side, and Jace puts the truck into gear.

I fall back against the seat as we head on down the road, away from my apartment. I don't know where we're going, but I don't care.

I'm so fucked. My job will never be the same again.

Chapter Twenty

Soon the bright lights and strip malls of the city give way to rolling countryside. No one speaks as we trundle down the dark, two-lane road, the way lit only by the truck's head-lights. I catch Leon glance at me out of the corner of his eye, then turns his gaze back to the road.

The truck slows and we turn right, the corner marked only by a huge oak tree. Up ahead I glimpse a small house—a log cabin, really—that looks like it has one, maybe two bedrooms in it. Where are they taking me? Finally I have the sense to be worried.

"Hey." Leon brushes my knee with his hand. "We've got you. Okay?"

Whatever is ahead of us, I know Leon won't lead me wrong.

The truck stops at the house, and Leon gets out of the driver's seat. He walks around to my side and opens the door, but before I can get out, he's lifting me up into his arms.

We don't head toward the house, like I expected. Instead, Leon starts down a small path around the side of the house, toward the tree cover. I grip his arm, wondering where he's taking me.

"Shh." He takes my hand and holds it tight in his. "Our house is just a little farther."

The path continues through the forest until we reach the base of a hill. There, shockingly, is a big door built into the hillside, with a wooden structure seated around it that seems to be a part of the landscape itself. Leon nods at the door, and Quinn quickly runs to open it for us. Then Leon carries me inside.

I'm too numb to really appreciate where we are. The walls seem to be made of dirt and rock, held up by bare wood beams. There's a big table on the left with four chairs next to a surprisingly large kitchen. On the right are two couches and a television, a big flat screen which strikes me as odd against the clay wall behind it. There's a fireplace, too, but it's not lit.

When we step inside and Jace closes the door behind us, Leon starts assembling logs and tinder in the fireplace. Quinn takes my hand and leads me to one of the couches.

All my thoughts feel sluggish. "He saw us." I drop my head into my hands, feeling the tears return as I think about his face, that awful grin, the way he cornered me against the wall like he knew that he'd won. "He knows now. And he's not going to let me forget it."

Next to me, Jace snarls in a way that's distinctly animal. "Fucking asshole."

"I should buy a cobra so I can put it in his bed," growls Quinn.

I'm too tired to even laugh. Jace wraps his arm around me as the fire crackles to life, and this time, I let him hug me. Now I just feel exhausted, like all the life has been wrung out of me. I don't even have the energy to worry about tomorrow.

Eventually, I find myself drifting off, the weight of the

world crushing me. I hear hushed whispers, and a voice that's distinctly Eli's. I want to open my eyes, to apologize to him for today and give him a big hug, but I'm too exhausted.

I feel someone carrying me, and by the scent, I know it's Leon. There's a creak as someone opens a door, and then I'm set on what must be a bed, and a pillow is tucked under my head. Then something soft, so soft, lies down next to me.

"Go to sleep," a deep, husky voice says. I can tell it's Leon, but different. Changed.

Another body curls up behind me. "We've got you, Tiff," says Jace, low and thick, like he has rocks in his mouth.

And so, I obey and tumble away into the abyss.

My phone alarm startles me awake. I'm surrounded by the softest, warmest fuzzy blankets that have ever existed, and I have to wriggle to get my hand into my back pocket, where my phone is buzzing against my butt.

I hold it up, blinking bleary eyes at the screen. It's time to get up and go on my run. Or that's what my brain says until I take in where I am. In front of me is a big wall of white, and it groans as the alarm continues going off. I finally have the sense to silence it when the wall moves.

"Tiff?" It's Leon's sleepy voice. My eyes travel up the broad, thick chest that seems to go on for miles, to his neck, to his face.

In his werewolf form, Leon is snow white, with the same blue eyes that he has when he's human. His snout is long and pointed, with a wet black nose at the end. His lips peel back in what could be either a snarl or a smile when I look up at him, and I choose to believe it's a smile.

"Hi," I manage to say.

Leon's big, furry arms wrap around me and drag me in close to his chest, while his wet nose burrows into my hair.

"Good morning," he murmurs, his voice chalky and thick like it was last night. On the other side of me, someone else is moving. I feel clawed hands, enormous ones, slide over my hip.

"Do you feel any better?" asks Jace's deep voice, and when Leon releases me, I turn over to find a thick, gray pelt. When I look up, a big werewolf face is peering down back at me, and I know by his glittering eyes that it's Jace.

"I..." I fumble for my words, still groggy. "I think so?" My face feels tight after crying so much last night.

"Maybe you should call in sick to work." It's Quinn this time, and I finally sit up, wondering exactly where I am.

The room is huge, and so is the bed. Morning light streams in through a high skylight overhead. Quinn is sitting up like a dog waiting for dinner, while Jace and Leon are both sprawled across it—all of them in their werewolf forms.

"I can't." I rub my eyes and look down at my phone one more time, knowing I don't have long to get home and change before work. "He would kill me."

"Then quit." Leon sits up next to me, towering over me. Holy shit. He's even bigger than Jace or Quinn—truly monstrous. "That piece of shit doesn't deserve you."

It just makes me want to cry all over again. I don't have a choice, and I really don't want to explain it to them.

Pulling away from the fur pile, I climb off the huge bed. It's definitely big enough for three full-grown werewolves and one... me.

"Sorry," is all I can say as I tuck my phone back into my pocket. "I have to go."

Quinn frowns and gets to his feet, too. He stops me with a clawed paw on my shoulder. "Wait. Are you sure? That was a really bad panic attack last night." He leans down so his big muzzle is in front of my face, and he licks me across the cheek. "We're worried about you."

I push him away.

"I'm fine." I have to keep my resolve hard and unyielding, or else I'll never leave this warm, wonderful place. "Can you take me back to the restaurant so I can get my car?"

That's when the door opens, and someone walks in. It's Eli, in his human form, dangling my keys.

"We got it for you last night." He tosses them to me, and I barely catch them. I can't read the look on his face. Unlike his brothers, Eli seems to keep his feelings much closer to the chest.

"Thank you." I grip them tight in my hand. "I appreciate that."

Eli just nods.

Jace leads me back to my car, leaving the others behind at their odd house-in-the-hill. My sedan is parked out front of the cabin right next to the Lupine Landscaping truck. He doesn't seem at all worried that someone might see him in his werewolf form.

"I'm sorry things went so sideways last night," Jace says, bringing up one of his enormous hands to my cheek. He pulls me in for a hug, and reluctantly, I accept it. Once I'm buried in his gray fur, though, all I want to do is stay. His huge paws roam down my sides, over the wrinkled edges of the dress I wore yesterday. It felt so cute at the time, and now I wonder just how much my makeup ran last night.

When I tense up under his hands, Jace leans back and peers down at me. "Tiff..." He strokes my cheek with one huge, clawed paw. "I hate seeing you hurt like this. Please don't go back to that office today."

I don't want to go, either. I don't want to face Mr. Bosley

after last night, but I can't leave until I have another option lined up or I won't make rent next month.

"Thank you," is all I say in answer, putting my small hand over his big one. "Thanks for being there for me last night."

Jace nods slowly, but his eyes are concerned. "I'll always be there for you." He rubs his cheek against the top of my head. "You're mine, as long as you'll put up with me and my inane jokes."

I can't help a sniffle, because they're all so sweet, so kind and genuine, that I don't even know if I deserve them. Jace licks my cheek, clearing away my tears.

"Put up with you?" I ask with a shaky laugh. "You're the one who has to put up with me."

"Never! I..." Jace halts for a moment, then takes a long, deep breath. He crouches down in front of me, so we're close to eye-level, and briefly touches the tip of his wet nose to mine. "I love you, Tiff. You could ask anything of me, and I'd do it for you."

My heart stutters in my chest at these fully vulnerable words. I just want to cry all over again, but I settle for throwing my arms around him and hugging him with all my might. Big arms loop around me, and Jace brings me in as close as he can. I giggle a little when I feel something rather large and wet nudge at my belly.

"Sorry," he says, voice muffled by my hair. "I guess hugging you turns me on."

As tempting as it is to ask him to take me right here, I have to get to the office and face whatever is waiting for me there.

Of course I want to leave my shitty job—but I don't have that kind of luxury.

Eventually Jace lets me go, and he watches me as I get in my car and back out, heading off down the country road.

I'm not sure what I was expecting to find at the office, but it's not what I get. When I deliver Mr. Bosley's coffee, my hand shaking and my breath already growing shallow, he just grins at me. It's an eerie, too-wide sort of grin that looks unnatural and dangerous on him.

"Good morning," I squeak out. A few seconds pass, and when he doesn't answer—still smiling—I scurry back to my desk and plant myself in the chair.

God. I think this is even worse than the alternative I had imagined. Is he just going to wear that knowing, shit-eating smile all day?

I try to focus on my work, but it's impossible. Luckily, I'm ahead on things, so while Mr. Bosley's hiding in his office, I flick mindlessly through my social media. I have a friend request from Quinn, which makes me giggle under my hand. His profile picture is of himself in sunglasses, arms over two pairs of shoulders whose owners are off-screen, standing in front of a gorgeous mountain backdrop. I accept the invite, of course, and start browsing through his photos. He definitely likes to take selfies at the beach, and usually drags one of his brothers into the frame, all covered in sand.

This is just avoiding the problem, though, of what to do about this fucking job. I turn over Beatrice's warning in my mind. I'll never be able to find another gig like this, with a good salary, dental insurance, and a 401k. But after last night, it's feeling more and more like I'm a bug being ground under a boot.

I need to escape, or it'll crush me.

I look up my title of executive assistant on Job Finder, just to see what's out there. Most of the positions listed require a bachelor's degree, and every job description makes me cringe —there's no way I know how to do all that stuff—but I read through them anyway.

I guess I should start writing a résumé. I may not be qualified for any of these, but there's no harm in trying. Not when this is the alternative.

At closing time, I decide to pack up and leave, even though Mr. Bosley still hasn't left yet. I thank every star in the sky that I didn't have to face him again after this morning, and he decided to keep a low profile in his office. I couldn't stand that grin of his any longer. He wouldn't have the gumption to give me a smarmy smirk like that if Leon and Jace and Quinn were there—no, he'd cowered in front of them like a spineless rodent.

I'm so dazed on my way home, remembering that rather wonderful moment when the guys told off Mr. Bosley that I don't notice the black SUV behind me until I'm nearly to my apartment.

Oh, shit. Not this again.

Chapter Twenty-One

Fuck. I squint into my rearview mirror, trying to make out who's driving the black car behind me, but the windshield is too tinted. What do they want?

Hastily I take a right instead of a left, away from my apartment. Maybe it's just a coincidence that it looks like the same black car that followed me before, but the last thing I need is to show them where I live.

I keep driving, taking random turns. The car continues following me, mimicking each one, but keeping a good distance behind me as if they think I haven't noticed them yet. I'm starting to panic, wondering where I could go that they wouldn't tail me. What would they do if I stopped? Would they jump out of the car and swarm me?

Then I remember: the guys are working in the next neighborhood over. Surely if I can find them, I'll be safe from whoever is on my ass.

Immediately I hang a right in the direction of Work Street. The SUV continues following as I pull into the fancy neighborhood, driving straight for the house with the Lupine Land-scaping truck parked outside.

I sigh with relief that it's still here. Leon, Jace and Quinn will know what to do.

But when I pull up, there's only one person there working. It's Eli, with his short-cropped, dark hair, leaning over a shovel.

I hurriedly park next to the truck, then watch in my rearview mirror as the SUV continues past me with a *vroom*. When they're gone, I exhale a long breath and drop my fore-head against the steering wheel.

"Are you okay?"

I didn't realize my window was down until Eli peers into it. He has that same inscrutable look on his face as he did this morning—and the same one he had yesterday when he found Quinn and me together in the princess's castle.

My anxiety, which is already on high alert, has now decided that look of his is certainly because he hates me.

"Y-yeah." I sit up straight in my seat and force on a smile, even though the panic is still boiling underneath my skin. "Everything is fine."

"Then why are you pulled over to the side of the road looking like a ghost?" He furrows his brow.

"That car was following me. The black one." I peer into my side-view mirror, just in case they made a loop.

"Following you?" His frown gets deeper. "Are you sure?"

"I know. It doesn't make sense. Why would someone be following *me*?" A shiver ripples down my spine. "They did it a while ago, too. Same car. I thought it was weird then, but for it to happen again today..."

I trail off. I must sound like an idiot. I'm not special enough for someone to be following me, I know that.

Suddenly, Eli opens the door to my car, and I'm tempted to reach over and yank it closed again. I realize that I'm scared right out of my skin, and adrenaline is coursing hot through my veins, so even Eli is making me want to flee like a rabbit. But he settles in my passenger seat anyway.

"Is that why you came by?" he asks. "To get them off your tail?"

"I thought if I stopped near other people, they would piss off," I say, clenching my hands on the steering wheel to stop them from shaking.

"You hoped Leon and the others might be here?"

I nod slowly, feeling like I'm stepping into a trap.

"I see." Eli looks out the front windshield. "And were you disappointed to find it was just me?"

Now, surprise seeps in through my fear. Is Eli offended? I think I've said the exact wrong thing.

"I'm actually glad you were here," I say. And that's the truth. I remember the day when I met them, and Eli was the one who led me to the truck bed to sit down. He seemed to know what I was feeling, and how to help me through it. He made sure that I had space to think when Leon and I had conflict. Even though we didn't leave it on the best terms on the mini-golf course, I also felt like he understood me—like perhaps he even struggles as much as I do with his own emotional turmoil.

"Hmm." Eli continues looking straight ahead. "Well, looks like your tail is gone now, so you can probably head home if you want." He reaches for the door handle to let himself out. "I'm just cleaning up here because I drew the short straw. I'm sure if you needed company, you could go find my brothers at Lucky's."

Sure, seeing the others sounds good, but now that Eli's here, I don't want him to go. I want to understand what happened yesterday, why he left in such a rush. I'm definitely not ready to drive again; my hands are still trembling, and my heart is speeding along like a runaway train. I think I might get into a wreck if I tried to get myself home.

"Can I just stay here with you while you clean up?" I ask at last. His eyebrows rise almost to his hair.

"You want to hang out here?" That frown deepens. "I'm getting dirt everywhere."

"I probably shouldn't drive for a while." I'm afraid of saying what I want to say: that I want his company, that I want to understand him and find out how to repair the bridge between us. But what if he rejects me? I can't take that right now. "It would be nice to talk to you until I calm down."

"I see." His mouth opens like he's going to continue, then he closes it again. It seems like Eli is trying hard not to say all the things he wants to, and I wish I could tell him it was all right to speak his mind, and I'm not afraid of how he really feels about me. It would hurt my feelings to hear out loud, but I can bear it if it means I know the truth. I'd prefer that over perpetually wondering.

Eventually, Eli gets out of the car. "All right." He turns around and walks away without sparing me another look. "I'll be about half an hour, so you can hang out until then."

I emerge from the car, too, and head over to the work site, where the guys have dug a trench and are filling it with wooden squares.

"What are those?" I ask, peering down into the trench.

Eli sighs as he gathers up tools. "Frames for pouring concrete."

I get the sense my question annoyed him, so I don't say anything else as he works. The thick muscles of his back flex as he picks up heavy bags and carries them to the truck bed, tossing them into the back. Not sure where else I belong, I open the passenger side door and flop down on the seat, just watching him as he wipes the sweat off his forehead. Even though the sun's gone down, it's still pretty warm out. If he's losing all that moisture, he must be getting dehydrated.

I look around for a water bottle, but there's nothing in sight, so I head over to my car to grab mine out of my bag. When I approach him with the water bottle, Eli glances up. For a split second, I see the sweet, friendly guy who first said hello to me.

"You're sweating bullets," I say, handing him the bottle. "And you need to stay hydrated."

He glances down at the bottle, then back up at me, one eyebrow arched. After a moment of hesitation, he flicks back the lid of the bottle and chugs it down.

"Thanks." He hands the empty bottle back to me. "I'm gonna be wrapping up here soon."

I'm not shaking anymore, and I think I'm good to drive home given I don't run into any more creepy black SUVs on the way.

"Right. I'll go, too. Thank you for keeping me company." I glance up at him. "Can you, um, not tell Leon and the others about this? I don't want them to worry."

He quirks an eyebrow. "You want me to keep it a secret that you're being followed?"

I swallow. "Yeah. Just between us? For now. Until I find out what's going on. I know they'll freak out."

Eli considers this, then nods. "I won't say anything. They would probably overreact, like they always do when it comes to you."

I don't know why, but that sounds like a dig.

When neither of us speaks further, I hop out of the truck and shut the door behind me, wishing Eli hadn't put up such a tall, firm wall between us. All I want is to tease apart the confusing edges of him and figure out what's inside. I wish I could undo what happened, and we could start over.

It hurts that he won't look at me the same way now. I sniffle as I head back to my car.

"Tiff." Eli's voice takes me by surprise. "Did work go all right today?"

"Huh?" I ask stupidly. When I turn around, Eli is leaning on the bed of the truck with a dark look on his face.

"Today," he says. "After what happened last night at the restaurant."

I shudder just thinking about arriving in the office this morning. "It was... fine. My boss didn't say anything to me, which is maybe worse. He just had this horrible grin on his face the whole time." I wrap my arms around myself. "He's going to hold this over me forever."

"What's your boss's name?"

The question is so out of left field that it takes me a few seconds to process what he's asking.

"Oh, um," I stutter, "it's Mr. Bosley."

Eli shakes his head. "His real, full name."

Why does he want to know? Eli's expression is intense. I think if he were in his wolf form, whatever that looks like, his mane would be bristling. What's on his mind? He's so opaque.

"Orland. Orland Bosley." It really is the world's worst name. "Why?"

Eli ignores my question. "What has you so scared of a guy named 'Orland'?" His tone makes me flinch.

Why is he being so... I don't know, *mean*? He must really find me distasteful.

Fine. If he's going to be like this, I'm not going to stand for it.

"Oh, besides the fact that he's my boss?" I shoot back. "That he's the guy who writes me a check every two weeks?" All my bottled-up fear and frustration bursts out of me as anger. "The guy who could decide at any time to fire me, and then I'd be without that paycheck and unable to pay my rent? Yeah, I don't know why I'd be scared of *that* guy."

Eli's mouth tilts down at my answer, but he doesn't have a quippy response. Good. I don't need him telling me to quit, too —as if it's that easy to snap your fingers and get another job.

"He's done a number on you," Eli says at last, and this time his voice is much softer. "How has this man convinced you that you're not worth more?"

"It's just life to have a boss you hate." I shove my hands into my pockets and look down at the ground. "That's how it is when you work for other people."

Eli studies my face. "All right," he finally says, and I didn't realize how close he had been until he steps away, grabbing a shovel and tossing it into the back of the truck. "If that's how you feel. I'm going to head home for the night."

It's so dismissive that I flinch.

"Oh. Okay." I start heading back to my car. "Thanks for, um... being here."

"You can count on me." Strangely, it doesn't sound sarcastic. "Take care of yourself."

I'm sad to drive away with Eli still thinking I'm weak, that I let some asshole like Mr. Bosley control my life. I probably care too much about his opinion, but at the same time, it hurts to know that somehow, I've ruined whatever chance I had at a relationship with him, even just as friends.

I spend the night watching reruns and wishing I'd had the nerve to ask Eli what I could do to fix things between us.

And what does the driver of that black car want with me? Whatever shit Mr. Bosley is getting into, I just hope it hasn't dripped off his roof and landed on me.

Finally, I give up and flick the TV off around ten. When I head to bed, I get a text from Leon.

> Thinking of you. Hoping your day was okay
> with Mr. Fuckface

I smile down at the message. He's truly a good guy, and I'm lucky to have him.

> Something weird was going on. He didn't
> seem to care about me at all

There's a pause before I see the three dots.

> Maybe he knew we could beat him up before
> he had time to call the cops ;)

I laugh outright at this, imagining Jace, Leon and Quinn roughing up Mr. Bosley. It brings me immense joy, actually, so I continue imagining it as I head off to bed.

Chapter Twenty-Two

I'M NOT AWOKEN BY MY ALARM, BUT BY A PHONE CALL. WHEN I groggily open my eyes and fish my phone off the bedside table, I find it's Mr. Bosley.

"Hello?" I ask sleepily. It's only six in the morning, and I'm not even due in for another three hours.

"Ms. Dockett!" His frantic voice nearly blows my ear off. "I need you to go into the office right away and call the police!"

I sit up in bed. "What?"

"Did you not hear me?" he roars. I pull the phone away from my face and cringe. "Go and call!"

"O-okay," I manage. "I'll get dressed right now and head over."

I throw on my nearest clean clothes and quickly neaten myself up, using some dry shampoo on my hair, and hurry out the front door. I wonder what happened that Mr. Bosley needs the police?

He could have just called them himself. I groan as I get into the car, still trying to shake off sleep.

By the time I get to the office, there's only one or two other cars in the parking lot. Neither of them is the black Escalade, thank goodness.

Once I'm inside, I call the police phone number. Since it's before business hours, though, I get sent to a non-emergency line, which then goes to voicemail.

"Damn it." I guess I'll need to call 911 if I want real help—but is whatever happened to Mr. Bosley serious enough for that? He didn't sound like he was injured or in immediate danger.

Then the office door bangs open, and the devil himself steps inside. Mr. Bosley's not wearing a tie, which is highly abnormal, and his shirt is wrinkled with the sleeves halfway pulled up. He sees me on the phone and stops dead.

"Put it down, Ms. Dockett!" he hisses, and I just stare at him, unsure if I should obey his previous order or his current one. *Do what he says.* "Ms. Dockett!"

I slam the phone down. "What's going on? What do you need the cops for?"

Mr. Bosley closes the door and locks it behind him, then creeps over to my desk.

"There are people after me," he says quietly. "That woman isn't named 'Mrs. Smith.'"

No shit, Sherlock.

"When I woke up, half of my beautiful yard was torn out, like someone went on a rampage with a tractor." He leans in closer and whispers, "It's a message, I'm sure of it."

Instantly I think of the black car. Was that a *message* from Mrs. Smith, too?

"Fuck," I hiss, and Mr. Bosley gives me a surprised look. "They're the ones who have been following me!"

"Following *you*?" He shakes his head. "You couldn't possibly interest them." He stands up straight again. "I'm not going to let this slide, though. That bitch can't intimidate me.

But we're not going to involve the police, either. If it's who I think it is, then we have to resolve this ourselves."

We? I'm not sure what part he thinks I play in this, but I want to get as far away from it as possible.

"Okay," I say, leaving the phone. "What are you going to do?"

"I'm going to fight back." Mr. Bosley glares at me. "I'm not going to let myself be bullied by some... some..." He splutters as he searches for an insult, but he must not be able to think up anything good because without another word, he spins around on his heel and storms back out the way he came.

That was strange and unusual. Now I'm at the office and it's not even seven o'clock.

I decide to head home, take a shower, and get ready like I normally would. It's been too long since I was able to go on a run, and I wonder briefly if Mr. Bosley would even notice if I didn't come in again today.

After getting fully ready for a normal day, I return to the office to find it empty. As I expected, my boss doesn't come back.

I wonder what he's doing to get his revenge on Beatrice. I have a feeling that he's far, far deeper into something nasty than he wants to admit. I just hope that by extension, my shoes aren't also covered in shit. I've done too many things over the last few weeks I surely shouldn't have, and a shiver ripples across my skin at the idea I might have been a part of whatever scheme Mr. Bosley cooked up.

The invoices. The inventory. The fixed spreadsheets. Fuck.

I'm ahead on my work, so I decide to start an investigation. I need to know what Mr. Bosley's been doing, and how I might now be caught up in it.

I spend most of the day looking through the files for whoever this *Beatrice* is. I flip through paper after paper, searching all over for her name. Surely, he must have some evidence somewhere about who this woman is.

Instead of finding the incriminating document I'm hoping for, I stumble across even more invoices. One in particular shows a huge shipment to one of our warehouses, and a name I don't recognize as the warehouse manager, though I'm pretty sure that guy's name is Doug.

Then, a little farther down, there's yet another shipment. And another one.

I don't know a lot about the business, but I've picked some things up during the years I've worked for Mr. Bosley. The biggest orders he ever makes are ten or twenty units. These show hundreds of units, delivered to an address I don't recognize. All of them have been billed and paid for, even though the orders add up to hundreds of thousands of dollars. I didn't think Mr. Bosley had *that* sort of raw cash on him, and I know the business hasn't been growing nearly fast enough to justify that.

What is he doing? Is he funneling money for her? Are these shipments even real?

My phone buzzes, and I look down to find it's Leon.

Hey love, can I take you out to lunch?

I check my watch, and even though it's about one o'clock, I don't think Mr. Bosley is coming back. I desperately need a break from whatever is going on here, so I gratefully accept.

Sure. I'd like that.

Leon asks me to meet him at the food truck pod, and when I show up, he kisses me with surprising ferocity. When he puts me back down again, he points out all his favorite places to eat. It's too far for me to get here from work and back on my usual lunch hour, so I've never tried it before. But today I doubt anyone will even notice I'm gone.

"So how'd you get the time off to go out with me?" Leon asks, sipping his drink and making a lot of noise doing it. It's funny how the werewolf side of him still fully exists when he's in his human form.

"Oh. Apparently, someone vandalized Mr. Bosley's house." I narrow my eyes and lean forward. "He thinks someone's after him. First, he had me call the cops, then told me not to call the cops. He was furious. After that, he just left and didn't come back."

A strange look crosses Leon's face—almost like he's not surprised to learn this information.

"Leon?" I ask, a nervous tone to my voice. "What do you know about this?"

When he turns away and rubs the back of his head, I know something's wrong. What has he done?

"Leon," I repeat. "Tell me what's going on."

"It wasn't me," he says at last, still not making eye contact. "It was Eli. He was gone last night. Took the truck and just left. When he came back, he was covered in dirt. We grilled him, and he confessed that he went wolf at your boss's house and, uh, trashed it."

My hand flies to my mouth. Fuck. "*Eli* did this?" I repeat, still not sure I understood him properly. The realization crashes over me that Eli has just set off a potentially terrible chain of events. "Mr. Bosley thinks that the scary lady is after him, that it was some kind of message from her. He said he was going to stand up to the 'bullies,' whoever they are."

Leon's eyes go wide. "Wait, what? Some scary lady is after your boss?"

I nod quickly. "There's been a car following me, too. I think it's related. It happened the night that Mr. Bosley asked me to —" I stop myself. I can't possibly tell Leon what he asked me to do—and what I did.

"He asked you to do what, Tiff?" He's stern now. "Are you involved in this somehow?"

A whimper comes out of me against my will. "I think I might be. He had me 'fix' the books. He also had me sign for some big orders, which I never do. And then today I found these receipts that didn't make any sense. Hundreds of units delivered to the warehouse, but I saw no evidence that they ever showed up."

I collapse to the table, realizing just how epic of a fuckup that was. Beatrice must have known, somehow, that I'd been pulled into his lie, and now she's keeping tabs on me, too.

"Money laundering." Leon has a look on his face like he could kill. "Your boss pulled you into his money laundering scheme."

Money laundering. So much more makes sense now. Oh, shit. I can't believe I fell for it, that I let Mr. Bosley bully me into becoming a part of this.

I'm so stupid.

"But how did Beatrice know that he asked me to sign off for him?" I ask helplessly.

"Maybe she bugged your office." Leon's eyes are daggers now. "He's being watched, and so are you."

"That means they know he's coming to pick a fight now because of Eli." I feel the telltale clench in my chest, the tightening of my throat. "Is she part of the mob, Leon? Are they going to kill me?"

Leon reaches across the table and covers my hand with his. "Hey. Tiff. Come back to earth for me." He lets out a deep breath, and then sucks it back in, reminding me that I need to breathe. I close my eyes and attempt it, counting between inhales and exhales. But I can't tamp down the rising fear that Eli has royally fucked over not just my boss, but me, too.

"Why?" I demand. "Why did Eli do that?"

"Why?" Leon looks confused by my question. "Because Mr. Bosley's an asshole, and he deserved it."

I gape at him. "That doesn't mean he should have gone beast on my boss's house!" I'm breathing too fast. "And why Eli? He hates me."

Leon looks at me like I have antlers. "He doesn't hate you. Not at all. Why would you think that?"

The panicky tears are breaking free. "It's obvious! The way he acted yesterday, like I was a huge pain in his ass." I sniff.

"Yesterday?" he asks.

"When they were following me, I went to the work site and Eli was there. He was..." I scramble for the right word. "I don't know. Mad at me, or something."

Leon just shakes his head. "It's not what you think, Tiff. Eli bonded to you that day, too, you know. He's just afraid. He struggles to tell people how he really feels."

But I don't care that he's *bonded* to me. "Eli could have just told me," I say, trying to hold back the sob threatening to burst out of me. "Why did he have to go and do this?"

"To show you he cares."

It's so idiotic, but somehow, I believe it. That's why he asked for Mr. Bosley's name last night—he was planning this all along.

I pull out my phone, anger sweeping through me. At least

anger is better than panic. "We're going to work this out. Right now. Eli has to confess to Mr. Bosley what he did before it's too late."

Leon chews his lip as I type out a frantic message to Eli.

> Why did you go after Mr. Bosley last night?
> Are you nuts??

My food gets cold while I wait for his response. Leon sits there silently, clearly ashamed of his part in keeping this from me.

Finally, an answer appears.

> I did what needed to be done. He has no right to treat you like that.

I groan in frustration. Now Eli has created an even bigger problem, one that could potentially backfire on me in a dangerous way.

> We have to talk. Now.

He responds immediately.

> I'm at the state park. Meet me here?

It's a strange place, but it will be neutral ground. I wonder why he's there. I used to go to the state park almost every weekend to hike and enjoy nature.

> I'll be there in 20

If Leon were in his werewolf form, I think he'd have his tail between his legs the way he demurely takes my leftover food to the trash.

"I gotta go," I tell him sternly, heading for my car. "I have to fix this mess."

He grabs my hand one more time before I can go. "Tiff."

I'm angry, but I have to relent a little at the sullen look on his face. He pulls me into a tight hug.

"I'm sorry for not telling you sooner."

I sigh and hug him back. I can't resist how sweet he is, how good he smells, how comfortable he makes me feel.

"I think I love you," he says at last, tucking my head under his chin. "Actually, no, I know I do."

He's confessing this to me now? As soon as he says it, though, I'm certain that I feel the same way. Maybe he made a mistake, but I can't stay mad at him.

"I love you, too." I bury my face deeper in his chest. "I know your heart is in the right place."

"I understand that you're furious at Eli, and you have every right to be—but the two of you are more alike than you think." He lets me go and kisses me on the forehead. "And don't let that stupid fuck of a boss of yours scare you. We have your back. Okay? You're safe as long as you're with us."

I sigh and lean into him, hoping he's right. But can my sweet, good-hearted werewolves really protect me from whoever is after Mr. Bosley and the hellfire he's brought down on us?

Chapter Twenty-Three

WHEN I PULL INTO THE PARKING LOT AT THE STATE PARK, THE picnic tables are full of families having lunch or taking breaks from swimming in the lake. Beyond the picnic area, though, are miles of untamed forest. I know the trails well, and even when the lake is busy, I'm usually alone when I go out hiking. Sometimes I'll just take off into the woods with my compass, if only to enjoy the sense of pure wilderness all around me. It's quiet, peaceful, and beautiful, and it's often the only way I have to de-stress after a long week at work.

As I park, I spot Eli sitting on a bench, his shoulders curled and tense. When I get out of my car, his head jolts up, though he still has that flat expression I can't read.

"Tiff," he says. I stop a few feet away, and he doesn't try to bridge the gap between us.

"Eli." I sit down carefully on the other side of the picnic table. There's such an intensity in his dark eyes that I have to look away. "What are you doing here, anyway?"

"Clearing my head." He turns and gazes out into the trees.

"I love it out here. Sometimes I like to just get lost in the woods until I come back to earth."

I know what he means. It can be really centering to escape the city and simply breathe in the scent of the trees.

Maybe Leon's right, and Eli and I are more alike than I thought.

"You've created a huge mess," I say at last. Right now, the park doesn't make me feel *peaceful* in the least, because all I can think about is what damage he's done.

Eli shrugs like it's the most inconsequential thing in the world. "The fucker deserved it."

"You don't get it," I say, biting my lip. "Mr. Bosley—he's caught up in something bad. Something that could come back and bite *me*, too."

His hard expression falters. "What do you mean? Does this have to do with that car following you?"

I explain everything: the strange woman making frequent appearances at the office, and what I suspect Mr. Bosley has been doing for her. How my idiot boss is now probably putting his life at risk doing something stupid, like confronting whoever is in charge of this operation, because of Eli's little escapade last night.

The longer I talk, the more drawn Eli's face gets.

"That woman is dangerous," I tell him. "I'm sure of it."

"Jesus, Tiff," he says, massaging his temples. "And you helped him with this?"

I frown. Why don't any of these guys get it? "I didn't have a choice. It was that or lose my job."

"No job is worth this." He reaches across the table to put his hand on mine, but I pull it away. My anger rises like a flame.

"You don't get to tell me that," I snap. "You have to come

clean with Mr. Bosley, Eli. He's going to get himself in trouble. They might even..." I don't want to think about it.

"So what?" Eli stands up, furrowing his dark brows. "He's the one who got himself into this mess! It's not your responsibility to get him out of it again."

I could just smack him right now. How does he not realize that he's only made a big problem much worse?

I get up to my feet, too, because I'm tired of letting other people intimidate me. All the anger that's been festering inside me, that's grown every time Mr. Bosley insulted me or demanded I defy my own moral compass for him, is sprouting to the surface.

"Don't you get it? Whatever happens to him"—I jab a finger into Eli's chest—"it'll blow back on me, too!"

"Then we'll protect you." He lowers his head toward mine, speaking quieter. "I'll always protect you, Tiff."

It sends a shiver rolling across my skin. Eli inhales deeply, his nostrils flaring. He smells like sweat and pine trees, and it's so intoxicating that it's maddening. I put a hand on his chest and push him away, but he's like a wall of bricks. Maybe his build is more slender than his brothers', but Eli is still far taller and stronger than I am.

"Why?" I hold my ground, even though he's so close to me —so, so close—and it's filling my head with all sorts of thoughts I shouldn't be entertaining. "You made it clear I don't mean anything to you."

The growl that comes out of him is most certainly not human.

"You mean *everything* to me," he says in a low, rumbling voice.

I gape at him. "Then why?" I ask. "Why did you treat me like you couldn't stand me?"

Eli's eyes are wide, like he doesn't understand the question. Then, with clear shame on his face, he looks down at his feet.

"I didn't know what to do," he finally answers. "When I saw how close you were with Quinn, how comfortable you already felt with him, I felt like I'd lost a race. Like my brothers already reached the finish line while I hadn't even realized it started yet."

"It's not a competition," I say, throwing my arms in the air. "There's no race. You could have stayed when we all went on a date, you know. We could have gotten to know each other better. Instead, you've made me think I did something wrong all this time."

Eli's shoulders rise to his neck, and he keeps his eyes anywhere but mine. "It was too much pressure. I move at a different speed. And I thought that since I wasn't like them, you wouldn't be interested in me. I didn't want to fall for you if you weren't going to return my feelings."

I shake my head, finally understanding. "So what are you saying? Do you like me, Eli?"

His mouth falls open. Then he snaps it closed and frowns deeply.

"*Like* doesn't begin to describe it," he says, almost dangerously. "I know who you are. I know *what* you are."

All the hair on my skin stands on end. "And what's that?" I ask, voice wavering.

"Mine. My mate." He steps closer to me, lowering his head so his mouth drops to my ear. I don't move a muscle as his breath tickles my cheek. "And a wolf protects his mate. From everything."

Just the words make me twitch between the legs. Warmth is pooling in my belly at the low, seductive lilt of his voice. "You can't protect me all the time."

"Yes, I can." The words come out in a rumbling growl that

no longer sounds human. "Because when I drag you back to our den, we'll all be there to make sure nothing happens to you."

His mouth trails down from my ear to my throat, never once touching me, just gusting his breath across my skin. The sensation sends a sharp bite of pleasure rippling downward, and I squeeze my thighs together.

Eli sniffs the air and groans. "Is that right?" His hand drifts around my back, still hovering an inch away from my shirt. Then his fingers duck under my hair at the nape of my neck. "Am I turning you on, little rabbit?"

As if his words have taken on a life of their own, I feel my very blood pulsing in my veins. I want to tell him he can't shut me up and end this conversation just by being sexy. I want to push him away and yell in his face. He has to fix this, some-how. But it's like he's put me in a trance.

"W-we shouldn't be doing this," I say, my voice unbearably weak. "Not while Mr. Bosley—"

"Fuck Mr. Bosley." He leans down and taunts me with another not-quite-kiss on my neck. "You and I have unfinished business, and that's much more important to me. You're all I'm thinking about right now."

The only thing I can focus on is how much I need his mouth to finally taste my skin, how much I need his hands on other parts of me.

"I know what you want," Eli murmurs. I can feel him changing, his claws tangling in my curls. "I can smell it on you."

His nose grazes over my shoulder, and then he scrapes me there with his teeth. My back arches, my hips sliding back against his.

"Eli, there are people everywhere."

But I don't want him to stop, either. My heart is beating

madly, as if I could run a mile. I want to kiss him and I want to flee at the same time. Eli is beautifully, wonderfully dangerous. He understands me, and he destroyed for me. I know now that no matter what, I'm safe as long as I'm with him.

"Is that it?" he asks. "You want to run and hide where no one can see you? Let out all that anxiety until I catch you and rip all your clothes off?"

"Yes," I whimper. I want to give him control, but in a very different way than Leon takes control. I want to escape the whole tangled web of Mr. Bosley's bullshit, to forget all about my shitty job and let Eli fuck all the tension out of me.

He runs his hands down my thighs, digging the claws of his other hand into my jeans.

"You want to run away from the big, bad wolf?" he asks, still gripping my hair, breathing against my neck, and I can't help the moan that falls from my lips.

I nod rapidly. I want to find the high he's promising me, far away from all these people.

"Then go." Eli releases me. I find his canines have grown even longer, even sharper. He licks them, as if he's ready to tear out my throat, and that makes all the blood in my body run even hotter. "Run and hide, little rabbit, so I can find you again."

I know these woods, probably better than he does. A thrill runs through me. I can weaponize all this fear, all the anxiety I've felt since Mr. Bosley called me this morning, and use it to fuel me.

Maybe then I can lose myself in Eli, instead.

My breaths speed up, and without thinking twice, I turn around and run.

I sprint past other picnic tables, where people give me odd looks as I blaze by. Once I'm through the picnic area and surrounded by tall trees, I dive off the main path, because I'll be much too easy to follow if I take it. I careen between trunks, my legs finally recognizing what I'm asking of them. My muscles come to life and speed me into the forest.

From far behind me comes the sound of footsteps, the crunching of pine needles and twigs. A loud howl echoes through the woods, and I know I'm no longer being chased by a man, but by a creature.

I push my legs even harder, my feet pounding the forest floor as I take a quick left turn, then keep going. That heat in my abdomen hasn't cooled—if anything, I'm even hotter, even wetter between my thighs, thinking about what Eli might do to me when he finds me. He is truly a beast right now, something feral and hungry. And he wants to eat *me*.

The ground slopes upward, and my breaths come harder. My thighs burn as I try to keep my pace going uphill. I'm dodging fallen logs and zigzagging between tree trunks when a roar echoes through the air. Instead of two feet crunching the forest floor, now I can hear four bounding through the trees behind me. They're growing closer and closer, and a manic laugh comes out of me.

I think, perhaps, I've always wanted to be chased. I've been training for this for years without even realizing it. All my anxiety about Mr. Bosley has drained away, turning into raw fuel.

I take another sharp turn and keep going, my lungs burning, my chest aching. My legs are losing strength quickly, and now my heavy breaths can be heard everywhere.

Suddenly, there's a low growl from behind me, so close it could practically be on top of me. I don't have time to dodge or duck before something heavy slams into me, catapulting me to the forest floor. My hands skid across pine needles and dirt, and all the air rushes out of my lungs.

"Caught you," Eli's gravelly voice says.

Something massive is holding me down with sharp claws, its body weight keeping me from escaping, no matter how much I scrabble with my hands and twist my body. The more I wriggle, the more those claws dig into my shirt and jeans, and the monster on top of me snarls. My fear and my arousal all mix together, driving me absolutely wild. I'm so painfully wet that it's sticky between my thighs.

"Keep struggling, little rabbit," Eli tells me, lowering his drooling mouth to my ear, "and you'll awaken the beast more than you already have."

Droplets of saliva fall onto my cheek, dripping down to the forest floor. I moan as those clawed hands rake down my sides, chewing into my clothing. He licks the side of my face, that hot tongue leaving a trail along my cheek and ear. I gasp as his huge hands find my ass, squeezing it tight. I buck, pushing my hips against his paws.

"Should I rut you right here on the ground?" he asks, panting into my ear. "Or should I take you on my cock against this tree?" He tears into the fabric of my pants with an audible *rip*.

Oh, I kind of liked those.

He drags his claw between the cheeks of my ass, down to where I'm moist and needy, and cups my pussy in his paw. "I think you want me to mate you right here, in the dirt." There's even more ripping as my thighs open of their own accord, exposing me to the air.

Yes, that's exactly what I want: to be fucked by this monster, right here out in nature, right where we belong.

Chapter Twenty-Four

SOMETHING HOT AND SLICK RUBS AGAINST MY ASS, AND LIQUID drips onto my back. I don't have to look to know it's Eli's massive cock. He groans and reaches under my hips to yank my ass into the air.

"What do you think, little rabbit?" he snarls, his tongue laving across my neck, tasting my sweat. I shiver and wriggle, my pussy clenching and unclenching. "Should I put all of my cock inside you? Should I fuck you until you beg me for mercy?"

"Please," I moan into the ground. I need it, now, or I might just cease to exist. "Please, big bad wolf. Right here."

His groan is deep and low, rumbling in his chest. He pushes his cock down between my cheeks, and then it slips between my folds, gliding easily along with how slick I've become.

"So wet for me," he murmurs, that wide head already pressing into me, insisting I open for it. Like this, my elbows and knees in the dirt and my legs askance, I'm spread so wide that my pussy easily parts for him.

"Yes, Tiff," he grunts, trying to squeeze in even more, but his cock is so fat and swollen that I don't think I can take it. Panting, Eli reels his hips back, and with a heavy grunt he thrusts in, hard.

That strangely shaped head burrows in deep, reaching into me and filling me so full that it's obscene. I jerk against the ground as Eli thrusts again, and I'm moaning into the pine needles at the cataclysm of sensation.

His tongue swipes across the back of my neck, his teeth grazing over my flesh.

"Your feet wanted to run, but your sweet little pussy wanted this, didn't it?" he growls.

I try to answer with a *yes*, but then he sinks that cock into me again, his furry legs crashing into mine, and all I can do is let out a cry instead. He reaches in so far that he brushes something sensitive, but it doesn't matter, not like this. Eli slams in again and again, clutching my hips in his claws and digging them in with every movement. I'm splintering apart, each harsh pump making my breasts press harder into the ground as tendrils of fierce pleasure lance out across my body. I'm moaning in time with Eli's rough pants, his drool dripping onto my neck and back. His fangs tangle in my hair as he tries to hold on to me, to keep me pinned underneath him as he takes me. Claims me.

Mates me, as he put it.

Eli lets out a guttural snarl, then suddenly his huge hands are around me, and that thick cock slips out of me with a wet sound. He pulls me up off the ground, into his arms, and I can't believe he can cradle my whole body without difficulty.

"I want to look at you as I make you mine," he says, voice rumbling low in his chest. I nod in frantic agreement, only wanting him inside me again.

Now that I can finally see him, I'm surprised to find a huge creature with black fur, not a speck of color on him. He looks like the night incarnate.

Eli shoves me up against a tree trunk, and I'm glad I still have my shirt on as the bark bites into my back. He pins me there, one clawed paw gripping my side, the other one curled under my ass. I wrap my legs around his waist, desperate to have him inside me.

"Eli," I whimper, my hips bucking.

"Needy rabbit." His wide lips peel back in a grin, revealing two rows of white fangs. "You want my cock? My big werewolf cock?"

"Please." He's slick with me, so his shaft slides easily along the outside of my pussy. "Fuck me, please."

With a grunt, he positions his hips and glides back inside me, burying himself deep.

"Oh, god," I moan, my head falling back against the tree.

The tips of his claws bite into my butt as he thrusts in again, lighting up every nerve ending inside me. Soon I'm clinging to Eli like I'm caught in a storm, my face buried in the soft fur of his chest and my hands gripping his mane. He keeps me aloft with just his hands as he fucks me harder, his panting growing more frantic with every pump. I feel like I might just tumble off the edge of the earth into the abyss.

"I can't wait to feel you come around me if you're already this tight," Eli says, grunting as he shoves himself inside me again. He reaches so far in that the swollen bump of his knot butts up against my spread pussy, which is already strained just to take his cock. When he pulls out again, he teases just the edge of me before plunging himself in. I'm practically vibrating with the sheer avalanche of my pleasure, of his knot pressing at my entrance. I sense my whole body clenching as that swollen lump at the root of his cock nudges me again and again.

"Someday you'll take my knot." The rigor of his thrusts almost pushes me down onto it, but my channel is too tight, too close to my eruption, and Eli groans. "Not today, but soon, when we've used this sweet pussy enough."

One claw dips into the collar of my shirt and pulls, so the fabric splits right down the middle. Eli snaps my bra next, and it tumbles away. When my breasts are bared, he pulls one into his mouth, that huge tongue curling around my nipple. White-hot energy fills my veins, driving me nearly to madness. After he finishes tormenting my nipples, still thrusting wildly inside me, Eli opens his huge jaws and wraps them around my face, as if he might tear my head off my neck. He slips his long, thick tongue into my mouth. It's so much bigger than mine that when he jams it down my throat, I nearly choke. Drool dribbles off his fangs, down my face, and now I'm sobbing out my bliss while his tongue muffles me. His hips jerk, and that powerful cock drives into me again, the shaft even thicker, even more swollen than before. He tears his mouth away from mine, his heavy pants turning my cheeks hot.

"I'm going to fill you with so much of my cum," he snarls, his thrusting growing uneven and fierce. "You'll smell like me for a week." That fattening cock stretches my edges as far as they can go, and lightning strikes me from above.

I cry out as my climax erupts, and I clamp down hard on Eli. The skin on his snout bunches up in a fearsome growl as he drives into me once more, and he ejaculates so hard I can feel warmth filling every crevice in me. It slides down my thighs before dripping audibly onto the forest floor.

We remain like that, my face pressed into his fur, his softening cock still inside me while one of his arms curls around my back to protect me from the tree bark.

Panting, Eli lowers me to the ground. The feral madness in

his eyes has quieted, and he looks sated as he slips out of me. My feet are wobbly, but he catches me as I pitch forward.

Eli chuckles. "I'm surprised you could take me," he hums, wrapping those big, furry arms around me. "Quinn must have prepared you well."

It sends a shiver through me, and the big creature buries his snout in my hair. He inhales deeply, and then suddenly sweeps me up into his arms.

"Where are we going?" I ask, clinging onto him, still completely naked with my clothes lying in shreds on the forest floor.

"Somewhere I can fuck you more," he says as he jogs off into the woods. "Until it's dark and no one will see two naked people coming back to get their cars."

We're lying on a bed of moss by the side of a clear, burbling creek when the sun starts to set. Eli gently lowers my legs as he withdraws his slick cock from my soaked, battered pussy. I can't keep track of how many times he's spent himself inside me. My thighs are sticky with him, and it burns as it runs down my ass in a stream. I think we fucked so hard that I might be paying for it tomorrow.

The big black wolf settles next to me, curling one arm around me and drawing me in close to his chest. While we spoon, he rests his chin on the top of my head and curls his haunches underneath my legs so I'm fully ensconced in him, keeping the cool evening air off of me.

"Thank you, Tiff," he murmurs into my hair, scattering it with his heavy breaths. "I'm sorry it took me so long. I didn't know how to rise above the noise and show you what you mean to me." A low growl rumbles in his chest. "But when I saw how your idiot boss was treating you, I had to do something."

I stroke his big arm, down to the clawed paw smoothing over my belly rolls. "I think I get it." Deep down, Eli has a sensitive soul, and he didn't know if he could handle the rejection. "It's hard to show our feelings to other people and risk being hurt."

His relieved breath ruffles my hair. "Thank you. For forgiving me." He brushes one claw over my bare, peaked nipple and huffs. "And for everything else, too."

I giggle. Perhaps I've been preparing to be chased through the woods my whole life.

Something wet and long gently prods my backside, and when my hips instinctively grind against it, Eli groans.

"Your smell is incredible," he murmurs, cupping my big breast in his huge palm. "It just makes me want to mate you over and over again, until you have my pup inside you." His paw slides down my belly to the hair between my legs, where he spreads my thighs apart. That heavy cock of his slides between them, the head nudging at my entrance again.

I laugh. "I don't know if I can take any more," I say, even though blood is already rushing down to my abdomen. "I've never been fucked like that in my life."

"Just one more time?" he asks, dragging his tongue over my earlobe, which sends a shiver down my spine. I tilt my hips so the head of his cock starts to slip inside me, and Eli grunts, gripping my flesh tight.

"You know I'm on the pill, right?" I ask him. "There aren't going to be any *pups* here."

He squeezes me even harder as he slides in deep on his first thrust.

"For now. But I'm going to practice as often as I can."

This time, the way he takes me is slow and loving, his paws

memorizing every part of me. He bundles me up close as he nurses another powerful orgasm out of me, his sharp teeth gripping my shoulder without breaking the skin.

I still couldn't take his knot, but he didn't seem worried about it.

"Leon will know how," he says with a surprising certainty. "And it will be so, so good when it fits."

I can barely walk by the time a now-human Eli and I return to the parking lot. He kisses me goodbye at my car, and I grab a blanket out of the trunk and wrap it around me before driving home.

Chapter Twenty-Five

WHEN I REACH MY APARTMENT, I TAKE A LONG SHOWER, THEN treat the scratches on my back and hands with some Neosporin. They're not bad, but you don't get away from a forest fuck without a few scrapes to show for it.

There's a text waiting on my phone from Leon.

I'm glad you and Eli worked things out

We certainly did.

Me, too

Did anyone follow you home?

I smile down at my phone.

No, I was alone

But that reminds me that there's still the matter of Mr.

Bosley. I can't possibly tell him it was Eli who vandalized his house and risk the cops coming after the brothers. I consider calling my idiot boss to try to convince him not to do whatever foolish thing he's got planned—but if I were to hedge a bet, the damage is already done, probably long before a werewolf pounded me into the ground out in the woods.

I want to say that I'm sorry about it, that I should've done something when I found out what Eli had done. But I can't bring myself to care.

Mr. Bosley's the one who made me sign those incriminating order forms, who made me "fix" the spreadsheets. He made sure my name was all over his dirty business.

Whatever trouble he's gotten himself into, he can get himself out of it again. He's not my responsibility.

The next morning, I get to the office right at nine, but I have to unlock the door to get in. I flip on the lights, deliver Mr. Bosley's coffee to his desk, and settle down in my chair.

It's almost ten when he finally comes in, hair disheveled and clothing askew. I've never once seen my boss look so unkempt.

I raise an eyebrow as he walks past me without acknowledging my presence. Once he's in his office, though, I get a call to the phone right away.

It's from Mr. Bosley. Who's in the next room.

"Um, hello?" I answer.

"Talk quietly," he whispers through the phone. "The office is bugged."

So Leon was right. A prickle of fear raises the hair on my neck.

"Why?" I whisper back into the receiver. "Who would do that?"

"I think I've made a mistake, Ms. Dockett." His voice goes even quieter, and cold dread fills my veins.

"What did you do, Mr. Bosley?"

He inhales sharply, then says, "I kicked the hornet's nest."

I hold the phone very still, wondering what he's done now.

"Are the hornets coming for you?" I finally ask in a hushed voice, covering the receiver with one hand.

Through the glass window into his office, I can see him shaking his head.

"No, Ms. Dockett. They're coming for *us*."

Oh, fuck.

I slam the phone down and get out of my chair, throwing my purse on. I am not going to get pulled into whatever hurricane Mr. Bosley has set into motion. However he managed to piss off Beatrice, I don't want to be here when she comes for him.

"Ms. Dockett!" He throws open his office door as I head for the exit. "Where are you going?"

"I'm not going to stay here and wait for them to show up," I say over my shoulder.

"You can't go." His voice drops lower. "You're just as involved in this as I am now. Your name's all over the files."

"Because of *you*!" I spin around, my fear and rage twining together into something even bigger and uglier than either of them. "You're the one who sucked me into this! What, you had me sign those orders so you'd have someone to blame?"

Mr. Bosley splutters weak objections, but I know I've caught him. He set me up. He wanted to pin it on me should this exact thing happen.

"Those three big guys of yours," he says quickly. "That's where you're going, right? For protection?"

I hadn't thought about it yet, but that's exactly where my instinct is driving me. The landscapers' den out in the countryside is the only place I could possibly feel safe from the storm that my idiot boss has brought down on top of us.

"Yes." I pull out my phone and start typing out a quick text message to warn Leon I'm coming. They're probably at the work site this time of day, and I hope they're willing to meet me.

"Take me with you!" Mr. Bosley claps a hand on my shoulder and squeezes. I wrench away from him at the sudden contact, feeling as if I have slime all over me where he touched me. "Please, Ms. Dockett. That woman is dangerous, and she's going to be after my skin now."

I freeze. Mr. Bosley might be the biggest asshole I've ever met, but that doesn't mean I should leave him to the wolves, so to speak. I don't want his blood on my hands should Beatrice decide to take severe action.

But he's the one who painted a target on himself. If she's after him, taking him with me could mean leading her straight to the brothers, and I can't do that to them.

I turn to my boss, clenching my phone tight to steel myself for what I have to say.

"Go to the cops, *Orland*. It's not my job to help you get out of this giant hole you've dug for yourself." I head for the door, clutching my purse to still my hands. "None of this was ever my fucking job. You took advantage of me, you used me, and now you're going to pay for what you've done—*by yourself*."

Mr. Bosley stares at me, open-mouthed. "Ms. Dockett," he says in a warning tone. "If you leave me here, you're fired."

I expected it would sting, that it would unleash another wave of panic to know I'd be losing my job.

Instead, I feel nothing. Eli was right. He doesn't deserve a second of my pity. This man has only ever done damage to my life, treating me worse than an object, abusing my better nature. Now he's pinning his idiotic crimes on me, when I've never done anything but try my best at this job.

Now, I am fierce and clawed. I tamed a werewolf yesterday. I have people in my corner, my friends and my lovers both, who will help me if I fall. I've been hiding myself for too long, making myself smaller so other people will be happy, when the truth is that they'll always be impossible to please.

Maybe it means sacrificing the regular paycheck and the healthcare, but I refuse to get caught up in this nightmare Mr. Bosley's created for himself. No fucking job is worth this. It's too bad it had to get to this point before I woke up, but there's no one to blame but Mr. Bosley for taking advantage of me.

"Fine," I say at last, turning to face him. "Then fire me. I'm done being your punching bag."

My boss blanches. "Ms. Dockett—"

I jab a finger into his face, and he leans away from it, eyes wide.

"Shut up!" The words come out sharper and louder than I expected from myself. "I'm fucking tired of you. Of this job. You've treated me like shit since the day I started."

I feel like a volcano about to erupt. Or maybe I'm already erupting, and all my pent-up hurt and rage is too much to hold inside now.

"I'm not going to take it anymore. Go turn yourself in, and maybe the cops can protect you from whatever hell you've pulled down on top of us."

"Your name is all over the documents," Mr. Bosley says, but he sounds pathetic, even to me.

"I don't care," I hiss back. "I'll tell them you made me do it. In fact, I should have reported you already."

He narrows his eyes. "You have no proof."

I'm done arguing with him. I turn around and head for the office door when my phone buzzes in my hand.

It's Leon's reply.

> Come to the den right away. We'll meet you there

I exhale a breath of relief, then head to the door.

"Wait!" Mr. Bosley takes a few steps to follow me, his expression pleading. "Come on, Ms. Dockett. Please. I can't go to the police. They'll throw me in jail. And if I don't, Beatrice will find me no matter where—"

"I'm done with this," I tell him firmly. "You can deal with the consequences of your own actions, on your own. At least you'll be safe in jail."

Saying these words, a powerful sense of relief floods through me. No more speeding to the coffee shop, hoping I don't get into a wreck. No more walking on eggshells, praying I don't upset Mr. Bosley. No more of him breathing down my neck and watching my every move like a hawk, waiting for the moment to strike and bring me down a peg.

Mr. Bosley stands there, mouth hanging open, as I stride out of the office and slam the door closed.

If the office is bugged, then Beatrice most likely knows where I'm headed. And surely if she's as competent as I think she is, she already knows about the brothers, too. I hope I'm not leading all five of us straight into a trap by finding refuge with them.

I'll always protect you. I have to believe Eli when he said it. I have no other choice.

I drive as fast as is safe out of town, down the long country road that will take me to the brothers' place. I can only hope that whatever is coming for me, they can handle it. *We* can handle it, together.

When I arrive, the Lupine Landscaping truck is parked beside their spare car. I pull in next to it, and when I do, Leon, Quinn, Eli and Jace are already waiting. They surround me as I get out of my car.

"Fuck, Tiff," Leon says, dragging me into a firm hug. "What has that asshole done?"

I bury my face in his firm chest. "I don't know, but whoever he pissed off... I doubt they're going to just let me off the hook, not with how much I've seen." All the invoices, all the orders, have passed over my desk.

Someone pats my hair. When I look up, I find Quinn smiling at me confidently. "Don't worry. They won't get past us."

I want to believe him. I have to believe him.

We walk to the den, all four of them clustered around me like a battalion. As I close my eyes and breathe through all my fear, all my worry and anxiety, Eli takes my hand in his and squeezes it.

"Thank you for trusting us," he says quietly. "If there's any night that something like this should happen, well, I'm glad it's tonight."

I blink at him. "Why? This could be really bad, Eli."

He just grins, then tilts his head up to the sky and points. "See that?"

The moon is round and full tonight as it rises, a glowing silver disk floating above the earth. I nod. "A full moon?"

Then it clicks. They're fucking *werewolves*.

Jace smirks. "It gives us strength," he says with a sultry lilt to his voice. "Oh, and it makes us really, really horny."

I have to laugh at that. "Isn't that the same as any other day?"

Leon snickers behind me. "You have no idea."

Chapter Twenty-Six

I WAS SO EXHAUSTED AND MISERABLE THE LAST TIME I WAS AT the brothers' house, I barely got a look around. This time, though, I can take in what a marvelous place it is.

"This is amazing," I say, spinning around to take in the high, dirt-packed walls, the cozy lamp lighting, the wide open living room big enough for, well, four full-grown werewolves, with plenty left over.

"We built it ourselves," Quinn says, chest puffing out. "Took us a few years to carve it all."

I can't believe they did this on their own.

Jace grins. "And the great thing about it is we can, uh, expand it as much as we want."

The brothers all exchange looks I don't understand.

Eli grabs my hand and leads me to the hallway branching off the main room. Curious what he has to show me next, I trail after him while Jace, Quinn and Leon follow behind us.

"Then, down here," Eli says, "is where we really live."

The hallway is tall but fairly narrow, and high sconces cast a dim orange light. It's so cozy, like a hobbit's house.

The first room I'm shown belongs to Jace. A low, wide bed is covered in music magazines, and three different guitars hang on the wall. He doesn't seem ashamed of how messy it is.

"You can play?" I ask, tucking my hands behind my back as I examine the guitar.

Jace shrugs shyly. "A little. I need to practice more."

"I'd love to hear you sometime."

This lights Jace up all over. He pulls down the bill of his cap, flushing.

"Any time you want," he answers.

Across the hall is Quinn, who has walls papered over with posters. There's stuff *everywhere*. I'm kind of impressed at how much he managed to fit into this one room.

"Why do you have a poster of Gordon Ramsey?" I ask, tilting my head as I stand in front of it.

"He's an amazing chef," Quinn says, as if this is an obvious reason to have a big framed picture of Gordon Ramsey in your bedroom glaring down at you. "It's inspiring! I want to impress him."

"Quinn's the best cook of the house," Leon says with a chuckle. "So clearly that poster is working."

We continue on down the hall and this time, Eli leads me into his room. It's the darkest, with very little decoration. His blankets and pillows are all deep, muted gray, and it's clean and neat—though that's probably easy when you're a minimalist to this extent.

"You don't have much stuff," I say as we stand in the doorway.

Eli shrugs. "Don't need stuff." He loops an arm around my back and ushers me inside. "Stay here? I have something for you."

Curious, I wait patiently as he opens the bottom drawer of his dresser and rifles through clothes, all neatly folded, looking for something. Then he pauses, and pulls out a small, leather-bound notebook. He returns to me while the other three brothers wait in the doorway, knowing looks on their smug faces.

"Tiff." Eli stops in front of me, then takes my hand in his and presses the book into my palm. "Once upon a time I wrote down what I wanted in my someday-mate, what I dreamed of having."

I wonder what's in here that means so much to him. I take the book and open it to the first page. There's a dedication written there.

To the one who will have my soul forever.

Already my heart is thudding hard in my chest as I flip to the next page. Written on it is a poem, clearly crafted by a much younger Eli.

I hope that whoever you are, you know what my family means to me.

I hope that whoever you are, you can love me past my mistakes.

I hope that whoever you are, you shine like the sun on a rainy day.

I know that whoever you are, I will be by your side until I die.

It's so sweet that tears threaten to spill out of my eyes. I throw my arms around Eli, holding the notebook firmly, and kiss his cheek. He's stiff with his surprise until he relaxes into me and hugs me back.

"Thank you," I say, my voice shaky. He nuzzles me with his nose, breathing me in. "I want to be all of this for you."

"You are," he says, wrapping my hands around the notebook and pressing it firmly into my chest. "You don't even have to try."

Eli's still holding my hand tight in his as we continue the tour. The hall is long, as if there are more doors missing, rooms that will someday be built. Then we stop at one final door.

"And this is me," Leon says, tapping it. The others stand back as he pushes it open, and I step inside.

This is where I slept the other night, when the brothers brought me home with them. It's bigger than the other rooms, and his bed is massive. It takes up a good chunk of the room, leaving space only for a pair of overstuffed chairs and a dresser. A high skylight brings in fresh sunlight, which is fading with the afternoon. They've truly created something remarkable here.

Leon's eyes are on me while I take it all in. Then I turn to him, and he stoops down to kiss me. Holding me tight, he lifts me up off the ground, and instinctually, my legs wrap around his hips. He groans into my mouth, and I feel his sharp canines brush against my tongue.

"Tiff," he says in a husky voice. "I hope you know what's coming tonight."

Hands trail over my ass, and I find Jace behind me, his chin resting on my shoulder as Leon peppers kisses across my face.

"My blood is burning for you," Jace murmurs to me, nipping the shell of my ear. "I need you."

Together, Jace and Leon set me down on the bed. Quinn is hastily taking off his clothes, and I'm surprised to find he's already quite hard. He grins widely at me, his mouth shifting and contorting as he starts to change. The snout comes first, and then the ears, as his body grows bigger and bigger. His tail makes a *sloop!* sound as it emerges, and Quinn lets out a little moan as his hands become paws and his nails grow into claws.

"Does it hurt?" I ask him, suddenly worried. I've never even asked before.

Quinn shakes his head. "No. It's just..." He reaches down

with one paw and grasps his thick, shining cock. There's already pre-cum dribbling from the tip, and he drags it along the shaft. "I really, really want to fuck you. And I'm working very hard right now not to tackle you to that bed."

Leon holds up a hand to Quinn. "Stay there," he says in that booming voice, the one that no one can resist. Quinn freezes in place. "It's been too long. *I* will take her first."

The others all reluctantly nod, and between my legs, my pussy pulses.

Leon stands in front of me, then places one knee on the bed and leans forward until his face is inches from mine.

"Tiff," he murmurs, raising his palm to my cheek. He strokes it, slowly and gently, even though I can tell by the fire in his eyes that he wants much more than that. "Every instinct in my body is telling me to claim you right now, for us. Regardless of what's happening out there in the world."

Now that all of us are here together, I want that, too. Instead of answering, I peel up my shirt by the hem, then toss it to the side. Leon groans as he takes in the sight of my tits, pressed together by my bra.

Eli climbs onto the bed, and makes his way behind me, until he's kneeling at my back. He unclips the bra, and I let it fall from my shoulders, then he flicks it away. While Leon stares at me, his mouth open, Eli reaches under my arms to cradle each of my breasts in his hands. A groan trickles out of him.

"Damn," he murmurs into my ear, rolling my nipples in his fingers until they're taut and hard as beads. "I can't wait to fuck a pup into you someday, and watch these get even bigger."

The dirty talk takes me by surprise, but then again, I'm also not surprised to hear it from Eli. I could tell by the very first poem I read that having a family means everything to him. And it's like Leon said—it's in their very nature. If I'm really their mate, like they say I am, then all of them will want to have kids in the future.

I wonder how that works.

Eli nibbles on my earlobe, cradling me to his chest, while Leon leans down to unzip my skirt and pull it off, followed by my underwear. Quinn is watching from behind him, stroking his extra-large werewolf cock. Jace simply has his arms crossed, a grin playing at the side of his mouth.

Leon surveys me up and down. "Now, spread your legs."

My body listens before my mind even considers the words, and my thighs open wide. He nods in approval, then kisses his way down from my sternum to my pelvis, where he pauses at my bush and hums. His long tongue darts out, and he swipes it eagerly over my pussy, from slit to clit. Leon's whole body shivers.

"Damn," he murmurs, licking his lips. "I almost forgot how fucking good you taste."

From somewhere behind him, Quinn whines.

"You'll get your turn," Leon says over his shoulder.

Unperturbed, he dives back into my pussy, thrusting his tongue inside me, then lapping at my clit again. He torments it greedily, sucking on it and flicking it, circling it and then smothering it, until I'm moaning and writhing with my head in Eli's lap. He pets my hair as I come apart in his arms, and Leon wrings my orgasm from me like a wet rag. I'm lying there panting, my body limp, when Leon's voice echoes through the room.

"Get in my lap, love," he says, those blue eyes focused steadily on me.

As if of its own accord, my body listens, and Leon folds his legs in front of him. I bracket his hips with my thighs, his cock now squeezed between us. A groan falls from his lips.

"I can't wait to be inside you," he murmurs, curling his

hands under my ass. I flex my thighs so I'm above him, and he's positioned right underneath me, right where he needs to be—because I can't wait, either. I want to be joined with him again, to show him how good I am, how safe he makes me feel.

"Leon." I lower myself ever so slightly, so only the soft, wide head of his cock is touching me.

He smiles back at me, and even though he's trembling with his need, he's gentle as he cups the back of my head, threading his fingers through my hair.

"I'm so glad you jogged by that day," he says, so softly only I can hear him.

"So am I. Even if you weirdos howled at me."

My arms embrace his neck as I sink a little lower, so he's wedged between my soft folds, almost inside me. Leon groans as I finally welcome him, my wet channel eagerly sucking in his head, and then his shaft. I hover there, our bodies only partially connected, as he cradles my cheeks in his hands, then kisses me. It's a soft, slow kiss, full of so many unnamed things. I forget about everything else in the world besides Leon's mouth, and how beloved it makes me feel.

I slide down on his lap and take the rest of him into my body. We both moan at the same time, finally united. Where his hands were, there are now claws poking into my flesh, holding me as close to his body as I possibly can be. They trail up and down my back as Leon kisses down my neck. Once again, I sit up high, and with him holding me stable, I sink back down, moaning Leon's name into his shoulder.

Behind me, I sense Eli crawl closer, as if I have an antenna tuned in to each one of them. As I rise and fall on Leon's lap, gasps and moans tumbling from my lips as he finds his marvelous place inside me, Eli maps out my spine with the pads of his fingers. He leans forward until he's breathing against my ear, and holds each of my ass cheeks, lending his strength to me as I take Leon harder and faster.

"Tiff?" he murmurs to me, tracing his hand around to the tight hole between my cheeks. "Let me touch you here?"

"Y-yes," I manage, and Eli looks pleased. He spits on his fingers, then brings them down to my tiny, puckered ass. Methodically, he teases it outside until he can fit one finger in, and the bliss that sweeps over me threatens to overwhelm all my senses. With Leon filling me full, Eli's hand is almost too much.

"I can't wait until I can fit here," he murmurs to me, dragging it around in circles, pumping in and out with the rhythm of Leon's thrusts. I gasp in surprise. He wants to put his cock *there*? "What do you think, Leon? Two of us inside her at the same time?"

"She'll be so tight," Leon grunts, and in response, he slams me down surprisingly hard on his cock. I whine as Eli pumps his finger faster, and then joins it with a second one, stretching me wider. It burns at the same time that it sends shockwaves of pleasure all the way to my toes.

"Yes," Leon grunts, gripping my hips to help me as my thighs grow tired. "Come around me, Tiff. Drink me up. Swallow me."

I can't help it. Eli's hand and Leon's incredible cock together finally break me, and my body clamps down tight around both of them as I cry out. Underneath me, Leon is fucking me harder, moaning my name. Then he growls, an animal sound, and jams himself deep. That knot of his presses eagerly at my opening, but I'm drawn too tight to take it. He tangles his hands in my hair and kisses me hard, pouring everything into his mouth and lips and tongue.

I can feel when Leon comes because he goes rigid against

me. He pumps once more before coming to a rest, panting. Then he pulls me against him, embracing me tightly and burying his nose in my hair.

"What a good girl you are," he whispers as he clutches me close. "Coming all over my cock like that. My sweet mate."

Chapter Twenty-Seven

WHEN MY BODY STOPS TREMBLING, LEON TILTS ME BACK AND lays me against Eli once more, his cock slipping out of me and spilling cum across the bed. I lie there, panting, my legs wantonly askew. Eli wipes the sweat from my forehead and grins.

"You know," he says, leaning down to brush his lips over mine upside-down, just a gentle whisper of a touch. "Only my wolf got to have you out in the woods. But I think it should be my turn this time."

Anticipation ripples out from the place our lips are touching, all the way to my toes. He was an animal in his werewolf form, fucking me against that tree. I wonder what human Eli is like.

He seems to understand just how overstimulated I am right now, because he takes his time, lowering my head to the bed, and then kissing down my chin to my throat, leaving warm splashes on my skin every place he touches me. When he reaches my breasts, he nips gently on each one, taunting them, teasing them. Then he sits up to take off his clothes, and I help him, because I want to see him.

He's gorgeous, in a special Eli way. I love how his hair is even darker than his brothers', and his eyes are like warm chocolate pools. I lose myself in them as he cages me in his arms, letting me feel the weight of his body on top of mine. He drags his hand down between my legs and just ever so slightly brushes the pad of his finger over my clit, which causes my body to twitch and jerk.

"Perfect," he says, sliding his hips down so they're resting at the juncture of my thighs. His cock is alert and seeping with his excitement, the excitement he carefully hides behind his stern face. But I want to see him come undone again, to go wild.

So I wrap my hand around his cock, then circle his hips with my legs and pull him toward me. He enters me in one wet, fluid motion, and Eli gasps, gripping the blankets tight in his hands.

"Oh, fuck," he moans, his way eased by all the cum Leon left inside me. He fills me up on that first thrust, burying himself in me. His dark eyes are even darker now, consumed by the black pupil at the center. He turns his head away, like seeing my face is too much for him.

"Eli," I say quietly as he withdraws, then slides in slowly, firmly, as far in as he can before his knot meets my entrance. "Look at me."

I hold a hand to his cheek as he glides into me again, and he lifts his eyes to meet mine. There are so many deep, soft emotions in them as he continues his progress, his knot pushing me apart with each thrust, that I have to hug him tight against me.

"Tiff." He leans his forehead against mine and sighs as we join again. "You feel amazing. Like nothing else in the world."

Those dark eyes remain fixed on me as he leads me slowly, like a horse to water, toward my orgasm. With each gentle stroke, his thick knot asks me to spread wider and wider, one millimeter at a time.

"Yes," Eli murmurs, caging my head in his arms. He kisses me hard and deep while that thick, fat bulge slides farther into me. "You're taking me so beautifully."

"Are you ready for Eli's knot?" Leon asks, pushing a curl of hair away from my face while Eli gently, slowly fucks me. "Can you let all of him inside you?"

I nod rapidly, eagerly, and Eli moans as even more of him pushes through. The stretch feels like heaven, and it's lifting me higher and higher into the sky, gentle as a hot-air balloon.

"Little rabbit," he whispers, kissing my cheeks, my nose. "I can't wait for you to come apart."

At last, he eases through, and then his whole knot is encased in me. When he moans, it's a full-throated sound.

"Ah, Eli!" I cry out as he reels his hips back to pull his knot free, then buries it inside me a second time. Then a third time.

"Good girl," Leon croons, wiping some sweat from my forehead as Eli continues his slow, steady thrusts. "Now come around his cock. Drench him."

My voice is stolen from me as my body obeys. This orgasm is bottomless and full of love, just like Eli is. My cry is trapped in my throat as he sends me flying off the edge. I cling tight as he tenses up above me, trying to push through my climax, but I can tell by his open mouth that he's failing.

He buries his face in my neck, pumping his hips furiously as he empties everything inside me. I writhe as he jams himself in one more time, my pussy clamping down hard around his knot.

Finally, Eli collapses, barely holding up his big chest with one arm. I squeeze him close in the embrace of my legs, relishing the feel of him stuck in me, all his warm cum still inside me. He traces my cheek with his hand, and a sigh of contentment tickles my face.

"I'm glad I could have you like this," he says, just for me. "I want to be with you in all the ways I can."

"Damn," Quinn says. Gently, Eli peels us apart, and Quinn, in his big, brown werewolf form, is watching us hungrily from the floor beyond the bed—and stroking the huge, pink cock that extrudes from the furry pouch around his big balls. "That... that was..." He groans as he strokes faster. "So fucking hot."

Poor Quinn, the inexperienced and sexual creature that he is, has been waiting for so long. Eli gives me a knowing smirk.

"Do you want Quinn's big werewolf cock?" he asks me. "Have I loosened you up enough for him?"

I nod furiously. "He'll fit." Just thinking about it, I clench around Eli, and he squeezes the flesh of my shoulder with his teeth.

"Do that and I'll have to fuck you again," he mutters. Eventually, when his knot comes down, he slides out of me. A warm gush follows it.

"Thank you," he says. "For trusting us enough to come here. For being with me." With a final kiss, he helps me up. "Now I think someone is waiting for you."

Quinn is sitting on the floor, his tail wagging wildly, his cock thick and heavy. When I open my arms to him, he leaps onto the bed on top of me.

"Tiff," he hums, licking my face. Dribbles of his cum fall to my belly. "God, babe, I need to be inside you. Please."

I kiss the tip of his nose. "I'd love that."

With a snarl, Quinn grabs me around the middle with two firm, clawed paws and throws me onto my belly on the bed. I let out a squeak as he grips my hips and pulls me up onto my knees so my ass is in the air in front of him. He groans, kneading my generous flesh in his claws.

"Oh, fuck." The slippery head of his huge cock is already nudging at my opening. He slips in easily, thanks to Eli's knot widening me, and those claws dig even deeper. "You feel incredible."

Quinn pants, his slobber falling onto my shoulder as he tries desperately to hold himself back.

"It's okay," I tell him, pushing my hips against his so he slides even further in. He rewards me with a groan. Then Quinn lets out a furious roar and slams his cock in, burying it all the way inside me. His knot butts right up against my pussy, and he grinds it against me. He drags his tongue from the back of my neck down my spine, leaving a trail of saliva behind.

"How is your pussy so good?" He reels his hips back, then thrusts in, yanking a cry from my throat. Quinn drops forward, supporting himself with one arm while he fucks me. His teeth graze the back of my neck, my hair, tangling in it. He huffs hot breath on my skin while he pumps inside me again and again, that swollen cock demanding I open for it, and my body gratefully accepts. The shape of his cockhead, so different in his werewolf form, carves a vicious path of pleasure through me with every stroke. I bury my face in the blankets as I start to shiver and shake all over, so sensitive from my last two orgasms that I can barely stand it.

"Please," I sob. "Please, Quinn."

He huffs against my back. "Please what, baby?" He pumps even faster, even harder, and I cry out, my whole body tensing and vibrating with the power of my unfurling climax. "You want to come? You want me to stuff you full?"

I nod helplessly, needing more, and more, and more. With a guttural snarl, Quinn shoves his cock deeper, that massive knot of his pushing even harder on my pussy. I whimper, feeling a burning stretch.

"Quinn," Leon says in a warning tone. Panting, Quinn pauses. "She's not ready yet."

"But—"

Leon growls, and Quinn hastily retreats. Instead, he fucks me with just his shaft at an even more brutal pace, until I'm screaming, ripples of agonizing bliss spreading across my body.

"That's right, babe," he growls into my ear. "Come all over me. Give me another one so I can fill you all the way up."

When my orgasm hits me, it's like a tsunami, bowling me over and hurling me down into the sand. Behind me, Quinn moans raggedly, and his cock swells up even bigger, shoving through my tight channel, over and over.

"Oh, god," he grunts, his claws nearly biting through my skin. He snarls as he hits his own climax, shoving himself so deep his knot is frantically trying to push through.

Finally, Quinn comes to a panting rest. He drags his paw tenderly down my back, over my ass. Then he nuzzles my hair with his nose as I collapse to the bed.

"Someday I'll fit my knot into you," he rasps in my ear. "And then I'll fuck you with that, too."

The suggestion makes me shiver all over. Gently he withdraws, and his cum gushes out of me onto the bed. I'm not sure I'll be able to move after that absolutely thorough claiming.

Quinn chuckles at my dazed expression. "Sorry, Jace," he says. "I wore her out."

I raise my head to find a big gray werewolf crouched beside me. Jace slips his furry arms around me and pulls me into his lap. There he cradles me, his cold, wet nose nudging my cheek.

"Is that right?" he asks, one paw tracing over my belly. "Are you tired?"

I try to shake my head, but truthfully, I'm exhausted after everything that's happened over the last few days. I don't know if there's even one ounce of strength left in my body.

With great care, Jace lies me down on the bed next to him, spooning me with his much bigger body. He pulls me into his arms, enveloping me. His cock has extruded from his sheath, at half-mast against my ass, but he doesn't move to use it. Quinn in his werewolf form, and Eli and Leon in their human forms, all climb onto the bed around us.

"I'm really glad I saw you at that bar," I tell Jace, covering his huge hands with my small ones around my middle. I loved how his face lit up whenever he told a joke, how the time flew by when we stayed up late chatting.

He tightens his grip on me and sighs with his head tucked over my shoulder. "Me, too. You mean everything to me."

I shift my legs so that his cock slides down, between the cheeks of my ass. Jace groans involuntarily, his hips jerking against mine. Reflexively, my thighs part, and soon Jace has slipped between them. His shaft glides easily over my pussy, which is soaking wet. Jace grunts against me, thrusting again to apply even more friction against my clit. I'm still high on sex, and my body is so well-used that I buck against him.

"Oh?" Leon asks, lying down in front of me. He props himself up on one elbow, then trails his hand down from my sternum to my nipple. "Are you ready for Jace's cock now, love?" He leans down to bring my breast into his mouth and sucks, sending another jolt through me.

"Lean forward, Tiff," says Jace, all his usual playfulness gone, "and spread your legs."

I do as I'm told, leaning closer to Leon and turning my body so I can open my thighs for him. This way, Jace's cock slips between my wet folds, and he groans. Gripping my flesh, he angles himself so the tip sweeps past my entrance. I moan as it slicks over that divot again, and again, then finally dips inside me. I'm so covered in cum that it's easy for me to take him, but Jace moves slowly anyway, only teasing me with the head as he grips his cock with one clawed hand, guiding it inside me.

It takes nothing for him to thrust in.

I let out a cry, and Leon holds my hands in his while Jace pumps his cock into me a second time. In his werewolf form, Jace is big, and the friction of him inside my tight channel is bringing the coals of my pleasure back to life. I thought I had nothing left, but I was wrong.

Leon grins as Jace moves in and out of me, making a wet slurping sound with every pump of his hips.

"Do you like that, love?" Leon asks, scooting in even closer to me so he can palm my breast in one hand, my belly in the other.

"Yes!" I'm aching with my need to orgasm again, but I've had so many that I have to reach for it. As if he can read my mind, Leon traces his hand down to where Jace is sliding in and out of me, and gently brushes his finger over my clit.

"You're taking Jace's big werewolf cock so well. What a good girl."

My entire body spasms. Again he rubs me, and again Jace's cock plows into me, and my legs are shaking violently with my need. White fur is spreading across Leon's body as he watches us, as he touches me, and he pulls his hand away as it transforms into a huge paw with long claws. Growling, he wraps his hand around my neck and pulls me in.

His huge jaws open and his tongue darts into my mouth. This wrenches a groan from my throat as that thick tongue explores me, tentative, while Jace's cock rams into me over and over. I buck against him, desperate for more.

When Jace slides in deeper, so does Leon's tongue, down my throat. Drool coats my cheeks as Jace's breaths come in heavy pants.

Whereas my orgasm with Quinn was an avalanche, Jace is nursing something else in me—a small flame that's slowly growing, building and swelling, with every thrust.

"Tiff." Leon pulls his face away, fangs glistening with his drool. "Will you tell us... Will you tell us that you'll stay? That you're ours?" His gravelly voice is tinged with uncertainty. "Please."

Maybe it's just the endorphins flowing fast through my veins, but I can't imagine anything better. Staying here, with them? With Leon and Quinn, Jace and Eli?

"Yes." When the word tumbles out of me, Jace groans and sinks his cock even deeper. "Yes!" I imagine sleeping every night, surrounded by them, and my peak pounces on me. I cry out, burying my face in Leon's soft chest, fisting my hands in his fur. Jace groans as he thrusts faster, spreading my bliss like hot oil across my body.

"You feel so fucking good," Jace whispers to me, clutching me closer as my orgasm tears me to pieces, then puts me back together again. "I'm going to pump you so full, Tiff."

And he does. He lurches as his cock grows, as he fucks me harder and faster.

"Oh, fuck," Jace moans. As he swells, my pussy resists, and I careen straight over the cliff. Jace jerks again as he spurts inside me. More and more of it fills me, until each of his mad thrusts is splattering cum down my legs.

At last, Jace's movements slow, and he bundles me up as close to his chest as he can, both of us breathing hard.

"Soon, you'll take Leon's knot," he says, and the aftershocks make me tremble. He groans as I clench around him. "But only when you're ripe."

"Ripe?"

"Ready for us. Ready to carry our pups." He licks my ear. "Our mate."

Soon, Eli and Quinn are on the bed, too, each of them resting their heads on me.

"Okay." Sleep clouds my voice. I think I've agreed to both marriage and children in one breath, and I don't mind it at all. To be loved by all four of them, forever...

"Our queen," says Quinn, running his claws through my hair. "We found her."

I've finally discovered where I fit, and I don't even realize it when I fall asleep.

Chapter Twenty-Eight

LEON SITTING UP JERKS ME AWAKE. HE'S IN HIS HUMAN FORM now, but you can see the wolf inside him by the way he leaps off the bed, tense and alert.

Nearby, Quinn groans. "What's going on?"

"I hear something," Leon says. In a moment, the others are on their feet. "Someone's outside."

All four brothers stalk to the bedroom door, hands curled into fists. I pull a blanket off the bed and wrap it around me, following behind the four rather naked men.

Outside the house, though, there's no sign of anyone or anything. The full moon shines down, beams of silver light sneaking through the trees. It's chilly, too, so I pull the blanket tighter.

Leon sniffs the air. "Come on out," he growls. "I know you're there."

From between the darkened tree trunks emerge six men dressed in black suits. They're silent on their feet, and each of them has one hand poised on what's clearly a gun.

Horror fills me. "Wait!" I reach out to grab Leon. "Those guys are armed!"

Leon just snorts. He curls his arm around my back and pulls me to his side. "Don't worry." He turns back to the men. "Are you sure you want to trespass on our territory?"

"Sorry to intrude," says a woman's voice. "But we have to tie up some loose ends." She's the last one to appear out of the shadows.

"Mrs. Smith?" I ask, dumbfounded. But now her hair is down, and she has a gun of her own in hand. "What are you doing here?"

"I tracked your car." She quirks an eyebrow at me. "So there are four of them now?" she asks. With a sad shake of her head, she says, "I don't want to have to do this, especially not to all five of you. I wish you'd been alone, Ms. Dockett."

I back up, but Leon tightens his arm around me.

"Do what?" I ask, my voice tight. But I think I already know the answer, because why else would she be here with a battalion of armed guards?

She means to kill us.

"Clean up this mess. It's already been such a long night." Beatrice sighs as if this is all very tedious. "I wish Orland hadn't pulled you into this because you seem like a nice girl, Tiffany. But here we are."

I'm wishing that now, too. "Where is Mr. Bosley?" A stone settles in the pit of my stomach. "Isn't your problem with him? I haven't done anything."

A faint smile crosses her face. "Oh, he's not a problem anymore."

My throat goes dry. She can't be saying what I think she's saying.

"You..." My blood feels cold, and goosebumps spread down my arms. "You murdered him?"

Beatrice frowns. "What a harsh way of putting it. That makes me sound so cold-blooded, Ms. Dockett."

She killed my fucking boss, and she's talking about it like she put down a rabid dog.

"And now I'm next?" This is how it ends? That's too stupid. I refuse to die for Mr. Bosley's scheme.

"I told you to quit your job." Beatrice narrows her eyes. "Now you know too much. And that idiot Orland made sure your name was all over everything."

I pull Leon closer, because now I'm terrified for him. If she wants to take me out, then that means they're all in danger, too.

The six suited men step forward, snapping their holsters open.

"As if." Quinn laughs, tilting his head up to the moon. "Nice night tonight, isn't it?" Beatrice furrows her brow in confusion, and a wide grin crosses Quinn's face. "Full moons are omens, you know. A lot can happen on a night like tonight."

And then he changes. Brown fur erupts across Quinn's body, and there comes the sound of creaking as his bones elongate, making him taller and taller until he's long past his usual werewolf size. I can only stare, my mouth ajar as his face stretches out into a snout and his lips peel back in a sneer. His tail emerges with a *pop!* and unfurls behind him as he stands there, eight or nine feet tall, like a true monster.

Our visitors gasp at the immense werewolf in front of them, and a few of the men murmur, slipping their guns from their holsters. For all of Quinn's confidence, they're *armed*. What chance do four creatures, made of flesh and blood, stand against bullets?

Even Beatrice is taken aback by what she sees. She eyes Quinn up and down.

"Some rather special boyfriends you found, Ms. Dockett. Just when you think you've seen it all..."

Quinn laughs, and it's a feral sound. "You haven't seen shit, lady."

He squares his body, his claws extended, and poises to lunge.

"Quinn," I whimper, reaching for him. "Don't!"

A safety clicks. There's a sudden flash of movement, and one of the men screams before any shots can be fired. Quinn has gone from standing next to me to being on top of his victim, pinning down the man's body with one huge paw, his jaws wrapped around his throat. Leon pushes me behind him, and soon he's changing, too. In the darkness, Eli's black shape is like a shadow flying through the air as he tackles two of the other men at the same time. He's enormous now, rippling with barely restrained muscle, as if he's been pumped full of blood. I've never seen anything so monstrous, the personification of death itself.

Air rushes past me as Leon joins the fray, a massive white beast full of teeth and claws. He slashes with one huge paw, sending a man flying and slamming into a tree, his body falling to the ground.

Jace leans down to me, huge and gray, his eyes twinkling. He licks my face. "Don't worry. These guys can't stop us."

A gunshot rings out, and Leon howls.

"No!" I cry out, moving to run toward him, but Jace holds me back.

"Stay here," he says firmly. "Leon will be fine." I have a hard time believing that as red drips down Leon's bicep, and he turns on the man who shot him. The white wolf leaps, ripping the gun out of the man's hand—along with some of his arm.

I scream as blood sprays.

"Oops." Leon tosses the dismembered arm away. "Don't know my own strength."

There's another gunshot, but Jace has already bridged the gap to the man who fired, and the shot misses him. Jace grabs his victim by the waist and hurls him into the last man standing, the two of them colliding with a loud *thump!*

Beatrice's face has gone from smug to utterly slack. Her eyes travel across the chaos, each of the brothers holding down one or more of her men. Then her gaze reaches me.

"Not quite the mouse I thought you were," she says, a ghost of a smile tweaking her lips. "But you're a reasonable woman, Ms. Dockett. Maybe we can find a middle ground." It's the first time I've heard uneasiness in her voice.

Eli stands tall, ready to pounce on her. I hold up a hand to him. She might have killed Mr. Bosley, but I don't want any blood on my own hands.

"What sort of middle ground?" I ask.

"You don't tell anyone about me," Beatrice says, talking too fast. "You pretend you have no idea what happened to Orland. And you let us go."

I arch my eyebrow. "That sounds like mostly favors to you," I say, taking a step toward her. I come to Leon's side, gesturing to his injured shoulder. "When you've already drawn blood."

She shudders. "Right. Sorry about that." She looks around at the four werewolves, then at her men groaning on the ground, one of them clutching his stump of an arm. "But you got what you wanted, didn't you? It looks like everything worked out in your favor. Now just let me go, and I won't come back here. I'll tell my boss to leave you alone."

I'm really tired of other people telling me what to do, then walking all over me and expecting me to simply tolerate it.

"Why should we let you leave?" I ask her, fury bubbling up inside me. "You came here and tried to kill us. And now you want mercy?"

Quinn snarls, all the hair on his body standing up on end. The wheels are turning in Beatrice's mind as she realizes just how dire her situation is.

"Okay," she says finally. "Okay. I'll pay you, all right? Everything I owed Mr. Bosley, we'll give it to you." She gauges my reaction, but I keep my face carefully schooled. "And we could give you protection. I could get you a better job."

But I don't want any favors from this woman. I just want to be left alone, to live my life in peace.

"No." I'm tired of this. "We'll let you go. You won't tell a single soul what you saw. You'll give the payment to Mr. Bosley's wife, you'll scrub my name off everything, and I'll send you the hospital bill." I narrow my eyes at her. "And you won't suck any other innocent people into your fucking schemes."

Beatrice nods with relief. "Thank you." She straightens her back. "It's nice to see you stand up for yourself. I hope that continues."

Carefully, Eli, Jace, and Quinn release their captives, but Leon looks ready to end the man he has pinned down.

"Let me kill one of them, Tiff," he growls. "Just one. So they really don't come back."

The moon must be driving him to rage. I scratch behind his ear, and he leans into my hand.

"No." I tug on his fur. "Leave him. She understands, and won't ever show up here again." I glance at Beatrice for confirmation.

"Yes, of course," she agrees.

With a growl of disapproval, Leon relaxes his grip around

the man's throat and backs away. The one who lost his arm moans as the others help him to his feet. All of them stumble away into the woods, Beatrice giving me one last nod.

"I'm glad you found what you were looking for," she says, glancing at each of my werewolves, then back at me. "Who knew."

She follows her henchmen off into the darkness.

When she's gone, I rush to examine Leon's wound, all my adrenaline at last catching up to me.

"This isn't good," I mutter, pressing my hand to the bullet hole to staunch the bleeding. "We should take you to the hospital right now."

He just turns and smiles at me. "Don't worry, love. It's a full moon. I'll be fine."

"Fine?! You were shot!"

Jace chuckles as he shrinks back down to his human form. "Really," he says, pushing my hair back from my face and kissing me on the temple. "We're more resilient than you think."

Leon gets to his feet, towering over me in this new, full-moon form. Then he leans down and slides his arms underneath me, lifting me up.

"Leon!" I cry. "Your arm!"

He licks my cheek. Then he nods to the others. "We'll be back."

"Go on," says Quinn, flapping one big paw at us, "and work off all that heat in your veins."

Jace snickers as Leon turns around and trots off into the woods, clutching me tight to his chest.

"Where are we going?" I ask as I cling to him, the trees whizzing past us.

"To clean me up." He nuzzles my face. "And if I don't fuck

you soon, I'm going to go find and murder each one of those guys just for looking at you."

I grin and pet the side of his face. "Aw. I've never had anyone offer to kill for me before."

Leon's fangs flash in the moonlight as he grins. "I'd do anything for you, Tiff."

Chapter Twenty-Nine

LESS THAN A MILE FROM THE DEN, THERE'S A WATERFALL LEON claims brings fresh glacier water down from the mountains. The waterfall gathers in a pool at the bottom of the cliff, where it then trickles away in a creek.

Leon sets me down on the edge of the pool and then climbs in, his wet fur turning dark gray in the water. There's just enough moonlight to see by as I drop the blanket and step into the pool beside him. The water is freezing cold, so I swim quickly towards him to soak up his body heat.

With a chuckle, Leon pulls me in against his soft chest. In his lap, between my thighs, his furry sheath is parting for that bright pink cock. But he just remains holding me, tucking his snout over my shoulder.

"I never expected getting involved with you would lead to a confrontation with the mob," he says, chuckling in his deep, rumbling werewolf voice.

"I'm so sorry." My shoulders curl tight around my neck. "I should never have done what Mr. Bosley asked. This is my fault. The fact you got hurt is my fault."

Leon's snout bunches up with a snarl. "That's not true at all. You didn't know what he was up to. You were doing your job."

I shake my head. "I knew it was wrong. I was just too scared. I was a coward. And now Mr. Bosley's *dead*."

With a deep sigh, Leon rests his big head on top of mine, stroking his soft palms down my back. "You have no responsibility for that, Tiff. He did it to himself. And he tried to frame you!" He growls. "You don't owe that asshole anything. He should have gone to the cops, like you told him."

I know he's right. I close my eyes and try to accept this. Maybe Mr. Bosley didn't deserve to die, but his fate isn't on my shoulders, either.

Turning around in Leon's lap, I take a good look at his wound. I bring water up to his shoulder and dump it over him, cleaning the blood on the outside away. When I've finished, something hard and metal falls out into my hand. I blink as I realize it's the bullet, and the tip of it is completely crushed.

"Hit the bone," he says, taking it to set it beside the water.

"Your *bone* stopped a bullet?" I gape at him. "And your body somehow ejected it?"

He grins and shows me his shoulder, where the dark pink wound has already stitched itself back together.

"The full moon. Werewolf stories always make it out to be this bad, scary thing. But the moon is special to us." He bares his fangs in a smile. "It makes us even more who we are. It intensifies all of our natural abilities."

"I certainly did like how, um, horny it made all of you. And the way you fought back there..." *Cool* seems like too weak of a word. It made me feel. Safe. Protected. Awed. "Amazing."

Leon grins as he squeezes the folds of my belly with one big paw. "Thank you, love."

I run my hand through his wet scruff, up his snout to his

ear, and tentatively scratch just behind it. Leon unexpectedly moans, his head leaning into my palm while his cock swells up underneath me.

"You like that?" I ask, scratching a little harder. Despite his injury, he's curling into me, his hands tightening around my body so his claws brush my skin.

"It's so good, Tiff," he says, nuzzling my palm. "You know just how to touch me."

So that's his weakness. I tuck this information away for later.

His cock is full now, jutting up between my thighs. He rocks his hips slightly, and I squeeze my legs together around it.

"I've been waiting for the right moment," he says, lazily dragging a claw through my wet hair. "It's special for me to claim you in this form."

I can't help but smile. I had a feeling. "You wanted me to agree to stay with you first, didn't you?"

He nods. "I was afraid of getting too attached. Once I commit, that's it. That's everything. That's all of me, forever."

These four brothers have such big hearts. I'm lucky, so lucky, to have found them.

"I understand." I stroke his long snout, snuggling against his warm, furry body, absorbing every inch of him. "It's forever for me, too."

Leon shifts in the water so now I'm up against the shore of the little pond. As he crouches over me in his super-sized full moon form, I have the sense to wonder if he'll even fit inside me. His cock is big, bigger than any of the others, and his knot is swollen and red.

Leon must be able to read my uncertainty, because his lips peel back, revealing his fangs.

"Don't worry. I'll be preparing you to take my knot someday." He lifts my hips in the water so his cock is positioned at the crux of my thighs. I don't know how these four have made me so needy, but I'm already clenching, thinking about what he'll feel like. "What a good girl you are," he says, pressing just the tip of himself into me. "Take my cock, just like that."

The stretch, even at this depth, is unbelievable. I moan and twitch as he pushes further in.

"You feel amazing, Leon," I whimper as he thrusts a few times, just with his tip, widening me for him. His tongue hangs out of his mouth as he stares into my eyes.

"Are you mine?" he asks, teasing me even more ruthlessly. "Please, tell me you're mine, love."

"I'm yours," I say in a whine. "I'm all yours."

It's what he wanted to hear. That monster cock slides in deeper, and I think I might be at my physical limit. Every nerve ending in my pussy is responding to him, firing off pleasure all across my body as he sinks further in on every stroke. He blots out the moon, as big as he is, and his fur is silhouetted in bright silver. He's beautiful, I think, my white wolf.

"Tiff," he moans, settling fully inside me, the bulge of his knot just beyond my edges. "Fuck. You feel so perfect."

He fucks me long and hard like that, panting my name, burying his tongue in my mouth. I don't even feel the rough stone against my back as he snarls a feral snarl, his huge hips snapping against mine with every thrust. When he comes, he comes so hard that I feel it jettison deep inside me.

While we lie there in the water, panting, Leon brushes one paw down over my breasts. "Tiff."

My eyes flutter open. "Yes?"

"I love you."

I touch my nose to his. "I love you, too."

When his wound is fully healed, Leon picks me up out of

the water, drapes the blanket over me, and carries me back to the den.

The next day, I head home to my apartment, and it feels strange that I'm not in a rush to shower, dress, and get to work on time. I stand inside my front door, wondering what on earth I'll do with myself now.

I need a new job, for starters. I guess I'd better start looking a little more seriously. I doubt I'll be getting any severance, because Mr. Bosley is, unfortunately, quite dead.

He shows up on the news after his wife reports him missing, and the authorities begin the search for him—or his body. The cops call me down to the station to interview me and find out what I know. I play dumb, saying that Mr. Bosley was behaving erratically over the last few days, and then simply didn't come to work one morning.

When they ask where I was, I'm forced to confess I was with my "boyfriends." The cops arch their eyebrows, but after a quick call to Leon to confirm, I'm released without further suspicion.

I thank my lucky stars.

A few days later, Mr. Bosley's body is pulled out of the bay in a nearby city, with a cause of death of drowning—clearly intentional. I think that's a horrible way to go, even for that asshole. There's an investigation, but I'm not brought in for questioning again.

I get the sense that whatever evidence existed with my name on it... Beatrice took care of it, like I told her.

When Aisling and Hannah see Mr. Bosley's face on the news, they both frantically text me to meet up. They need all the sordid details.

"I can't believe he was actually *murdered*," Hannah says, her eyes huge as we dig into some wings. "I've never known anyone who was murdered!"

"What are you going to do about your job?" Aisling asks.

"I've been looking." I shrug. "There's not much out there right now that I'm qualified for."

My friends frown in unison. "You're under-selling yourself," Hannah says. "You're so much more qualified than you think you are. You basically ran Bosley's operation."

She has no idea.

"Hey." Aisling snaps her fingers. "What about that boyfriend of yours? Who owns the landscaping company? You complained a bunch last time that their business acumen is... lacking."

I stiffen up. Right. My friends still think there's just one.

"I wasn't being entirely truthful last time we talked."

"What do you mean?" asks Hannah. "About the boyfriend? Is he not real?"

I accidentally burst out in a laugh. "No, no. He's real. It's just, um, there's more than one of them."

At their wide-eyed, slack-jawed faces, I finally explain everything—minus the werewolf part. Hannah and Aisling are both completely silent until I finish the story about how Eli destroyed Mr. Bosley's yard.

"Did he drive a tractor over it or something?" Aisling shakes her head. "Insane."

"Sure," I say. "A tractor."

"That's incredible, Tiff." Hannah gestures to the waiter. "Can I buy her a beer, please? This girl has four entire boyfriends. Four of them!"

The waiter doesn't know what to make of this but gives a nod of approval before going off to retrieve my drink.

"Seems like a foregone conclusion to me," Aisling says after a time.

"What does?" I ask.

"That you'd run their business for them. These guys clearly have no idea what they're doing—and you do."

I blanch. "There's no way I could run a whole company!"

"Why not?" Hannah pouts. "I'm sure it would be a walk in the park for you after everything you did for Bosley."

I actually consider the idea. I know how to manage projects, true. I've handled ordering and inventory. Scheduling is second nature and communicating with clients was most of what I did for Mr. Bosley.

"They really do need help," I hedge.

"Exactly!" Aisling slaps me on the shoulder. "I bet they'd take you up on it in a heartbeat."

"And then you'd get even more hours with them," Hannah says, waggling her eyebrows. "I bet four guys take up a lot of your, um, *time*."

I think about the other night, when we all gathered on Leon's huge bed, and my face must turn red as a beet because my friends giggle.

"I'll pitch it," I finally say. It would be the ideal solution. "And see what they say."

I'm nervous when I bring the idea to the guys. Maybe they don't really need or want my help. What if I'm inserting myself somewhere I don't belong?

But after I finish my pitch, Jace is overjoyed.

"Holy shit," he says. "That's the best idea anyone's ever had!"

"You do know how to do everything we don't," adds Quinn. "Bookkeeping, organizing, tracking jobs and clients..."

"I know it would be like babysitting a bunch of idiots," says Leon, taking both my hands, "but we would absolutely love to have you take care of business."

Eli slides his arm around me. "Are you sure you want to commit to that, Tiff?" he asks. "It would be a shit show if we ever got audited."

Just the idea makes me shudder. "Oh, yeah, no. We have to fix that."

Quinn grins a doofy grin. "Please be our office manager, Tiff."

I didn't expect them to be the ones begging *me*. I hug all of them at once.

"Sure. I would love that."

"Thank goodness," Leon says with a sigh of relief. "We've been falling apart without you and we didn't even know it."

Chapter Thirty

When I meet my mom for dinner, Mr. Bosley's murder is all she can talk about. "He must've gotten caught up in something shady," she says, "or why else would he end up at the bottom of the bay?"

I shrug.

"Well, what are you going to do for work?" she asks. "Are they giving you severance?"

"Yes, I have a new job." I bite my lip. Am I ready to tell her yet?

"Oh, I hope they have good insurance." Rather than asking a single question about my work, she spends the rest of the meal talking about her upcoming trip to Mexico with her friends, and I don't have the courage to tell her the truth about the brothers.

Not yet.

Still, I find myself spending more and more time at their place. Most nights I wind up in a cuddle puddle on Leon's bed, thoroughly spent. There's very little reason to stay at my own apartment when I'm here working most of the day, and then spend my evenings having dinner with the guys and getting fucked until I'm dripping and utterly spent.

When I get home one night—and their den has started to feel like my own home—I'm surprised to find all the guys there. Eli sometimes has a pottery class, and Jace likes to go to the bar and watch sports, so it's unusual for all four of them to be there at once.

The moment I'm inside the front door, they all stand up.

"Uh oh," I say, hesitating in the entryway. They clearly want to talk about something important. The part of me that assumes the worst reflexively curls in, afraid of what they might have to say. What if it's over already? What if they've changed their minds about me?

"We wanted to talk to you." Leon grabs my hand, and just the feel of him helps settle my nerves a little. He kisses my cheek. "About what you want."

"What I want?" I'm mystified by the question. I have everything I could want right here, in front of me.

"For your life. For *our* lives."

The others have such hopeful, vulnerable expressions that all my nerves settle. Seeing this beautiful home they've created, looking at their faces, I think that this is where I belong.

"I want you," I say with certainty. I know there's a reason it feels so comfortable, so natural to be with them. This is the place I was always meant to find.

"Even this crazy life we have?" Jace asks, sliding his arm around my waist and bending down to kiss my cheek. "Four bozos with zero business acumen? Who are all just a bunch of big dogs?"

"Yes. Especially that." I lean into him. "Maybe it won't

make sense to people outside, but it feels perfectly right for me."

Quinn can't help himself and runs to wrap his arms around me. He kisses me deeply, and already, fur is spreading across his body.

He's such a horndog, and I love him.

"Then that room down the hall we started carving out?" Leon says. "It's yours, if you want it."

Move out of my shitty apartment that costs too much and live in this wonderful home of theirs? Twist my arm. "Yes. I do."

Eli's face relaxes with relief. Jace swoops me up off the ground, kissing me hard, wrapping my legs around his waist.

"Thank you," he murmurs, rubbing his face on my hair. "Thank you for being ours."

"Always." And it's true—I could never love anyone like I love these four perfect men.

It was an easy decision to ditch my apartment. There was nothing there for me but atrociously high rent, when I could be shacking up with my four mates in their beautiful underground home, instead.

I move into the new room the guys have carved out of the hill, right next to Leon's, bringing my bed, my desk, and my dresser with me. It's lovely to have my own space, but still be near all of them. We almost always sleep on the big bed in Leon's cavern of a room, the four of them curled around me.

Naturally, I get to meet their parents. Mr. Graham acts like any other dad in his sixties, with a bit of a beer belly. His hair is still dark, just like his sons, and thick across his body. I don't even have to be told to know he's a werewolf.

"Oh, I'm so happy they found you!" Their mother, Delaney, is sweet as a cupcake and has perfectly round cheeks. "I remember when their dad imprinted on me..." She swoons. "What a whirlwind romance! It didn't take long to know I was his mate."

They exchange a kiss, and behind me, Quinn makes a disgusted *blech!* sound.

If I'm going to do the job they want me to, I need an office, so my first item of business is to clear out the little cabin that acts as the "house" on the property. While the guys and their dad work on clearing away old junk and furniture, then repairing what's fallen apart over the years, Mrs. Graham helps me pick out a desk, a chair, and plenty of filing cabinets. I didn't expect how powerful I would feel getting to select what goes where and creating the most efficient workspace for myself possible.

"I knew it," she says after a while of us assembling the desk from terrible instructions.

"Knew what?" I ask, realizing I've put the wrong screw in.

"That they would all bond to one person." She shrugs. "They've just always been close, the type to share. It's not uncommon for siblings to bond to a single mate and form a pack." She grins. "I expect I'll have lots of grandkids."

A flush takes over my face. The plan is that once the office is up and running, and I've figured out the flow of things, I'll stop taking the pill. We still have to complete our ceremony, but we're waiting until the next full moon.

Tiff! You going to be done soon?

It's Quinn texting me. He's always so impatient for me to come play with him. He likes to roll around with me on the floor until he's good and worked up, and then he fucks me until I can't walk.

Eli's been experimenting with fingering me from behind while I'm bouncing on Quinn. We're building up to taking him there, and I'm thrilled and nervous. But oh, it feels so good when he does it.

Luckily, my body has adapted pretty well, and I've gotten back into running again. Now I jog through the beautiful woods that surround my new home, and sometimes I'll even catch sight of deer or a fox.

I sit back from the desk project and text a quick reply.

> I'll be back in a bit. Then you can even chase me if you want 😊

Quinn sends me a bunch of puppy dog faces, and I put my phone in my pocket to finish the desk. When it buzzes again, I assume it's one of the boys. But when I glance down, I find that it's a call from my mom.

Great.

I contemplate not answering. I haven't once felt bad about myself since I moved in with the guys, and I don't like the idea of what lies in wait if I meet with her. But I only hold out on picking up until the third ring because she'll get annoyed with me if I let her go to voicemail.

"Hey, Mom," I say, steeling myself for the worst.

"Hi there, honey. Are you feeling better this week?" She doesn't wait for me to answer. "I'm calling because I need to reschedule our usual dinner date. Can we go on Friday? Miriam wants to go to happy hour, and—"

"Sorry," I interrupt. "I have a date that night."

Maybe it'll get her off my back until I can figure out how I'm going to tell her the truth.

"So it's going well with the boyfriend, then?" For a second, I'm offended by the strength and volume of her surprise. "That's great, Tiffany." Then she pauses, and I can hear her thinking hard on the other end—which never goes well for me. "Is it serious?"

Well, Mom, I just moved in with them. They practically consider us married, and we're already talking about having kids.

"I guess so," I answer.

"Then I want to meet him!" She huffs. "Okay, instead of going out on Friday, bring your date to the house. I'll cook dinner. I need to know all about the man who is so lovely as to be getting serious about my daughter."

I frown at the way she says it, like I should be blessed to have a boyfriend.

It's a terrible idea. I could bring just Leon, but that would feel wrong. I'm mated to *all* of them, and each of them means the world to me.

But I have no idea what Mom will say when she meets them and I have to explain our unconventional situation. I suppose I have to rip the band-aid off sometime, and it's better she knows now than when I have to explain my baby bump has four dads.

"Okay," I finally say. "We'll come over on Friday night. But you'd better make a lot of food."

"Huh? Why?"

"A *lot* of food. Just believe me."

When I hang up, Delaney is watching me. "Your mother?" she asks, as if she could tell just by the sour look on my face. I nod. "You think she won't approve?"

"Oh, definitely not." I could laugh. "She doesn't think I can get one guy, not to mention four."

Oddly, this earns a mischievous grin from my new mother-in-law. "Then this will really stick it to her."

I decide then that I like her, and I think I'll be happy to become a part of their family.

The guys' eyes are wide when I explain what we're doing on Friday night.

"You want us to meet your mom?" Leon asks, mystified.

Jace rubs his forehead, brows creased. "All of us? Together? Are you sure?"

I frown at them. "Of course we're going together. What did you expect?"

Quinn, Eli, and Jace all turn to Leon. "Well, we thought you'd just bring him," Jace says.

"You really think I'd leave you out?" I pull Jace into a hug, and his hat falls off his head. "But I love you."

He chuckles, and his hand skates down my back to my ass. "I love you, too. We just thought it would be easier for her to accept one of us."

They might be right, but I don't care anymore about what's *acceptable* and what isn't. I almost got murdered by the mob, and my boyfriends are werewolves. My shitty job is gone and my boss is dead. I have nothing to lose, and I don't want to hide who I love. It's not fair to them or to me.

"Thank you," Quinn says earnestly. "For including me."

"I told Mom to make plenty of food," I say, "so hopefully she listens." I kiss Quinn on the lips, and he pulls me in, bending me backwards with the force of his answer.

"I say this calls for a celebration," Eli says, his body already starting to shift.

"What sort of celebration?" I ask, knowing exactly what he's going to say.

"It's time to catch the rabbit." He steps forward as black chest hair spreads across his body, turning into fine fur. So I turn around and sprint out the door at top speed, and four wolves howl behind me as I dart away into the trees.

When Jace, the fastest of them, catches me, he fucks me with my pants around my ankles.

Chapter Thirty-One

WE ALL PILE INTO THE TRUCK AND HEAD TO MY MOM'S HOUSE, where I lived my teenage years. She's since given away everything I had as a kid—without asking me, I should add—and converted my old room into an art studio that she doesn't use.

When we pull up to the curb, I get out first, because I'm expecting Mom to be waiting at the doorstep. Sure enough, the door flies open when the truck parks and she steps out.

"Oh, hello, dear," she says, much more warmly than she ever does when we're alone.

Jace gets out of the driver's seat, and Mom's eyes go wide.

"Wow," she mutters, gaze fixed on him. He's wearing a nice, tight shirt tonight with jeans that hug his ass and crotch in a rather mesmerizing way. He even left the baseball cap at home. "You really scored, Tiffany, darling."

"Um," I begin, when another door opens and Leon steps out. Then Quinn, then Eli, until all four of them are standing on the sidewalk behind me.

My mother is standing there, confusion written across her

face. "I thought I was meeting your boyfriend tonight, honey. Who are they? Have you joined a gang?"

I stare at her, then shake my head and walk over to Leon, who's already holding out his hand to me. I take it in mine.

"No, Mom." I inhale a deep, calming breath. I've practiced this in my head. I can do it. "I'm seeing all of them."

Quinn waves. "Hi, Mrs. Dockett! I'm really glad to meet you, I'm Quinn, and I've heard—"

"*Four* of them?" Mom asks, her eyebrows rising ever higher on her forehead. "That can't be right."

"No, she has it all correct." Eli takes my other hand and kisses me on the cheek, as if to prove his point.

"H-h-how..." Mom trails off, glancing between them and me. "I don't understand, Tiffany."

"Then how about you let us in and I'll explain?" I try to keep my game face on. Eli squeezes my hand to give me courage. "All of us."

Too flabbergasted to object, my mother steps aside at the door. Leon walks in first, keeping his hold on me, and I follow behind. The other three file into the house. I never thought it was particularly small before, but with all four of them here it feels shockingly cramped.

No wonder their den is huge.

"I don't think I have enough chairs," my mother frets. She's completely off-balance, and it gratifies me a little. She leads us all into the dining room, which was clearly set up for just three people.

"There are some folding chairs in the basement," I remind her.

"Oh, gosh, yes, thank you." Mom hurries away, leaving us standing in the living room.

Quinn gazes around at the atrociously outdated decor. Everything has flowers on it of some kind, and often the patterns clash. The room is cast in a yellow glow because of the gauzy curtains hanging over the windows.

"Charming," he says, inspecting the grandfather clock—one of many large items squashed into this little room.

Mom returns a moment later with more chairs, looking stressed and harried. "I don't think I made enough for this many people," she says, wringing her hands. "Maybe I should order pizza."

"It's fine, Mrs. Dockett," Leon says, stepping toward her. His voice has that eerie boom to it, the one he uses when he tells me to take my clothes off, or suck on his cock, or take a deep breath when I'm overwhelmed. "We're just here to meet Tiff's mother. That's what's important."

Her eyes travel from his boots, up his toned thighs to his thick chest, then to his face. She gasps when she sees his bright blue eyes.

"Wow, you have such dark hair, though," she says. Then she shoots me a deadly look. "Is this some kind of joke, Tiffany? Are you trying to make me look silly?"

"What?" I don't know what to say. "Why would I do that?"

"Four incredibly hot men." She gestures at them. "All of them? Dating *you*?"

I can't miss the way she says *you*.

"What do you mean by that?" Eli asks, taking a step forward so he's level with Leon. "You don't think Tiff deserves that kind of love?"

Mom stares at him blankly. "Love?"

I let out a deep breath. This is going off the rails, fast. "Let's sit down and eat," I finally say, hoping the guys will retract their claws. "Do you want me to help you get the food, Mom?"

As if startled from a daze, Mom nods hastily and leads me into the kitchen. The moment we're alone, she rounds on me.

"You have to be joking," she says, eyes narrowing. "You can't date *four* men, Tiffany. That's not how it works."

I return her look. "Why not? They all care about me." I hesitate. "They love me. And I love them."

Mom shakes her head like she's disappointed in me. Not that it would be anything new if she was. "I can't believe you. What will people think?"

"People will think whatever they want. It has nothing to do with me or the life I'm living." This is always how it is with her. What other people see has always meant more to her than my actual happiness.

"And what kind of life is that? Sleeping with four men at once. That's just not how society works." She rubs her temples. "I can't believe my daughter would be such a slut."

It feels like a dagger right through my chest that my own mother would use a word like that. Maybe she's right. My pulse speeds up, and my breaths start coming short and fast. What if what I'm doing is wrong? What if the life we've already started living, that makes me so happy, is corrupted?

I squash my eyes closed, trying to calm my pulse. No. Mom's wrong. What we have may not look like other relationships, but it means the world to me, and we've fought hard for it. I'm not going to let my mother and her opinions influence me. She's already beaten me down for too long.

I stand up straight. I took it from Mr. Bosley for years, and I've taken it from her, too, without argument. But I'm fucking tired of it. I'm tired of making myself smaller, of making excuses, of feeling bad about myself so she can feel superior.

"That's it," I say, drawing on all the confidence I've worked hard to build since our confrontation with Beatrice. I have Leon, Jace, Quinn and Eli to back me up. "We're going. Right now."

I turn around and walk back out of the kitchen without another word, to where the four brothers have seated themselves at the table. They all look up and cock their heads when I come in.

"Come on," I say, grabbing Quinn's hand off the table and pulling him along as I pass. "She doesn't want us here, so we're leaving."

"What?" Eli shoots the kitchen a dark look. "What happened?"

Jace and Leon, both perplexed, follow me to the front door.

"She told me in no uncertain terms that she doesn't *approve*," I spit out. "And I'm not going to spare another moment on her."

Eli doesn't follow us as we head for the front door. No, when my mom exits the kitchen again, he whirls on her with a furious expression.

"What did you say to Tiff?" he demands. Mom flinches at the tone of his voice, her eyes going wide. "What did you tell her to upset her like this?"

Mom's mouth falls open. "I, um..." She clearly doesn't know what to do with someone Eli's size getting in her face. "I just said that—"

"She called me a slut," I finish for her. I'm not going to shield her anymore, to downplay how much she hurts me. She can own up to her words.

Eli grits his teeth. "You what? You said that to your own daughter?"

Mom shoots me a helpless look. "Honey, that's not what I meant—"

"It is what you meant, isn't it, though?" I say. "You wanted to hurt me. To make me feel bad for how I've chosen to live my life. But I don't feel bad, not one bit." I twine my fingers with

Eli's. "I'm really happy, for once. I'm loved, and I have a cool new job managing their *very successful* landscaping company."

My mother blinks. "Oh, you're the manager now?" Her gaze becomes scrutinizing. "That's a lot of responsibility on just you."

"So?" I snap. "I'm good at it." Leon squeezes my shoulder, emboldening me. "No, I do a great job. I've been basically doing it for years for Mr. Bosley. I'm running everything now, and we have timelines, and we're writing up more accurate estimates, and..."

Mom holds up her hands. "Okay, I hear you, Tiffany."

"Do you?" I wouldn't need to be so defensive if she didn't always go on the attack. "I'm finally where I feel like I'm meant to be, Mom. And I don't know why you can't just be *happy* for me."

No one speaks as Mom stands there, frozen.

"Tiffany..."

"What? What else do you have to say?" I realize that I'm so worked up I'm panting. But none of the guys speak. They'll let me fight my fight with her. "What other nasty barbs do you have? What other holes can you poke in me to make me hate myself?"

My mother looks genuinely wounded. She opens her mouth to speak, but then studies my face, where I must be wearing all my anger and my hurt very plain, and she closes it. Instead, she gestures at the table.

"Come on. Come back inside." She gives me her best approximation of an apologetic face. "You know I didn't mean what I said, Tiffany. Sweetie."

I roll my eyes. Of course she's backpedaling. I've never talked to her like this in my entire life, and certainly not with four huge, hairy men at my side.

"Take a seat, please," Mom says to the guys. "Maybe we can start over? Hmm?"

Eli glances at me, and I know that whatever I say, they'll go along with it. I could walk out of here and let my mom believe what she believes—or we could stay here and show her that she's truly wrong about us.

"All right," I say finally, sitting down.

When we're all seated around the table, Mom serves what she has, asking lots of questions about where they work ("Oh, my, you're doing a job in *that* neighborhood? How lovely") and what kind of revenue they have. I explain what I'll be doing to manage the company.

"Wow," she says. "And you can handle all that, Tiffany?"

Quinn narrows his eyes. "She can more than handle it. She cracks the whip real good."

Mom blinks, and I laugh into my hand at the image of me with a whip.

"Really?" she asks. "My daughter?"

Leon crosses his arms. "Yup. She makes sure everything gets done on time, and she's really kicking ass."

I hate how surprised she is by this, but she doesn't make any further comments about it.

The rest of the dinner is, thankfully, uneventful. Mom does most of the talking, without once asking a question of any of them, and Eli rolls his eyes. Jace holds my hand under the table until, at long last, it's time to go. Mom doesn't remember their names, but she promises to learn.

"Will I have grandkids?" she whispers to me as we file out the door a few hours later. "How does that work?"

I shake my head at her. "I can't believe you. But yes. Eventually." I hop down the front step. "Bye, Mom."

In the car, Jace puts me in his lap, and wraps me up tight as the truck takes us home.

"I'm really impressed with you," he says, kissing the back of my neck. "I love how you told her off."

"It was super hot," Quinn chimes in.
I smile at them, my pack, my mates.

Chapter Thirty-Two

After a few months of our new life, I decide to stop taking the pill. I've talked it over at length with Mrs. Graham, who insists I call her Delaney, and she's more than happy to help in the office. Every morning since then, the guys have sniffed me, kneeling down to bury their noses in my crotch. During my last period, they all took turns devouring me and licking me up.

"It's a sign your body's getting ready for us," Jace said, palming my big breasts and sucking the sensitive nipples between his lips while Eli, crouched between my legs in his massive, black werewolf form, wriggles his tongue inside me. "You're making a new home for our pup."

Our pup. Whoever plants the baby, it will be the child of all five of us. Imagining one little kid with four rather big, hairy dads makes me giggle.

And then, one morning, I wake up curled into Quinn's side, his huge, furry arms clutching me close to his chest. We've slept in, and I can already hear the others bustling around the kitchen. When I move, he lets out a groan of complaint. Then, his ears twitch, and his eyes fly open. He sniffs the air.

"What's that?" he asks, a grin peeling his lips up on his long snout. His claws find their way down my hips, to my ass, where he stops to squeeze. I always sleep naked now, which means sometimes I wake up with a cock sliding between my thighs.

But Quinn's interested in something else. He skims his nose down my body, his nostrils flaring as he reaches the crux of my thighs. He pulls them apart and takes a huge whiff.

"Oh, fuck," he moans. "Smells so good."

He sits up and howls, making me slap my hands over my ears at the sudden noise. The door to the big bedroom flies open, and Leon, Eli, and Jace all come inside.

"What is it?" Leon asks.

Eli inhales sharply, then a wicked smile takes over his face.

"She's ready." He kneels on the bed in front of me and urgently runs a hand between my legs. "And on a full moon, too."

Quinn's mane puffs up. "Can we do it tonight?"

A pair of arms curl around my waist, and Leon leans over my shoulder, nuzzling my cheek with his. "This would be the perfect night."

Jace tilts his head at me. "Tiff? What do you think?"

Is it time to finally seal the bond between us? The conclusion feels foregone to me. I've never felt so loved, so cherished and happy, as with them.

"Yes." I rub my face against Leon's the way he likes. "I'm ready to do it. Tonight."

Again Quinn howls, and the others join in, until I'm laughing and begging them to stop.

"You still have to wait until I'm done at the office," I tell them, hands on my hips.

There's still so much to do going through past years' records and tidying things up, and I want to get everything squared away before a possible baby comes. I've set up a system that will make it much easier going forward to keep the finances in order, as long as the boys stick to their schedule. It's still tricky getting them through projects by deadline, but they're working on their time management skills.

That night we have a ceremony, just the five of us, under the full moon. On paper, I'm married to Leon, the leader, the alpha, but I know I'm bound to all of them.

When the words have been spoken, they all tilt their heads back at once, noses pointed to the moon.

"*Awoo!*" they howl to the stars. "*Awoo!*"

Quinn takes my hand and quietly leads me back to the house. We all make our way silently down to Leon's room, to the big bed.

When I'm bared to them, Leon traces a hand down my thigh, and he drops down into a low crouch to lick me there. Then, he opens his mouth, and I find his fangs are even longer than before.

"Tiff," he murmurs, dragging them along my soft flesh. "I want to claim you now. For all of us. Is this what you want?" His big blue eyes travel up to mine. "To be ours? To be our queen? To have us forever, and someday, have our pups, too?"

My answer comes out firm and decisive. "Yes." I've never been more certain of anything. "Please."

Leon opens his mouth and then bites down on my thigh, hard. It breaks my skin, and I yelp as blood wells up around his fangs. His eyes roll back in his head, and he groans as he licks it up. He looks like he's lost in a trance.

When he's finished sucking on me, Leon steps aside, and Quinn approaches me next. He crawls onto the bed in his big, awkward werewolf form, and lowers his head to the same spot.

There he licks up more blood, smearing it around with his big tongue. He lets out a hungry moan.

"Fuck," he mutters. "I'm so glad we found you, Tiff. I can't wait to spend the rest of my life with you."

"You, too," I say, running a hand down his cheek, then over his curly hair. "My big, sweet golden retriever."

His pulsing cock is leaking all over the bed. "Leon," he says, "please, I—"

"You'll have to wait," Leon responds firmly. With an obedient nod, Quinn gets back up. It's Jace's turn next.

"Beautiful Tiff." He runs his hands down my body, and when he reaches my mound, he glances over my pussy before traveling to the spot where Leon bit me. Then he prostrates himself in front of me and sucks on the bite, drawing my blood into his mouth. When he pulls away, his lips are red and his pupils are huge and black.

"Ever since that first date, I knew you were the one for me." He sighs with contentment and kisses me on the lips. I wrap my arms around him, remembering it fondly.

"I think I knew it, too," I say, as he kisses me again, then steps away.

"Eli," says Leon, nodding.

Eli turns me so I'm facing him on the bed, then gently pushes me down so I'm lying flat. Bending down, he brings my legs up over his shoulders, and kisses all along the inside of my thigh. When he reaches the bite, he pauses, and kisses there, too.

"Ours." He sips gently at the wound, then covers it with his hand. "I know I wasn't the easiest to wrangle, but thank you for not giving up on me."

I stroke his hair. "I wouldn't trade it for anything. It all happened how it was supposed to."

Eli sits up to strip off his shirt, then his jeans, and the

others all follow except for Leon, who sits down in a chair nearby, watching us.

"Eli," he says. "Go first. Make love to her. Show her what she means to us."

With a sharp nod, Eli runs his hand down from my breasts to my hips. There he pins my thighs down, spread wide, and drops his head between them. He licks me there slowly, tenderly, just flicking his tongue back and forth over my clit. He puts one finger inside me, lapping me and pumping me with it, until I'm moaning. Before I can finish, though, he pauses and withdraws.

"I want to be inside you when you come," he hums, kneeling between my legs.

His cock is hungry for me, dribbling white from the head. He eases his way inside me slowly, looking into my eyes as he does. He gathers me up tight in his arms and thrusts with a steady, languid rhythm, building me up slowly, brick by brick. The burn from the bite has morphed into something different, something delicious, that's making heat spread like wildfire across my body. Eli smiles that small smile of his as I creep closer to the edge, as each of his strokes rubs the head of his cock over my soft channel.

When I do reach my finish, it's powerful but quiet, and I wrap my legs tight around Eli's slim body, moaning and rocking. He kisses me thoroughly as it sweeps me under. He has such a tender heart, and I love seeing it filled up.

But I didn't take his knot, not yet. When he's ready to finish, Eli pulls out with a grunt and empties himself on my belly, gasping. Then he wraps his arms around me, hands tangled in my curls, and kisses me with all the soft love in his heart.

"Tiff," he says, nuzzling my nose with his. "I'm so glad we found you. Every single day."

I have to hold in the tears that threaten to flood out of me. I kiss him back before he pulls away.

"One," Leon says. Then he gestures at Quinn. "You're next."

Quinn frowns as he approaches the bed. "But I might not be able to control my transformation."

"You'll hold out as long as you can," Leon says, and Quinn gives a jerky nod. He climbs onto the bed, his cock already jutting out toward me like it's being drawn with a magnet.

"Tiff." Quinn sucks in a deep breath of air, bringing my hair to his nose. He moans. "You're so perfect for us. And fuck, you smell so good." His lips are more urgent as he kisses me, until he wrenches his mouth away from mine and travels down my chest, where he tweaks my nipples with his teeth.

"Quinn!" I grab his hair as he sucks on them, and he starts to pump his hips against me, telling me what he's about to do.

"I need to be inside you," he whimpers. "Please."

I widen my legs, and he bites his lip as he fists the root of his cock.

When he sinks into me, he feels like heaven. Quinn holds onto his transformation as he drives himself deeper inside me, but even in human form, he can't help his panting. He sits back, hiking my thighs up over his arms, and starts to lose control. Soon he's fucking me so deep that his knot nudges at my entrance. He groans as I clench him, thrusting harder.

"Please," he says helplessly. "Please, let me knot her, Leon."

"No," he snaps back. "Only I will fill her up."

Quinn manages to hold himself together until I'm moaning and squeezing him tight. As my orgasm approaches and I clamp down even harder, Quinn lets out a groan. His body erupts with fur, and a huge tail emerges from behind him. As his nose and mouth elongate into a snout, he's shoving through my orgasm, his cock growing even bigger inside me, building me up higher. I scream as I fall over the edge. Gasping, Quinn yanks himself out and empties his load on my belly, right on top of Eli's. He pants, dripping drool on my face.

"You always feel so good," he whispers, nuzzling my nose with his big, wet one. I stroke his furry snout.

"So do you. Perfect."

Licking my face, he backs away.

"Two," Leon says. Then he nods at Jace. "You. Shifted. I want you to loosen her up for me."

Jace nods in assent, and I'll never get used to watching them transform. Gray fur ripples across him, and he starts to grow, his jaw stretching into a muzzle, his body rising higher above me until I'm enveloped in his shadow. Claws emerge from his hands, and his thick cock is even bigger now, pulsing with its need for me.

"Are you ready to take me?" Jace growls. He climbs onto the bed until he's crouched over me, his cock dripping. "Is your pussy stretched out enough for me yet?"

"Yes," I say, my hips already rising toward his. "Yes, I am."

With a snarl, Jace flips me over, gripping my ass in his claws. He teases at my entrance with that massive head, and thankfully, Quinn already opened me up while he was inside me. Jace's thick cock slips in, and he groans as he drops his snout to my hair. He huffs against my neck.

"Fuck, you're still so tight, though," he says, sinking in only an inch or two before pulling back out. "And you feel so good, it's going to be hard not to give you my knot."

"Only me," says Leon.

Jace's amazing cock pulls me even wider as it dips further in, and soon, he can't control himself any longer. He shoves into me, filling me up, asking my pussy to accommodate him. My face falls to the bed as he moves faster, fucking me harder.

"I have to get you nice and ready," he growls, stopping momentarily to drag his cock around in circles. It fires off bursts of pleasure, making me tense up all over. His knot just teases me as he starts again, pounding into me with so much vigor that I slide across the bed.

This time, as I climb through the sky toward my finish, it's so abrupt and powerful that I scream. Jace howls, his voice rattling the very walls. He takes me harder, fucking me through it and spinning it even wilder, until suddenly he pulls out and snarls. Something hot and wet splatters across my back, dripping down my ass. Behind me, Jace is panting as I flop down to the bed, boneless.

"Three," says Leon. Then he stands up from his chair and carefully takes off his clothes, while Jace licks me and crawls off the bed. All three of them watch as Leon transforms into his enormous, white wolf.

When I face him, those blue eyes bore into me. He stalks toward me, his cock drooling thick, white pre-cum.

"I'm going to fit my knot into you," he tells me as I roll over onto my back so I can look up into his face. He opens his maw and his tongue dives into my mouth, filling up my throat. He pumps it inside me, licking every crevice. Then he pulls away roughly and lifts my hips so he's poised right at my slit. "And then I'm going to come inside you, and put a pup in you." His claws drag down my belly, indicating exactly where that pup will grow.

I nod feverishly. "Get it all inside me," I tell him, running my hand down the soft fur of his snout. "Where it belongs."

With a roar, Leon presses his cock in, and though his is bigger than the others, I'm so wet that it slides through. He buries himself deep on his first thrust, and I cry out as it finds its place inside me.

"God, Tiff," he says through gritted teeth. "I love you. I love you so fucking much."

I run my hands up his cheek, to his ears, where I know he

adores being scratched. When I tease him with my nails, Leon moans with pleasure.

"I love you, too," I whisper back.

Leon grits his teeth and, gripping me tight, he pulls all the way out. Then he dives back in again, whispering my name. He does it over and over, taunting my nipples with his claws, burying his tongue in my mouth, drooling all over me. When I'm moaning and crying, I feel him slide in even deeper—and his knot starts to press at my stretched skin.

It triggers a mountain of sensation as it tries to fit inside me, but I'm still too tight. There's no way that massive thing will slide through, no matter how much Leon opens me for him. I'm just human, after all. But he tries again, and again, and as I get even slicker and wetter, my body swallows more and more of it with each stroke.

"Take my knot, love," he croons, pushing harder and harder. "Open up for me."

"I'm trying." My voice comes out a whimper. There's no possible way. Tears work their way free from my eyes at how much overwhelming bliss is cascading through me. It's almost too much for my body to hold.

"Don't come yet," Leon instructs in his deepest voice, and my body obeys, my climax hovering just on the edge of my reach. He pushes in again, that thick lump squeezing through, until at last, my pussy finally gives way.

Leon buries that massive knot inside me, and I scream when I take it.

"Oh, Leon," I moan, burying my face in his furry chest. Leon reaches around me, gathering me up in his arms, as he starts to move.

"What a good girl," he says as he rocks me. "How perfect you are, so tight for me. Taking my knot so well. I can't wait to watch you get big and round with my pup."

Every single stroke is incredible, like nothing I've ever felt before. There's a wet squelching sound as the knot slips in and out, triggering a rush of sensation each time.

"Leon!" I cry out, writhing underneath him, my hips bucking with every thrust.

"Now, love," Leon murmurs, his mouth at my ear. "Now give it to me."

As if on command, my climax rushes over me, powerful and fierce. I clamp down tight, and in response, Leon groans. He's so deep that I can feel his cock brush my most sensitive place, and the pleasure and pain meld together into something indescribable.

Then, Leon swells thick and heavy inside me. The knot grows fatter, and my tight pussy strains to take it as another, sharper orgasm washes over me. I sob into his fur as he pets my hair.

"I'm going to fill you up so full," he says, holding me close. Even his voice is husky as he drives in, and I feel a burst of hot liquid filling me up. That knot is so huge that with my pussy clamped down tight around it, it can't move. My channel strains, holding so much cock and cum inside it that a burst of pain echoes through my body. I curl tight against Leon and he strokes my head.

"It won't last long, love," he says, nuzzling me. He smooths a hand down my body, over my belly, which is swollen from how much of his cum is inside me. "I promise."

He holds me while I whimper. Jace, Quinn, and Eli get on the bed, all of them now transformed. While Leon's cock remains locked inside me, they begin to lick me all over.

"You're so beautiful, Tiff," Eli says, running a claw down my cheek. "Holding all that inside you."

"What a wonderful woman," Leon murmurs, resting his huge head on top of mine.

Soon, the swelling in Leon's knot goes down. When he gently he pulls himself free, there's a wet *pop!* and all his cum sloshes out, dripping down my thighs and my ass.

Eli brings me into his arms while Quinn pulls my legs apart and licks my abused pussy. Jace pats my belly and kisses my forehead.

"And once you've had Leon's pup," he says, "then I'll fill you with mine."

My body shudders in anticipation.

We fall asleep like that, curled up together, waiting for what the future will bring.

Chapter Thirty-Three

LEON WORKS HARD TO PUT A BABY INSIDE ME, SOMETIMES snatching me right off my feet after work and dragging me into the woods. If I've been too busy to get a solid run in, then I'll make him chase me as far as I can before my thighs are slick and I desperately need him inside me.

Leon growls as he transforms, towering over me, his tongue lolling out as his cock gets pink and swollen. Often he simply picks me up, holding my legs apart as he drives it into me, bouncing me up and down in his arms until I'm screaming. He always jams his knot inside me by the end, working me into bigger and bigger orgasms that nearly make me black out, until he's huge and trapped inside me. Then his cum spurts into me, filling me up until my body can't take any more.

Every few days, I get out another pregnancy test, then we all crowd around and watch as the results appear in the window. After two months, finally, it comes up positive.

All four of them howl at once, making me squint. Then Leon picks me up and swings me around, my legs wrapping around his hips as he kisses me. When he puts me down,

Quinn twirls me by one hand, surveying me from head to toe with a huge grin on his face.

"I can't wait," Eli whispers in my ear, approaching me from behind and winding one arm around my middle. "Your belly will look so good all full of pup."

I look around for Jace, but he's missing.

"Where did Jace go?" I ask, furrowing my brow. I want him to celebrate this moment with us.

Suddenly, he appears in the bathroom doorway, carrying a pint of ice cream.

"I'm ready," he says, holding it up with a spoon like a pair of handguns. "Whatever weird cravings you have, I'm on it."

I love them all so, so much.

When I tell her the good news, Mrs. Graham is ecstatic, and grabs me in a big bear hug that reminds me of her sons. She starts making all sorts of plans—baby showers, caregiving schedules so that I still have uninterrupted time in the office, and an online cart full of baby clothes and toys.

Of course, I text Hannah and Aisling right away. My mom can wait. They're both over the moon, though they lament that they already don't see me as much as they used to.

Having four husbands will do that to you!

Hannah answers with a series of laughing faces. Aisling sends four eggplant emojis, and then a baby emoji.

Telling my mom is a little more arduous of a task. I know what kind of questions she's going to ask, and I don't want to answer them.

"We'll be there with you," Jace assures me.

Quinn nods. "And I bet she'll be stoked to find out she's going to be a grandma."

Finally, I arrange the dinner, which Mr. and Mrs. Graham insist on holding at their home. It's the parents' first time meeting, and I expect Mom to say something snarky or biting.

To my surprise, though, she holds her tongue. If nothing else, my mother is intent on impressing other people, and that works to my advantage as she puts on her most polite face with Mr. and Mrs. Graham.

Before I can even get a word out about the baby on the way, though, Mrs. Graham hugs my mother for all she's worth.

"Congratulations!" she says, a smattering of tears in her eyes. "We get to be grandmothers together!"

My mother's mouth falls open as Mrs. Graham releases her.

"Nobody's told her yet, Mom!" Quinn says, giving his mother a stern look.

"Oops," she says, winking at me. "Sorry."

"You're having a baby?" Mom asks, glancing at each of my wonderful partners.

"Yes, Mom. I am." I sit down firmly. "But let's eat before the food gets cold."

They fall into easy conversation talking about all the things Mrs. Graham has planned for the baby's arrival, from the color of the crib to the caretaking schedule. Mom critiques how many vegetables I'm eating, insisting that babies need lots of vitamins and minerals that only spinach and broccoli can offer.

Eventually, though, the question comes up.

"So," Mom begins casually, "who's the lucky guy?"

In unison, Leon, Quinn, Eli and Jace all tilt their heads.

"Lucky?" Eli asks, narrowing his eyes. "We're all lucky."

Mom shakes her head. "I mean, who's the father?"

I cover my face, because I'm already blushing madly. I don't want to tell her our plan.

"Me," Leon says easily, sliding his chair over to put an arm around my shoulders. "I went first."

My mother blinks. "First?"

"The next one's mine," says Jace. "You know. If Tiff decides she wants more."

I grin at him, thinking about him fitting his thick knot inside me and filling me up.

Maybe I am grateful for this conversation as Mom's face goes pale.

"Next one...?" She looks among all four of them, and then her eyes dart over to me. "You're going to have four kids?"

"At least!" pipes up Quinn. Eli smacks him on the arm. "What? There are five of us. We can handle it."

"Plus me," Mrs. Graham says cheerily.

Mom just nods along, but she's clearly holding plenty of commentary inside. I just roll my eyes and lean into Leon's shoulder while he gives me more mashed potatoes.

"She's right," he whispers in my ear, making all the hair on my skin stand on end. "Be a good girl, and eat some more so you can feed our pup."

Of course I do, knowing exactly how he'll reward me later.

I didn't think it was possible, but once I'm pregnant, the guys are hornier than ever—and strangely, so am I. They don't tell you that besides the cravings for red meat and mac-and-cheese-flavored ice cream, pregnancy sex is amazing.

The bigger my belly gets, the wilder Eli becomes in bed. He's obsessed with the idea of a baby on the way and has already started carving out the nursery. I have a feeling he'll be an intense dad. He's even written me a few lovely poems about all the memories he's excited to make.

Eli's still rough when it matters, but always takes care not to go too far. He loves to push me down onto my hands and knees, black fur spreading across his body as he grows and shifts into his impressive werewolf form. He fucks me with his tongue, beginning with my clit, then sliding down to worm it inside my pussy, where he groans in abject pleasure.

"I can taste pup on you," he growls.

He likes to keep going, tracing the outline of my puckered rosebud, then shoving that long tongue into it. Eli always wants to claim every last inch of my body. When I'm fully wet and ready, he grips my ass in his claws and thrusts into my pussy, that fat werewolf cock opening me for him. He's just as animalistic as he is gentle, taking his time to get deeper and deeper. Dropping onto his hands and knees on top of me, his hot breath tickles my neck, drool dripping down my back. Then he nuzzles me with his cool nose, cupping my belly with one huge, clawed hand.

Eli knows just how to nurse an orgasm out of me, where to strike with the sloped head of his cock, and he wields his power with relentless abandon.

"Please," I sob as he brings me almost to my peak, then slows down. "Please, Eli!"

"Begging?" he rumbles with amusement. "I suppose I should give little rabbit what she wants."

Then he takes me harder and faster until I'm careening into oblivion with him. Afterwards, he pulls me into his lap and curls his big, furry arms around me.

"Thank you," he murmurs. "For making all my dreams come true."

Eli's not the only one obsessed with how my smell has

changed. All it takes now for Quinn to turn into his werewolf form is a heavy whiff of me.

"Oh, god," he moans. "You're so fucking hot, babe."

When I know he's going to be home, I make sure to wear a dress and no underwear, because sometimes he'll surprise me. I'll be bent over in the living room, trying to figure out why the TV isn't playing Jace's football game, when Quinn comes up to me and reaches between my legs. He's almost always in his werewolf form at home, but he's careful to only use the pad of his big fingers to rub across my clit. Jace snorts from behind us as Quinn licks the back of my neck, and almost immediately I'm wet. He chuckles against me.

"Ready for my cock?" Quinn asks, grinding his length between the cheeks of my ass. He pulls up my dress, rubbing me harder and faster as he slides himself into me.

"You're blocking the TV!" Jace calls out. Quinn picks me up in one motion with our bodies still attached and carries me over to the couch, so we're really blocking Jace's game. He still lacks control, and sometimes spills himself early—but then he smells me again, and his cock is instantly hard and ready to fuck me a second time.

Somehow, he always manages to cook dinner afterwards, though if he can't change back, he's a little clumsy with the pots and pans.

Jace loves it when I come down to their work sites to check out progress. He sidles up to me, tipping his baseball cap and saying, "Ma'am," in a thick cowboy accent. I still adore the smell of his sweat, and the second I get turned on, he flashes me a knowing look. "Does the lady require some attention?" he says, sultry, and tugs me behind the truck so no one inside the house can see us.

Jace throws open the door to the back seat, then shoves the

front seat as far forward as it'll go before pulling me inside and onto his lap.

"Do you need a ride, miss?" He rolls his hips underneath me so I know exactly what kind of ride I'm in for. It's much easier for his knot to fit inside me now, and his eyes roll back in his head as he buries it as deep as he can.

"Jesus, Tiff," he groans, claws sprouting from his fingers as he grabs my ass. He always fills me with so much cum that we have to clean it off the seats with his shirt, and then I have the pleasure of watching him work without it.

Sometimes, they'll even fuck me together at once—Jace buried in my pussy while Eli takes my ass, and I've never come so hard in my life.

We sleep most nights in Leon's room, but as my body changes, sometimes I get much too hot curled up with a mix of men and big, hairy werewolves. One night I wake up sweating in the middle of the night, panting from a bad dream. I sneak quietly out of the room, slipping on a long shirtdress so I can get a breath of fresh air.

I love it out here, surrounded by starry sky and the scent of pine needles. I can't help but feel like it's where I was always meant to be.

"Hey, love."

I smile to myself as I sense Leon approach me from behind. He runs a gentle hand down my side.

"Everything all right?" he asks, pulling me in under his arm as we both gaze up at the sky.

I lean into him, letting him take some of the weight off my feet. "Just feeling funny. Had a weird dream."

"What did you dream about?"

"I was being chased, I think." The memory is a little fuzzy, like all dreams are.

Leon looks down at me and raises an eyebrow. "You love getting chased."

"Not by a T-Rex, though."

His laugh is big and boisterous. He kisses the top of my head, pulling me in even closer. "No T-Rex will get you while I'm around," he says. "Unless I'm the T-Rex." His hand tightens around me, squeezing my ass.

Before I know it, I'm on my back in the grass, Leon as naked as he was when he came outside. He yanks off my clothing and tosses it away, then kisses downward from my mouth to my belly. There, he pauses, and gently rests his head on it.

"Hey, pup," he says in a quiet, tender voice. "Can't wait to meet you." Then he covers my belly button with both hands. "Don't watch what I'm about to do to your mom."

Then he rises high above me, white fur erupting all across his body. He swells, bones creaking, eyes staying the same bright blue as he takes on his huge werewolf form. His pink cock is wet as it slides out of its sheath, hungry for me as it always is.

He works it slowly inside me, panting as he tries to control himself and take his time. But my body is hungry for him, too, so I snap my hips up into his big haunches, and he howls as he sinks deep inside me.

He fucks me under the bright night sky, chanting my name as his drool drips down onto my face. When I've come so hard that I'm seeing twice as many stars, he scoops me up into his lap, and holds me like that until I fall back asleep.

Epilogue

THE DOCTORS AND NURSES ARE MYSTIFIED BY THE FOUR MEN who all want to be in the room with me.

"Which of you is the father?" one of the nurses asks, blocking the door.

Eli, Leon, Quinn, and Jace all look at each other, perplexed by the question.

"All of us are?" offers Quinn.

In the end, only Leon is allowed in. If I'm going to be honest, it's probably the worst day of my life, those sixteen hours I spend in labor.

But the next one, where our first pup comes into the world, is probably the best.

The guys timed it perfectly so they have a few weeks off from work. With my new method of bulk ordering and charging higher per-hour rates, we've scrimped and saved enough that it's feasible, so we all get to bask at home with the new baby. Then we'll go back to work, me in the office with the baby, and them alternating days working outside and days spent at home.

Watching Eli playing with her, Quinn looking over his shoulder, and Leon fixing the crib, I know she's going to be the most spoiled kid who ever lived.

By the time May is two years old, she's become a well-oiled machine of terror and destruction. Her dads love chasing her all over the den until one of them catches her and she squeals with joy as she's thrown up into the air.

Jace sidles up behind me, winding one arm around my waist while Eli play-wrestles with her on the rug.

"What do you think?" he asks in a low tone. "Now that you've had one, do you want more?"

I giggle. I knew what I was signing up for.

"Yeah," I say, reaching up to kiss his cheek. "I do. But maybe we should wait for her first transformation?"

As if on cue, I hear a little howl. May has turned into a fluffy white wolf cub in Eli's arms. He squeals with delight and swings her around as she scrabbles with her tiny claws.

Jace snickers over my shoulder.

"Good," he says, his voice changing to become deeper, growlier. "I can't wait to knot you."

A shiver ripples from my throat straight to my pussy as Jace's arms become big and furry around me. I watch the others play, and I couldn't be happier they howled at me that day on my jog.

Thank you so much for reading!

If you enjoyed this book, please consider leaving a review! Reviews are incredibly helpful to indie authors like me in reaching new readers.

Get the extended epilogue on Patreon!

Ready for Jace, Eli, and Quinn to put their knots in Tiff, too? Read the extra smutty extended epilogues by signing up on Patreon! You can also find tons of exclusive NSFW artwork. Just visit my website at LyonneRiley.com!

Join My Newsletter!

For all the latest regarding books, and to get a FREE Trollkin Lovers novella, join my newsletter! You can also find signed paperbacks and artwork of your favorite books.

www.LyonneRiley.com

Also by Lyonne Riley

Trollkin Lovers

Stealing the Troll's Heart

Healing the Orc's Heart

Capturing the Orc's Heart

Charming the Troll's Heart

Keeping the Human's Heart

Finding the Troll's Heart

Tempting the Ogre's Heart

Enchanting the Ogre's Heart

Knowing the Ogre's Heart

DreamTogether Breeding Program

Bred by the Wolfman

Bred by the Dragon

Anthologies

The Monster Menagerie

Standalones

Prince of Beasts

Programmed for Love

My Minotaur Husband

Acknowledgments

First and foremost, I want to thank my Patrons for making this book a reality. I couldn't have gone on this fun, smutty adventure without you. All of your comments and encouragement made this possible.

I would also like to thank Rowan Woodcock for the gorgeous cover illustration, and all the little changes and additions he made to it along the way. Thank you to my dearest friend Ash Raven for your help designing the cover. To my critique partners, who gave me phenomenal feedback: You all make this possible. And of course, I want to thank my amazing spouse, who has always supported my dreams—and given me lots of inspiration for my characters' sexy adventures.

I couldn't have done this without the expertise of my fellow self-published romance authors. Thank you for inviting me into your circles and helping me through this process.

And thank you to my readers, who gave this book a shot.

www.ingramcontent.com/pod-product-compliance
Lightning Source LLC
Chambersburg PA
CBHW030612170726
48283CB00002B/565